IN PLAIN SIGHT

This Large Print Book carries the
Seal of Approval of N.A.V.H.

In Plain Sight

Fern Michaels

WHEELER PUBLISHING
A part of Gale, Cengage Learning

GALE
CENGAGE Learning·

Farmington Hills, Mich • San Francisco • New York • Waterville, Maine
Meriden, Conn • Mason, Ohio • Chicago

Copyright © 2015 by Fern Michaels.
Sisterhood Series.
Fern Michaels is a registered trademark of KAP5, Inc.
Wheeler Publishing, a part of Gale, Cengage Learning.

Wheeler Publishing Large Print Hardcover.
The text of this Large Print edition is unabridged.
Other aspects of the book may vary from the original edition.
Set in 16 pt. Plantin.

LIBRARY OF CONGRESS CATALOGING-IN-PUBLICATION DATA

Michaels, Fern.
  In plain sight / Fern Michaels. — Large print edition.
    pages cm. — (Sisterhood series) (Wheeler Publishing large print hardcover)
    ISBN 978-1-4104-7436-0 (hardback) — ISBN 1-4104-7436-4 (hardcover)
    1. Female friendship—Fiction. 2. Runaway women—Fiction. 3. Abusive men—Fiction. 4. Large type books. I. Title.
  PS3563.I27I5 2015
  813'.54—dc23   2015018486

Published in 2015 by arrangement with Zebra Books, an imprint of Kensington Publishing Corp.

Printed in the United States of America
1 2 3 4 5 6 7 19 18 17 16 15

I would like to dedicate this book to Julie St. George.

PROLOGUE

Five years earlier

Everything about Lincoln Moss shrieked money, right down to his monogrammed jockey shorts. He was still on the sunny side of fifty, the half-century mark, though just barely, with three short months to go till he hit the big five-o and moved to the shady side of the calendar. He hated the thought but was wise enough to know time was the one thing in his personal life that he could not control.

Lincoln Moss was all about control.

Time marched on, and time didn't care that Lincoln Moss was already a millionaire at the age of thirty-six. Time didn't care that Lincoln Moss became a multibillionaire at the age of thirty-nine, and time didn't care that Lincoln Moss retired at the age of forty-five with more money than God.

Time didn't care that Lincoln Moss had the President's ear and was welcome at

1600 Pennsylvania Avenue any time of the day or night. Time didn't even care that he was married to French model Amalie Laurent, dubbed the most beautiful woman in the world by the media and the face of the billion-dollar international cosmetic company *La Natural*. Owned, of course, by the very same Lincoln Moss.

Lincoln Moss, along with the current President of the United States, Gabriel Knight, a cousin three or four times removed, had grown up on the wrong side of the tracks, poorer than poor, often with not enough food to eat. Lincoln was the go-getter, the hustler, while Gabriel was the worrier of the duo, who went along for the ride. Lincoln's motto from the age of sixteen was "I want to be rich. I want to be powerful, and I won't stop until I achieve that goal." Gabriel didn't care about the money per se; he wanted to go into politics and be *somebody*. Lincoln promised his cousin and best friend that he would make it happen.

On Gabe's twenty-first birthday, Lincoln asked him if he would like to be President of the United States at some point. To which Gabe replied, "I think I could handle the office."

At that point in time, the bond between

the two men deepened even more, and both young men knew that nothing on earth could drive them apart. Nothing. They even did that blood-brother thing, where each of them cut the palm of his hand and mixed their blood. And the deal was sealed, as Lincoln said, "until death do us part." It's just like a marriage, he'd told Gabe, and Gabe had agreed.

Lincoln put his nose to the grindstone and within ten short years he was involved in shipping and leasing companies, diamond mines and oil. From there he branched out to banks and steel mills and dabbled in European car manufacturing. Because he was a pro at networking and knew how to schmooze, it wasn't long before he was making money hand over fist — so much money that it was hard to stay on top of it all. And that's where Gabe came in because he was a whiz with numbers. He invested the money, sought out small companies for Lincoln to buy out and build up and unload at ten times the buying price. In essence, Lincoln Moss, under Gabriel Knight's tutelage, became his own hedge fund. But the money he was investing was his own, not the public's. And money earned on those investments started pouring in so fast that even Gabe, financial genius that he was, had a hard time keeping up with the flow.

There had only been one disagreement between the two men, and that was when Gabe insisted that Lincoln buy a French cosmetic company called *La Natural.* Lincoln called it a dog of a company, selling cheap cosmetics, and on the verge of financial insolvency. Gabe countered that all they needed was a face for the company to send it off the charts. Lincoln continued to argue that owning a war-paint company did nothing for his image, much less his bank account. Gabe held his ground, and within three short years, the company was bringing in $10 billion a year under Gabe's sharp eye and expert management.

Lincoln Moss hung his head in shame, clapped his friend on the back, apologized for doubting him, and promised never again to underestimate his genius.

The $10 billion a year tripled the day *La Natural* engaged the new face for *La Natural,* a model by the name of Amalie Laurent. Lincoln had met her a year or so earlier, and on Gabe's advice, Lincoln wooed her, wined, and dined her, gave her everything a woman could want, then married her the day he turned forty-two.

The wedding was so over the top it was televised live all over the world. Women sat glued to their television sets admiring the top model's flawless beauty, which she said came from *La Natural.* There were those who said Princess Diana's wedding was tawdry compared to Amalie Laurent's.

A year to the day after he and his bride returned from their honeymoon on the island of Mustique, Lincoln got down to the serious business of grooming Gabriel Knight for the presidency of the United States. Two years later, Lincoln Moss announced to the world that he was going to manage Gabriel Knight's campaign for the highest office in the land. It took four years of steady-as-you-go politicking. He left no stone unturned. He worked tirelessly, campaigning seven days a week and making sure that all photo ops showed Amalie flanked by Gabe and himself. And that's how Gabriel Knight had sailed into the White House the year before Lincoln Moss turned fifty.

The media stewed and fretted when Lincoln was given no titles, no special perks, and all he would say was that he didn't want anything other than the President's friendship. They did notice, however, that Lincoln wore out the carpet leading to the Oval Office with his frequent visits. And they noticed when he sat in on briefings, not that he ever uttered a single word. Anytime a crisis threatened, Lincoln was the first one in the Situation Room. It was also said but not proven that the President and Lincoln had personal cell phones that not even the Secret Service was privy to. Then they started to whisper about Moss's little black book of secrets, but no one would or could confirm that there was such a book.

In the beginning, Ted Robinson and Maggie Spritzer of the *Post* very often wrote op-ed pieces and lengthy articles on Lincoln Moss as they tried to figure out if there was something no one was seeing besides themselves. As Maggie said time and again, "He's got to have something on someone, and I do believe there is a little black book," with which Ted agreed completely. From time to time, they questioned their own suspicious-reporter instincts and were inclined to give up their quest for a story when they couldn't come up with anything they felt was newsworthy. So they simply shelved the effort as they waited for a break, or, as Ted put it, a mistake on the part of Kingpin Lincoln Moss. It was just a matter of time, he said over and over, because everyone makes a mistake at some point. Ted was rarely, if ever, wrong. And when Maggie Spritzer agreed with him one hundred percent, you could take it to the bank.

And so they waited. Not too patiently but patiently enough.

And while they waited, Lincoln Moss went about his business of keeping his image pristine and making sure he made the front page of every newspaper at least once a week for something or other.

Lincoln Moss was a handsome, muscular, fit man. In his palatial home, he had a state-of-the-art gym and his own personal trainer, who lived in one of the cottages at the rear of the ten-thousand-acre estate. His chauffeur lived in another cottage. The day help — his housekeeper and butler, six maids, and the lawn and maintenance people — left the premises at six o'clock sharp every evening and didn't return until six o'clock the following morning. He was fond of saying to anyone who would listen that he paid out more in salaries in one month than some people made in their lifetime. Maggie Spritzer called it bragging rights. Everyone knew Maggie took no prisoners.

Lincoln Moss was also a snob. But not in public. In public, he was Mister Benevolent, Mister Congeniality himself. Something Maggie Spritzer and Ted Robinson saw through at their first meeting.

13

While the intrepid reporters were waiting for Moss to make a mistake, he was on his way home in the middle of the day to check on his beautiful wife and possibly have lunch with her in the garden. The bloom was off the rose, as the saying went, and Lincoln was the first to recognize that fact. He didn't love his beautiful wife. Never had. To him, she was just another possession. But he played the game, and the rules were all his because he was in total control. From time to time, he hauled Amalie out for the public to see and admire at some function or other at the White House. And four times a year he took her back to France, so she could do new photo shoots for *La Natural.*

The time was 12:50. He'd called ahead to the housekeeper to have lunch served in the garden and make sure his wife was seated and waiting for him when he arrived. He had dictated the menu in a rapid tone, then cut the connection. There was no doubt in his mind that his instructions would be followed to the letter.

Moss galloped into the house and took the elevator to the third floor, where he'd set up the master suite. He washed his face and hands, combed his unruly locks, then admired his good looks for a full five minutes as he turned this way and that to

make sure there was no excess flesh poking at his designer shirt. Mister Fitness Himself, thanks to a three-hour workout every morning and a twenty-mile run four days a week. The custom-made clothes completed his persona. He ate healthy, barely touched alcohol, and never smoked.

When he was satisfied with his appearance, he took the steps to the first floor. He walked at a leisurely pace through the solarium, then to the outdoor patio that led to a garden so rich with flowers one could get drunk on the scent alone. He rounded a path and saw his wife sitting upright at a small table set for two. She was wearing sunglasses.

Moss leaned over and kissed her on the cheek. She flinched as he sat down, but he pretended not to notice. He removed her sunglasses and tossed them on the ground. Then he stomped on them. "What did I tell you about wearing sunglasses in my presence?"

"You told me not to wear them, Lincoln. But I didn't think you'd want the staff to see what you did to me yesterday. Are you saying I made a mistake? If so, I'm sorry."

Moss looked at his wife with clinical interest as he dug into his lobster ravioli, which appeared as if by magic. "You need to eat,

Amalie, you're getting bony. I forgot . . . I'll have one of the maids bring you a new pair of sunglasses." Then he laid his fork down and stared across the table at his wife. Amalie met his gaze. "Are you telling me with all that makeup you have upstairs you couldn't cover up those bruises?"

"Perhaps tomorrow when the bruising turns yellow, it will cover it up. It doesn't work when it's dark purple the way it is now."

"Well, we're obviously going to have to call a meeting with our chemists and have them come up with something that *will* work. You need to eat. Don't make me tell you again."

Amalie dutifully picked up her fork and cut through one of the ravioli, hoping she didn't choke on it. Her neck was still tender from where her husband had tried to choke her just days ago. Somehow, she managed to chew the pasta and lobster to a fine mush so that she could swallow it. She sipped from her wineglass so the food would slide down her bruised throat more easily.

"What did you do this morning, Amalie?"

"Not much. A little yoga. I read the paper. I ordered some books online. I thought you might like Robert Gates's new book, so I ordered that for you." She popped the other half of the ravioli into her mouth, hoping it would go down as easily as the first half.

"What are you going to do this afternoon?"

Amalie wanted to scream at the top of her lungs, *I am going to plot your death in every way I can think of.* Instead, she said, "I thought I'd stay out here in the garden and do a little reading. I thought about a swim. The water in the pool is just perfect now that it's July. Unless there's something you want me to do."

"No. There's nothing. Eat, Amalie. You need to put those nine pounds you lost back on. I'll have the cook whip you up some nutritious milk shakes. You will drink them, won't you?"

"Of course." Amalie speared another ravioli and cut it in half. She managed to chew her way through it as she waited for whatever else was to come. She was so tense, she thought she would explode. She almost fainted in relief when her husband got up from the table and walked around to where she sat. He leaned over and nibbled on her ear. She flinched again, and he laughed.

"I'll see about getting you some new sunglasses. Have a nice afternoon, my dear." Amalie sighed heavily. Her shoulders

17

sagged, and her eyes filled with tears. She had to grab hold of the edge of the table when she felt her husband return and stand behind her chair to slide the glasses on and settle them behind her ears. "I'll see you at dinner. Dress nicely."

"I will. Enjoy your afternoon," she said woodenly.

The moment Amalie heard the engine of her husband's Porsche growl to life, she was up and off her chair and sprinting for her room. She banged open the door and looked everywhere for her maid, Rosalee. She motioned her to come closer and whispered in her ear. The little maid nodded and whispered back. They eyed each other, their eyes misting over at what Amalie had been going through for the last seven and a half years. And now, finally, with the help of the little maid, she was ready to bolt.

Both women blessed themselves, then hugged each other.

"Please, God, let Rosalee make it happen. Please, God!"

CHAPTER 1

The present day.

As the windshield wipers fought the waterfall of rain, Annie de Silva tried in vain to see where Myra was taking them. "This was not one of your better ideas, Myra," she grumbled.

"No, it wasn't, but you did agree, so keep quiet and let me pay attention to my driving. One more block, and we'll be there. Do you think you can keep quiet that long?"

"No one likes a smart-ass, Myra," Annie continued to grumble.

"You were the one who said you were sick and tired of being housebound because of a week of rain. You also said you were sick and tired of listening to Charles and Fergus babbling on about writing their memoirs that no one was going to read. Well, that's not quite true, you and I would be forced to read them." Myra laughed.

Annie gave up trying to see through the

driving rain and slumped back against the seat. "Men's memoirs are always boring. Now, if you and I wrote our memoirs, that's a whole other story. Ours would be runaway best sellers. Maybe we should think about that, Myra."

"Maybe we shouldn't, Annie. Okay, we're here. I think I changed my mind about a pedicure. I'm just going to get my nails done. If you want to go ahead with the pedicure, I'll wait for you. As it is, we don't have an appointment and are going in as walk-ins. Maybe they won't even be able to take us today."

Still grumbling, Annie said, "Trust me, we are the only fools out here in this weather. If the rain keeps up, we're going to need a boat to get around. Are we going to lunch after we get our nails done?"

"We can, but remember, we're in the village, not town, so we're limited as to where we can go. The Tea Shop is just two doors away. I don't want to drive any farther, Annie."

Annie pulled a face. "I'm up for a cucumber sandwich and some ginseng tea." What she really wanted was a footlong hot dog with sauerkraut, mustard, and raw onions, accompanied by a heaping pile of greasy french fries.

As though she read Annie's mind, Myra said, "Since our social calendars are empty, we can drive into town tomorrow and get that hot dog you are sitting there lusting for. We're going to have to make a wild dash for the shop. An umbrella isn't going to do us much good in this wind. You ready?"

Annie had the car door open and ran like the bats of hell were after her. She was drenched to the skin by the time they reached the Beautiful Nails shop. Both women barreled through the door. Five little Vietnamese women smiled at them. The shop was empty of patrons. The little women bowed the way they always did, and said in unison, "Welcome, Mrs. Ladies." That greeting was the extent of their English, along with, "Forty dollar, Mrs. Lady" or "Eighty dollar, Mrs. Lady" if they were getting a manicure and a pedicure.

Annie and Myra both dangled their hands in front of the women to signal they just wanted a manicure. More smiles, more bows, and they were seated at a double table facing the door.

As they were filed and buffed, Annie and Myra kept up a low-voiced conversation about nothing, the weather, the awful humidity that had preceded the awful rain that was to last another awful four days. "It is what it is, Annie. Like it or not, we can't change Mother Nature."

The front door suddenly blew open as a wet and bedraggled woman shouted loudly, "Myra! Annie!"

"Pearl! Is that you, Pearl?" Annie said, jerking her hand away from the little lady named Kime. "What are you doing here? What's wrong?"

"Charles said you were probably here. Hurry, you need to come with me."

Myra was off her chair and right behind Annie, wiping her nails on the leg of her pantsuit. She dug in her pants pocket for some bills and tossed them on the receptionist's desk. "We'll call for another appointment," she shouted over her shoulder.

The chattering in the shop was like that of a hundred magpies as the trio ran into the pouring rain to Myra's car.

"You better say something really fast, Pearl, or I'm going to fly you to the moon," Annie bellowed to be heard over the torrent of rain that was falling and flooding the small parking lot.

"Burn rubber, Myra!" Annie said, or we're all going to get pneumonia even if this is July. Put the heater on. Spit it out, Pearl."

"The clinic has been breached. That

22

means my underground railroad has been breached."

"Are you talking about the clinic Julia Webster set up before her death?" Myra asked as she pressed down on the accelerator.

"Yes! For God's sake, yes! What other clinic would I possibly be talking about? The one you and Annie keep funding, have funded all these years. I just found out early this morning. I don't know what to do. God, how could this happen? All these years, and nothing ever went wrong, and now, we've been breached. I just came from there. I shut the place down and sent the staff home. I was there since six o'clock this morning. It's after one o'clock now. I took the computers and as many files as I could load in my van. I didn't get it all, but what's left can't incriminate any of us. At least I don't think so. Lord, I am exhausted."

Myra screeched to a stop, looked both ways, and made a U-turn as she headed for the Good Samaritan Clinic. "We'll go there now and help you finish up." She pressed down on the gas pedal and roared down the road, all the while blowing the horn for the other drivers to get out of her way.

"Good Lord, Myra, when did you turn into Jeff Gordon?" Annie asked as she struggled to remain upright. "I didn't know you had it in you, old girl."

"There's a lot about me you don't know," Myra said through clenched teeth as she continued blasting her horn. Even she was stunned at how the other drivers moved to the side to let her pass.

"Did you hire any new people lately, Pearl? Could you be a little more specific?" Annie asked in a shaky voice as she watched the scenery pass in a blur of rain and backwash.

"No. Our last hire was two years ago. Everyone is vetted within an inch of their life. You know that. Number 9643 and Number 9644 didn't check in for the weekly check, which is mandatory. That has *never* happened before. I had one of our people check the residence, and both women are gone. I'm telling you, we're breached," Pearl cried hysterically.

"What about the women you help? Could one of them have turned on you?"

"Good Lord, no! When I put the call out, one of my people called me just as I got to the nail shop. Both 9643 and 9644 are missing. By missing, I mean they can't be found. They might be out shopping or visiting a friend, but I don't think so because they came to me together. If it were just one person, I wouldn't be so unglued. But not these two. I'm telling you, we've been breached," Pearl shrieked.

"Easy, Pearl, you're losing it here. Try to calm down. We're going to help. It might be a good thing for you to tell us who the two women that you think are gone really are."

"I can't do that, and you know it. Those names are sacrosanct. That's why it works. We go by numbers only, not names." She clamped her lips shut as if to prove her point.

"We're here, Pearl. Did you leave the lights on?"

"No. Maybe. I don't know, I was in a hurry. I wasn't exactly thinking about the electric bill at the time."

"Did you at least lock the door?" Myra asked as she stepped out of the car in rainwater up to midcalf.

"I don't know that either," Pearl responded as she dug around in the pocket of her slicker for a key ring. "Hurry, girls!"

Within minutes, the three women were in the lobby of the clinic, dripping water all over the tile floor. As one, they looked around. "It looks the same," Pearl said. "The door was locked, so I probably forgot to turn off the lights. I was under a lot of pressure."

"What about the drugs and stuff doctors use? Did you take those, Pearl?" Myra asked.

"I didn't even think about that. Like I said, I was panicked. My only thought was about the files and records. Of course, we have to take those. There are trash bags under the sink. Just throw everything in them. Don't leave anything behind. We also need Mr. Snowden to come in here ASAP and sanitize this place. I'll call him, and I have to update all the surgeons and nurses who work here."

"All right. While you do that, Pearl, Annie and I will start with the medicine room. Just so we're sure about what we're doing, we take everything, every scrap of paper, right?" Pearl nodded.

An hour later, Myra and Annie were both moaning and groaning as they carried bag after bag out to Myra's car.

The minute the last bag was loaded, Annie headed for the small kitchen and returned with three soft drinks. She handed them out. "I pulled the plug on the fridge and the microwave oven." She was one sip into her drink when Avery Snowden and three other men showed up. They were all dressed in white coveralls and carrying bins of what looked like cleaning supplies.

26

"Make sure you swipe everything, right down to the lightbulbs. We can't have even one fingerprint showing up." Snowden looked at Myra over the top of his glasses as much as to say, *Are you telling me how to do my business?* "Rest easy, we know what to do. Just out of curiosity, where are you going to store everything you took out of here?"

Pearl looked blank for a moment. She shook her head as though to clear away the cobwebs. "I was going to take it home and store it either in the garage or the basement," she said. One look at Snowden and his men told her that was not a very good idea. In short order, Snowden dispatched one of his men to unload Myra's car and instructed him to go to the village shopping area and take Pearl's car to an undisclosed location. "We'll return your vehicle to your driveway sometime this evening," he assured her. "I'll need your keys, Pearl." Pearl handed them over with a sigh of relief.

"We'll drop you off at home, Pearl, unless you want to come out to the farm. I assume you want to call a meeting and set up a mission."

Pearl rubbed her temples. She nodded. "As soon as possible. In cases like this, every second counts."

"Leave the soda bottles," Snowden barked. The women didn't need to be told twice. Within minutes, they were back in Myra's car and headed toward Pinewood. Annie made call after call, alerting the team that a meeting was set for five o'clock, with dinner to follow. Her last call was to Charles, informing him there would be guests for dinner. Per Myra's orders.

The moment the women hit the farmhouse kitchen, they all bolted up the back staircase to shower and put on clean, dry clothes. Thirty minutes later, less than fashionably dressed, they all sat down at the kitchen table to cups of wild blackberry tea with fresh honey.

"Talk to us, ladies," Fergus said as he continued to chop vegetables. "Charles and I can listen and cook at the same time."

They talked, and Charles and Fergus listened.

"This could truly be a disaster in the making. I can see why you are so upset, Pearl," Charles said as he waved a wooden spoon in the air.

"What you need to really look at is this. Was it an accident, or was it deliberate. You said all the people are vetted and trustworthy. If true, then how did this happen?" Fergus asked.

"I don't have a clue," Pearl wailed.

"Get a grip, Pearl. This is no time for you to fall apart; too many people depend on you. Now, like I said, get a grip. Drink your tea and explain to us how the clinic works. While Myra and I fund the clinic, it doesn't mean we know how it works. And that's your own fault, Pearl. You keep it all to yourself. There has to be someone else to help you carry the load. If something happened to you tomorrow, what would all those people do? Do you have a plan in place? You don't, do you? I can see it on your face. We understand the need for secrecy. We get it. All we want to do is help, and you keep blocking our efforts. I'm starting to think you don't trust anyone, even us," Annie said coolly.

Myra added, "And yet, where did you come the moment you sensed trouble? You came straight to us, yet you won't share the details. It's you who aren't *getting it,* Pearl.

"One other thing. Even when we had to enlist Jack Sparrow to help you, you still wouldn't share with us," Myra said, her annoyance and frustration evident to all but Pearl.

Pearl's shoulders sagged. She looked around at the others and nodded as she swiped at her eyes with the sleeve of her

29

sweatshirt. "I've learned over the years that the only person you can depend on is yourself. When I first embarked on this journey, I realized I was taking on the responsibility for women's and children's lives. Me. No one else. It's the only way it could work for me. I can't count the times I wanted to confide in someone, have someone pick up the slack, to help. I was afraid to take the chance. It's the way it has to be."

Myra eyed her old friend with narrowed eyes. "I am hesitant to bring this up, Pearl, but this is way too serious not to discuss it. What about your daughter? She's the reason you do what you do. We never discuss her because you said she was off-limits. If I recall correctly, and it's been years, so possibly I guess I could be wrong, but you did say you worried constantly that she would weaken and get in touch with her ex because she was so in love with him. So in love that she allowed him to beat her unconscious until she almost died. We sat with you, Pearl, in the hospital; we helped with your granddaughter; we were there for you every step of the way. Is it possible she's involved?" Myra asked.

Pearl reared back in her chair as though she'd been bitten by a snake. "I can't believe

30

you asked me that, Myra! My daughter! Never!"

"How do you know for certain, Pearl?" Charles asked gently.

"I'm a mother. I know. She's happily married now, and her new husband loves her daughter. She had a baby boy with her new husband. She would never jeopardize her new life."

"And yet you never told us your daughter got married or that she had a baby?" Annie said, outrage at what she was hearing turning her face rosy red. "Where does she live now? What's her new married name? What name did you give her when you got her a new identity?"

Pearl clamped her lips together, her eyes showing her misery. She struggled to take a deep breath but sobbed instead. No one rushed to comfort her.

Myra got up and walked over to the kitchen counter, where she'd tossed her keys. She picked them up and tossed them to Pearl. "Take my car. I'll pick it up tomorrow."

"Wha . . . what?"

"I want you to leave, Pearl. That means go. Take my car. I'll pick it up tomorrow."

"But . . . why . . . ?"

Charles moved then and opened the

kitchen door. Fergus was behind him with an oversize umbrella. He handed it over.

"Drive carefully," Annie called out.

Pearl whirled around. "No! This is wrong. I need you." She fixed her wild-eyed gaze on Annie and Myra. "My daughter is off-limits. I thought of all people that you two would understand. I know my daughter just the way you knew your daughters. It's all up here," she said, tapping her head. "I did not commit anything to paper or file or record. You have to believe me. Those women trust me. I have to honor that trust even if I end up finishing my days in a federal prison. Their lives are in my hands and only mine."

Charles moved forward and closed the door. Fergus reached for the umbrella. Myra and Annie moved and wrapped the sobbing woman in their arms.

"We're going to make it right, Pearl. All you have to do is trust us."

Pearl nodded.

CHAPTER 2

The gang started to arrive a little after four-thirty. While their greetings were exuberant, the usual upbeat tone was missing. Everyone was wet and soggy with just the short run from Myra's parking lot to the house. Four inside-out umbrellas were tossed in a messy heap at the top of the steps thanks to the gusty winds.

Inside, Charles and Fergus handed out towels and offered to throw jackets and shirts into the dryers. Everyone declined and just said to turn off the AC. Fergus obliged. Charles handed out cups of sweet apple tea, which the group guzzled before they followed Myra and Annie to the underground war room. Charles and Fergus brought up the rear, with a warning to Lady and her pups to watch over things topside.

Lady yipped and ran back to the kitchen and looked around for a spot that would allow her to see the monitor that controlled the electronic gates outside. Satisfied that she was in position, she yipped again, and her pups took up their positions and went to sleep.

Down below, Annie pressed the button on the specially built table in the war room. They all watched as the table separated, and new leaves settled into place to accommodate everyone in the room. Myra called the meeting to order the moment everyone was seated. She didn't mince words and got right to the point.

"The Good Samaritan Clinic has been breached. As you all know, this is the clinic Julia Webster founded years ago when we were all . . . ah . . . starting out. Pearl just found out this morning. Annie, Pearl, and I removed all the files that could possibly incriminate her and her organization. Mr. Snowden is securing all of the, for want of a better word, evidence, in a secure location. Pearl came to us because she believes that two of her . . . um . . . clients have disappeared. She assured us that everyone, that means the doctors, the nurses, the aides, has been thoroughly vetted. There is a possibility that the two women in question, and there are two, simply went somewhere and haven't gotten back yet. To be honest, I don't think anyone believes that, at least I don't. That's pretty much it in a nutshell. We're now open for questions."

Maggie scrunched her face into a mask of puzzled concern. "What does the clinic have to do with your supposedly missing two people? I say this with all due respect, Pearl, but are you sure you didn't jump the gun when you rushed to close the clinic?"

"I didn't see that I had a choice, Maggie. Not just because of 9643 and 9644 but for all the others who underwent surgery at the clinic. I had to think about all of them. I would rather have jumped the gun than not jump. In this . . . ah . . . line of work, you cannot leave anything to chance. Before and after pictures, medical histories, that kind of thing. Even simple surgeries require truth on the part of the patient. That's the only answer I can give you at this time, and if I had to do it over again, I'd do the same exact thing." Maggie unscrunched her features and nodded.

"How do you know for certain that the women are gone?" Nikki asked.

"They didn't answer their phones. We give all our people special phones, and they know that when they ring, they are to pick up immediately. It's mandatory to check in once a week. Both 43 and 44 failed to check in. We have strict rules about that. To date,

35

none of our people has failed in that regard. Until now."

"Did you go to where they live to check on them?" Alexis asked.

"I sent one of our people. She said everything looked normal, almost as though 43 and 44 went out for a walk and hadn't gotten back yet. The phones were in the kitchen on the counter. I will personally go shortly, but my gut is telling me they're gone," Pearl said miserably.

"Isn't it odd that two women came to you together? Is it a mother and daughter, two sisters, what?" Yoko asked.

"Yes, odd, but one helped the other, so it was only natural that we had to take them both to prevent any blowback on the helper. We've only had one other case like that over the years, and nothing went awry at that time. We really didn't have a choice," Pearl said.

"There's a first time for everything," Jack said. "Off the top of your head, what do you think? You've been doing this for a lot of years, Pearl. What is your gut telling you?"

Her eyes still wild and unfocused, Pearl looked around at the others and groaned. "My gut is telling me two of my people are in serious trouble, and since I have never had this problem before, I don't know what to do or think other than that I now realize I can't do this myself, and I need help."

"What do you want us to do, Pearl?" Dennis asked.

Pearl stared across the table at the young reporter she liked so much and respected. Her thoughts were all over the place. How did she go from being a Supreme Court justice to this place in time? One minute she was applying and interpreting the law, and the next minute she was breaking the law, knowing full well she could go to prison for the rest of her life. She'd done it all for her daughter at first as she tried to save her and her granddaughter from an abusive husband and father, and the whole thing had grown legs. And now she was totally in charge of her underground railroad, saving women's and children's lives. Finally, she found her tongue. "Help me. Do whatever you have to do to find out what went wrong. Rescue the women."

Kathryn massaged her leg as she listened to Pearl and the others. This weather was killing her, and she was in so much pain with her leg that she wanted to cry. Perhaps another place, another time, she might have held her tongue, but not now.

"Well, you see, Pearl, here's the thing. I'm speaking for myself right at this moment, but I can almost guarantee that the others are thinking what I'm going to say. I'm tired of your bullshit with giving your people numbers and not sharing their names with us. This is the second time you've come to us to save your sorry ass, and we stepped up to the plate for you. Not this time, Miss Supreme Court Justice. You give us the people's names and let us decide how to handle it. Secrecy is a wonderful thing, and in your case, I doubly respect it. But there comes a time when that doesn't work, and that time is now. I am not putting my ass on the line for you again. Either you tell us everything, or I am outta here. As in now."

"Kathryn is right," Nikki said, standing up as Kathryn struggled to get out of her chair. Yoko and Isabelle pushed back their chairs to follow suit. Alexis looked around and did the same thing.

Annie cleared her throat and pushed out of her chair, followed by Myra.

"I do believe this is what you call fish or cut bait," Fergus hissed into Charles's ear.

"I do believe you are right, my friend," Charles hissed in return.

And then they were all on their feet, ready to leave the war room.

"Looks to me like you're on your own, Miss Supreme Court Justice," Kathryn snapped. "What's for dinner, Charles?"

"Dinner! You're worried about dinner! I can't believe this!" Pearl screamed.

Kathryn, always the most outspoken, always the one who moved at the speed of light, whirled around, her face a mask of pain at the quick movement. "Yes, Pearl, I'm worried about my dinner. It doesn't pay to worry about you because you are a selfish bitch who only thinks of herself. I'm sorry I have to admit I know you. We all came here because you said you needed us. That's what we do, we help people who can't help themselves. If you can't trust us, Pearl, whom can you trust? All you want is someone to save your sorry ass, then to show your appreciation, you throw obstacles in the path of those of us who are trying to help you. Well, screw you and the horse you rode in on!"

The room and the mood turned ugly, as everyone started to talk at once. Dennis West moved closer to Harry, his idol and protector. He was almost certain the next step would be bloodshed, and he didn't want to be the one doing the shedding.

Tears rolling down her cheeks, Pearl knew she was beaten. Either she gave up her secrets or she would be left alone to deal with the immediate crisis. "All right. All right! Please, all of you, sit down, and I'll tell you who . . . who the women are." She closed her eyes, made the sign of the cross on her chest, and let loose with a huge sigh.

"Her name is Amalie Laurent. The other woman's name is Rosalee Muno."

The women, the guys as well, stared at each other, then at Pearl. "Are those names supposed to strike fear in our hearts? I never heard of either one of them," Isabelle said.

"Who the hell are Amalie Laurent and Rosalee Muno?" Abner Tookus demanded. The others shrugged, not recognizing either name.

"The name sounds kind of familiar. Are those maiden names or married names?" Maggie asked. She looked at Ted. "Did we ever do a story on either woman, an interview?"

Ted frowned. "Sounds familiar. I'd say yes, but I can't recall specifically." He looked at Espinosa, who just shook his head that he didn't remember either.

Dennis was already tapping in the names for a Google search. A moment later he said, "Laurent is the face of a French cosmetic company. *La Natural.* She's married to . . . holy shit, she's married to Lincoln Moss. Everyone in the entire universe knows who Lincoln Moss is. *La Natural* is the crown jewel of the man's holdings." He held up his iPhone so the others could see what he'd just seen. "There is nothing on the Muno woman."

One by one, everyone returned to their seat and stared at Pearl. "Talk!" Annie demanded in a voice that left no room for silence.

Pearl swiped at her tears. "Five years ago, Rosalee Muno sought us out. We had helped a cousin of hers a while back. She talked to one of our people and said she needed help for her employer, who was afraid to come forward. She explained that Amalie was married to Lincoln Moss, and as Dennis said, everyone in the world knows who Lincoln Moss is. He had, according to Rosalee, been beating and abusing Amalie for years. She said Moss would never let Amalie out of his sight, and there was always security around her. There was no way for her to get away. Rosalee said she was worried that Amalie was going to do something to herself because she'd finally given up.

"It wasn't easy, and I can give you the details later, but we managed to get her and Rosalee to safety. Rosalee didn't want to go into the program, but we convinced her, knowing what we all do about Lincoln Moss, that it was in her best interest to go with Amalie.

"Right off the bat, we moved both women to Boise, Idaho, by way of our underground railroad. They stayed there decompressing for eight months. Over the next four months we transported them through four different states, and they stayed one month in each state, so we could monitor Moss's activities — which, by the way, were none. A year to the day, both women signed in to the Good Samaritan Clinic for just enough surgery to alter their appearances. Amalie was particularly hard because she is so beautiful. She is still beautiful, but she no longer looks as she did when she lived with Lincoln Moss. Rosalee was easy. Over the course of the year, she dropped thirty-five pounds. She was a bit . . . ah . . . overweight when she came to us. We changed their hairstyles, hair color, the usual. Add giving them colored contact lenses, which doesn't sound like much, but factor in the minor surgery, and you're looking at entirely different individuals.

"During all of that time, we had speech therapists working with Amalie so she could rid herself of her French accent. She now speaks English better than any of us. But . . . if she stresses out, she reverts to French, which is not a good thing. She loves

American slang and excels at it. Rosalee was no problem even though she's of Mexican descent. She was born here, and English is her natural voice."

"After the surgery, where did you put them?" Myra asked.

"In plain sight, in Arlington, Virginia. We had a little house we rented for the two of them. We got both of them part-time jobs, so they would blend in with the neighborhood. They drive ten-year-old Honda Civics. Rosalee works at Home Builders Depot part-time, and Amalie works in the local library part-time, in the reference department. They never go out to eat or to the movies or anyplace where they can be scrutinized. No one really pays attention to salespeople or librarians. In their spare time, they do a lot of gardening, raise some vegetables, grow a lot of flowers. They painted and decorated the little cottage to meet their needs. They were happy. Truly happy. Rosalee even had a boyfriend of sorts, a young man she met at her place of work. Nothing romantic, just good friends. Yes, the young man was vetted up one side and down the other, and he is exactly who he says he is, a college student working during the summer to help with his tuition.

"There is no computer at the cottage. We

explained that the temptation was too great, that Amalie might want to contact her family, what's left of it, back in France, even though she said she wouldn't. She swore to us on her mother's soul that she would not use the computers at the library. We lied and told her we would be able to tell if she did. As far as I know, she honored the promises she made to us.

"They attend church services every Sunday and blend in well in the little community they live in."

"I guess you gave them new identities," Harry said. "What are their new names?"

Pearl swallowed hard. When Kathryn banged her fist on the table, Pearl almost jumped out of her skin. "Amalie is now Patricia Olsen. Everyone calls her Patty. Rosalee is Emily Appleton. Before you can ask, the young man she is seeing is Jason Woods. He is studying to be an engineer and works part-time at the Home Builders Depot. He'll graduate next spring, possibly as early as December of this year. Now you know as much as I know." Pearl sagged in her chair as fresh tears rolled down her cheeks. No one rushed to comfort her.

"Is there a landline at the cottage?" Charles asked.

"No. They just have the special cells we

gave them, and they are monitored. I haven't had a chance to check with our people. This all happened so quick, and the top priority was to clear the clinic. No one is going to talk, I can guarantee that."

Kathryn leaned across the table. "Now how hard was that?"

"Let me tell you something, Kathryn, it was damn hard. I feel like I betrayed my own mother. I gave my word; I took an oath to all the people I try to protect. With my life if I have to. Don't you dare judge me. Don't you dare!"

"I would never judge you, Pearl. That's for you to do yourself. By not talking, you are the one who is putting the lives of your people in danger. We were not asking you to announce anything to the world at large, just to the people you came to for help. You did the right thing by telling us what we need to know," Kathryn said. Then, because Kathryn was Kathryn, she had to add, "Besides, it was time for you to come off that high horse you rode in here on."

Pearl didn't trust herself to say anything, so she kept quiet and simply nodded. She did, however, reach across the table to shake Kathryn's hand.

"Charles, for the third time, what's for dinner?" Kathryn demanded.

"Ah, yes, dinner. How does spaghetti and meatballs sound? Fergus made bread this morning, that crusty Italian you love so much, Kathryn. And fresh peach ice cream. I was up early this morning and at the farmers' market for the first load of peaches. I'm not going to guarantee the spaghetti and meatballs because Annie and Myra called in their order a little late in the day. I do guarantee that it will be tasty, though."

He looked at his watch, and said, "Fergus and I will go topside and you all can stay here and strategize if you like. Dinner will be in an hour."

The others looked at one another and by nods agreed to stay in the war room to talk and try to work out a plan.

Dennis West whispered in Harry's ear. "Harry, what do you think about Lincoln Moss?"

"What I think, kid, is the bigger they are, the harder they fall."

"Yeah, yeah, that's what I think too. Oh, boy, this promises to be a thrill a minute, don't you agree, Harry?"

"Oh, yeah," Harry drawled.

CHAPTER 3

Charles looked across the room at the bank of clocks that gave the time all over the world. It was 6:00 A.M. in Virginia. He was tired, but it was a good kind of tired. He and Fergus had worked through the night, with only two short breaks up in the kitchen for coffee, just to stay awake.

"I think we're done here, Fergus. We need to decompress, shower, snatch a few hours of sleep, eat something, and be back down here by ten. Does that work for you?"

Fergus sighed. Charles would get no argument from him. He was bone tired. He'd had no real idea until now how Charles and the Vigilantes worked. Now he knew what went into a mission, and he was glad to be a part of it. He crossed his fingers, the way he had when he was a child, that he could keep up. He stapled the last packet he'd just taken out of the printer and slipped it into a bright blue folder. They were ready to be handed out to the girls once the morning meeting got under way.

"You going home or staying here, Fergus?" Charles asked, as they mounted the moss-covered steps that let them out of the dungeon and up to the main part of the house.

"I'm going home. Annie went back home last night because she said she had a lot of thinking to do and wanted to sleep in her own bed. I'll come back with her for the meeting.

"Charles, do you think Pearl can hold it together. She seemed pretty fragile to me last evening."

Charles looked at his old friend, concern on his face. "I am . . . not exactly worried, but I must admit that I am concerned. If anyone can shake Pearl out of it, Annie and Myra can. What really concerns me is that everything is in Pearl's head. If anything were to happen to her, all her hard work would collapse, and I don't even want to think about what would happen then. I told Myra to try to convince her to call Lizzie Fox. Pearl trusts Lizzie. There has to be a legend so that down the road, if the unthinkable happens, the railroad and the people are protected.

"Pearl does not want to give that up. I get

that, but right now, she is not thinking clearly. If we're successful in this mission, then I think there is a very good possibility that Pearl will allow Lizzie to document everything. That's just my opinion, Fergus."

Fergus rubbed at the stubble on his cheeks as he stared out at the approaching dawn. "I know that Annie is worried. She was mumbling something about first it was Nellie, and now it's Pearl. You know Annie; when those bees in her bonnet start to swarm, you never can figure out what's going to happen. If she gets ticked off enough, she might shoot her."

Charles laughed.

"So, on that note, I will now take my leave. See you around ten. Don't start without us." Charles waved good-bye.

Feeling a nudge to his leg he looked down to see Lady, who was inching him toward the door. Her pups were right behind her. The last thing he wanted to do right now was to go outside with the dogs, but he did it anyway. All he wanted to do was sleep. "Make it quick, okay?"

The dogs were back inside within minutes, waiting for breakfast even if it was two hours early. Outside to pee meant you came in and got fed. The dogs sat on their haunches and waited expectantly as Charles sighed

49

and did what he had to do. He then bolted up the back staircase and headed for the shower. Myra could clean up the bowls.

Charles's last conscious thought as his head hit the pillow was that perhaps this mission was not going to be the slam dunk he originally thought it would be. When you take on a man like Lincoln Moss, all you could hope for was a lot of luck.

The July sun was bright at ten o'clock in the morning as the gang arrived almost simultaneously. They greeted each other in the parking area, then moved on to the back door, which Myra was holding open. More conversation ensued about the rain's finally being over, how everything looked so scrubbed and clean the way only Mother Nature could do it. The flowers looked perky, according to Yoko, and she bent down to snap off a bright yellow Gerbera daisy that she immediately stuck behind her ear. Harry grinned.

"Coffee, anyone? We have a little time before we have to be downstairs. Just so you know, Charles and Fergus worked through the night, snatched a few hours of sleep, and are hard at it again."

Annie poured coffee as the gang milled around. "I don't see Pearl," Kathryn said.

"Is she coming? Please, stop looking at me like that. I just said what had to be said yesterday instead of pussyfooting around. If you're upset with me, I can leave right now." She waited until everyone assured her that they agreed with her, at which point Lady barked, announcing Pearl's arrival.

By ten thirty, all the sisters and their counterparts were seated at the new table, which now accommodated all of them. Everyone appeared bright-eyed and expectant. Even Pearl looked refreshed, which was a relief to everyone in the room.

Charles and Fergus, his new right hand, were on the dais. The large screen came to life as Lady Justice beamed down on the occupants. For some reason, the women always smiled when she took over the room. Kathryn always saluted her, a crisp, no-nonsense salute that would have been the envy of any military officer had one been there to see it.

In front of each occupant was a bright blue folder. The rule was that you did not open your folder until Charles gave the word. That gave him the time to present his PowerPoint display, which made it easier to follow what was in the folders and generated fewer questions.

The overhead lights dimmed. The slide

show began. "This first picture is of Amalie Laurent. Also known as Mrs. Lincoln Moss. This is one of the professional pictures that are used by her husband's cosmetic company. As Pearl told us, she is the face of the company, which is the crown jewel of all his holdings. In other words, a multi-billion-dollar company. This next picture is of Amalie Laurent after her surgery, when she became known as Patricia Olsen. At first glance, it looks like the picture was simply tweaked. Look closely. Do any of you think if you had known the original Amalie that this new Patricia would fool you? Then ask yourself if you were her husband would this new picture fool you? We'll discuss this later.

"The next picture is of Rosalee Muno. I'm sorry for the grainy quality, but we have to work with what we have. She was, according to Pearl, Amalie's personal maid. In the original, she was on the plump side, plump cheeks, double chin, and around thirty-five pounds overweight. As you can see in the picture after surgery she looks very different. The plump cheeks are gone, the nose is thinner, and the double chin is gone, as are all those extra pounds. She's quite slim now. Her hair is also different, shorter, less curly, and a light brown. Ask yourself had you known her before the surgery, would you recognize her the way she looks today?

"The third picture is of Lincoln Moss, who needs no introduction. As you can see, he is a very virile man who is almost fifty-five now. I believe the term to describe him in today's lingo would be *ripped*. He sports a tan all year long. He is a sportsman, he sails, he snow skis, water-skis, hikes, runs, works out with a personal trainer. Doesn't drink or smoke. Knows how to make money. He's almost a standard fixture at the White House. He comes and goes as he pleases. It's rumored that he and POTUS have cell phones that no one else has. They can communicate with each other without the Secret Service eavesdropping. He and POTUS have been lifelong friends. It is whispered among many that Lincoln Moss is the real leader of the free world, not Gabriel Knight, our President. According to some, Moss made Gabriel Knight a very rich man by investing his money and making him a quasi-partner in *La Natural*. There seems to be a mixed opinion about who the real brainy investor is or was. Some reports say it was Knight, and others insist it was Moss. Neither man will confirm or deny, so that's where that's at. At least for now. In the end, I don't see it as all that important.

"Lincoln Moss likes to keep his life

private. Not much is available for public consumption on his marriage. There was a big hullabaloo when he married his wife because she was so gorgeous and photogenic. Now here is the odd thing about that marriage. Anytime in the past, when there was a White House function, Mrs. Moss was usually in France, where she was born and raised. Moss would say she had prior commitments, was doing photo shoots or traveling because she is the face of *La Natural*. I could only find two actual pictures of her at the White House. But she was there four times that are documented.

"It's also documented that Lincoln Moss travels frequently to France, sometimes three times a month. To see his famous wife, of course, the story goes. So that tongues didn't wag I have to assume. Mrs. Moss has never given an interview to anyone, not even to the French magazines or newspapers. I have to assume that's all part of her mystique. I'm told that it would be quite a coup to anyone who could land an interview with her. And the prize and price for the lucky reporter who managed to get an interview with both Moss and his wife would be the ability to pretty much name his or her own price.

"That's about all I was able to come up

with. Other than that the man is beyond wealthy. He's also a big philanthropist. As in *big*. People, and that means reporters, too, tread lightly around Lincoln Moss. If anyone gets too pushy or too inquisitive, they get a visit from some very important people and are pretty much never heard from again. I want to stress that while they are seen, they are not heard from again. The White House carries a really big stick, and if you're best buds with the big guy, you got it made in the shade. Plain and simple, Lincoln Moss is off-limits."

Nikki laughed out loud. "I think what you meant to say, Charles, is that Lincoln Moss is off-limits to the masses but not to the Vigilantes." The others hooted with laughter.

Charles playfully slapped at his forehead. "Whatever was I thinking? That's exactly what I meant to say."

"It's all right, dear, you were up all night working for us. We understand these little lapses," Myra said.

"We'll be starting out on the plus side. We have the power of the *Post* behind us. No one can shut us down, not even the leader of the free world no matter if his name is Gabriel Knight or Lincoln Moss."

This time the group clapped and hooted

their approval.

"Let's not forget Jack Sparrow, our friend at the FBI," Kathryn said.

"And our gold shields," Maggie chirped. She rubbed her hands together in glee. "Where and when do we start?"

"Oh, good Lord!" Pearl bellowed. "Look at this! Dear God, how did this happen?" She held up her phone to show the same picture of Amalie Laurent that Charles had just used in his PowerPoint presentation. "It was on the cover of this week's edition of that tabloid, *In the Know,* which came out three days ago. They have a circulation of around two million and are front and center at every checkout counter in every grocery store in the nation. I read that somewhere," Pearl said, panic ringing in her voice.

Annie let loose with a shrill whistle. The room went silent. "Just because Amalie Laurent's picture is in the paper doesn't have to mean anything. When it's a slow news day, they print my picture. Just to fill up space. I know how that works since I own the *Post.* Is there an article? What does it say?"

"I don't know; 390 just sent the picture."

Kathryn's fist slammed down on the table. "I thought we agreed no more numbers! Who the hell is 390?"

Pearl flinched as she looked around the table. They all wore the same expressions Kathryn wore. "Audrey Blake is 390. She was one of my first 'saves.' She's my third in command after 389, my second save. Her name is Beverly Hopkins," Pearl said as she saw Kathryn raise her arm to bring it down on the table again.

"Don't just sit there like some ninny, Pearl. Send her a text and ask her to send you the article or have her fax it here. You have the fax number." Myra looked at Charles, and said, "Give her the number again, dear." Charles obliged, as Pearl's nervous fingers tapped out a text.

Pearl read off the return text that said Audrey had to make a copy of the article, then she would scan it to Charles, who would then put it up on the big screen for them all to see.

Ten minutes later, they were all looking at the beautiful woman named Amalie Laurent, aka Patricia Olsen. The text was a rehash of her modeling career, her marriage to Lincoln Moss, and her passion for privacy. Then came the clunker in the form of a question as Isabelle put it. *Why would one of the most beautiful women in the world want to undergo plastic surgery to change her appearance? If true, who is going to be the next face of* La Natural? *Our intrepid report-ers here at* In the Know *want to know.*

The article went on to say that the thousand-dollar monthly bonus and a five-year free subscription to the paper for hot news would go to someone named Jane Petrie, but only when she submitted proof that surgery had taken place. Translation — before and after pictures that had not materialized as the paper went to press.

Readers were invited to call in, write in, or text if they had a sighting of the beautiful model. All sightings when confirmed would receive a year's free subscription to the paper.

"Who the hell is Jane Petrie?" Ted asked.

"I'm checking Google and Facebook right now," Dennis said, his thumbs flying over the small keyboard in front of him.

All eyes turned to Pearl. "Do you recognize the name, Pearl?" Myra asked.

"No. But that doesn't mean anything. Maybe it's a made-up name, which would make sense if she's selling confidential information."

"That makes sense," Jack agreed.

All eyes turned to Dennis, who was mumbling as fast as he was typing. "She's a nurse. She's single, and she works out of a registry that fills in for medical help on a temporary basis. She's twenty-eight. According to Facebook, she says she never married, and that's by her choice. Frees her up to take a trip to Europe twice a year. She lives in a town house in Crystal City and drives a Corvette. On-call nurses must make good money for her to afford her lifestyle. She graduated from Catholic University with a business degree but said that wasn't for her, so she then went to nursing school, and said it is very rewarding. She claims to be a health-food nut and also an exercise nut. Those are her words. Her whole life is here on Facebook. And here is her picture!" he said triumphantly. "I'm uploading it to you, Charles. You can put it on the big screen."

What the group saw was a smiling, attractive, young woman with short, dark hair sporting a sweatband and doing a stretching exercise with her foot up on a bench along the Tidal Basin.

"What's the name of the medical registry?" Myra asked.

"Around the Clock Medical Registry," Dennis responded.

"I know exactly what that is and where it is. Nellie used them for Elias when one of his caregivers would call in sick. No, they do not pay well. Nellie said she felt sorry for them and always tipped well. She did say she liked the people they sent to her," Myra said.

"Maybe Miss Petrie is independently wealthy," Alexis said.

"Nope. She said her father and mother are schoolteachers. She has no grandparents and comes from a big family, four brothers and two sisters. I don't see any extra money there. She must be getting it from somewhere else," Dennis said.

"Blackmail?" Espinosa said.

"Those tabloids pay big bucks for inside information. They might say they just pay a few thousand, but in reality try fifty thousand. We did a series of articles on tabloids about four years ago, right, Ted?" Ted nodded. "Tabloid journalism is nothing like the kind of journalism we practice at the *Post*," Maggie said virtuously.

Annie sniffed to show what she thought of Maggie's comment in regard to tabloid journalism. "I think I can personally guarantee this is the last picture and article you will see in that particular tabloid or any other tabloid for that matter. The minute Lincoln Moss finds out, if he hasn't already, it's history."

Charles weighed in. "I would not want to be Miss Jane Petrie right now. If she hasn't already been grilled to within an inch of her life, she will be shortly. It's a good thing, Pearl, that you cleaned out the clinic and sanitized it." The others nodded. Pearl just looked miserable.

"Which now brings up the question of did Lincoln Moss find his wife or did his wife leave on her own. The reason I say that is think about this. Amalie and Rosalee have to buy groceries. That's where the bulk of tabloids are sold. Do any of us really think that Lincoln Moss goes to the grocery store? I don't. I think, and this is just my own personal opinion, that the ladies saw the paper at the checkout stand and took it on the lam. All on their own. Possibly with the help of Rosalee's boyfriend, who works at Home Builders Depot, where she also works," Nikki said.

"Honey, I think you're right. That makes more sense than anything else we heard. That means to us, at least for now, that the two women are safe and not in Moss's clutches," Jack said.

Pearl sighed mightily. "I so hope you are right, Jack. But how long can they stay where they are without any real help? Think about the resources that Moss has at his disposal."

"*Think young,* people. Jason, that's his

name, right, doesn't think like we do? He and his friends are social-media fiends. They live on the Internet. They know how to do things and stuff that just boggles our minds, and they have a whole army out there just waiting to help them with a simple request," Jack said.

"Jack couldn't be more right," Abner Tookus said. "Y'all want me to hack into Miz Petrie's financials?"

"I thought you'd never ask," Annie drawled. "Do it!"

"What's our next move?" Nikki asked.

Charles cleared his throat. "I just made our next move. I sent Avery Snowden a text telling him to pick up Jane Petrie. Do not be surprised if she's gone and disappeared."

"Oh! A snatch and grab!" Dennis said, his eyes sparking with excitement.

"It's only a snatch and grab when you manage the grab part, kid," Ted said.

"Does that mean Petrie is in danger?" Dennis asked. No one answered him.

"I hope it does!" Pearl Barnes said spitefully. "I hope if she's guilty, she pays forever for what she's done. And all for money, so she can drive a Corvette and go to Europe twice a year! I'd like to see her tarred and feathered. Think!" she screeched. "Who else has she scammed or blackmailed? How many poor souls out there were at her mercy? She's a damn nurse!" This last was said as though that was the beginning and end of it all. Then Pearl shook her head and mumbled an apology everyone knew she didn't mean.

"Okayyyy, moving right along here, people. What's our next move?" Kathryn asked.

"I think we need to figure that one out. We are open to ideas, suggestions, and plans," Charles said. "The floor is open, people!"

CHAPTER 4

The gang broke for lunch at one o'clock. Charles left the group to their haggling and plotting to go, as he referred to it, topside to prepare a luncheon they could eat outdoors on the terrace. Fergus went along to help.

Left to their own devices, the group listened in awe as Abner rattled on about Jane Petrie's financial status.

"That was pretty quick, Abner," Ted said.

Abner beamed. "What can I tell you. When you're good, you're good, and I am *good.* The only thing I haven't done yet is to get her IRS file. The young lady is pretty much an open book. Doesn't appear to be hiding anything. So, sit back and listen up. Right now, as of today, Miss Petrie has thirty-eight hundred dollars in her personal checking account. Out of this account she pays a hefty mortgage of seventeen hundred dollars a month. She pays her utilities, cell phone, water, insurance, and a car payment that is nine hundred eighty-two dollars a month. Plus her credit cards. She has two, a Visa and an American Express that she pays off in full every month. Some months she takes it right down to the wire with an ending balance of five dollars. She deposits checks every three or four days. I assume paychecks from private clients plus checks from the Around the Clock Medical Registry. They usually run around seven to eight thousand a month. All of that in and of itself is not something out of the ordinary. What is out of the ordinary is her brokerage account, which is quite robust. She opened it three years ago with a deposit of thirty-three thousand dollars. All told, since she opened the account, she has made twenty-seven deposits, and the lowest deposit was for five thousand dollars. The highest was sixty-two thousand dollars, which was made ten days ago. Unusual amounts, to be sure, and all even amounts. Twice a year she takes out between five and seven thousand dollars, which coincide with her trips to Europe. She transfers the money to her regular account, then does the trip on her credit cards so she can rack up frequent flyer miles. On her return, she pays it all off. Right now, as of today, the lady has

$387,444.12 in her brokerage account. Not bad for a single, twenty-eight-year-old nurse.

"By the way, just as an aside to all this, Miss Petrie passed the security check the Medical Registry did on her when she signed on with them. She has a clean record as far as their records go. Not even one complaint. I checked her driving record, no tickets, no points against her license."

Pearl took a page from Kathryn's playbook and banged her fist down on the table. "That little sneak!" she bellowed. "Now what?" she demanded.

"You tell me," Abner shot back. "I'm just a hacker. What you do with the information is up to you. I laid it all on your doorstep."

"This might sound like a stupid question, but what does she buy on her credit cards?" Alexis asked.

Abner laughed. "The same thing all women buy. Clothes, shoes, handbags, cosmetics, and she buys a lot of *La Natural* products. At six hundred dollars a pop for some kind of magic eye cream that will reduce fine lines and wrinkles." Isabelle pelted him with a spitball. He laughed out loud.

"Send that all to Charles, and when he comes back, he can print us all a copy for our files," Annie said.

"Next!" Myra said.

"I think we should pay a visit to *In the Know* and see what we can pick up there," Maggie said. "How about if Nikki and Kathryn show up and say they have a sighting and are there to claim the prize. Its headquarters are in Alexandria. They can be there and back in a few hours, depending on how talkative the editor in chief is. If they don't get anywhere, then Ted, Espinosa, Dennis, and I can take a crack at them. Hey, you could do it right after lunch."

Nikki looked at Kathryn, who grinned. "Let's do it!" Kathryn laughed out loud as she bobbed her head up and down.

"Someone call Mr. Snowden. We should have heard something by now. Unless he called Charles personally," Myra said.

"I'll call him. He hates me," Jack said. "I won't let him slough me off either." The others sat back and listened to the one-sided dialogue that made some of them titter. The end result was Miss Petrie, according to Avery Snowden, left for Europe last night. And the reason he knows this is because he ran into Miss Petrie's neighbor, a studly young man who works out religiously at Gold's Gym who said he was house sitting until she got back. He said it was an arrangement they've had for a few years. He also said she moved her trip up early this summer because she normally didn't go till September. Said she needed a break from the horrible humidity and foul weather. Whatever the reason, she's gone. At least for now."

"Abner, dear, is it possible for you to . . . um . . . freeze Ms. Petrie's brokerage account?"

Abner smiled. "Is that a question or a suggestion?"

"Both!" Myra snapped, before Annie could get her tongue to work.

"No problem. Consider it done. I love screwing up everyone's paperwork as much as I love giving away other people's money." Isabelle blew him a kiss to show her approval.

Fergus appeared suddenly and announced that lunch was ready on the terrace. Everyone beelined for the stairs.

Lunch was BLTs, with the lettuce and tomatoes from Charles's garden, the bacon so crisp you could snap it in two. The tomatoes were vine-ripened to perfection, the lettuce crunchy, and it was all served on homemade sourdough bread. Pitchers of frosty sweet apple tea and lemonade were the beverages of the day.

Charles was about to make an announcement when Myra cut him off. "We know, dear, Jack called Mr. Snowden. Miss Petrie has flown the coop at least for now. What you don't know is that Abner checked her financials. Abner, tell Charles and Fergus what you found and what you did. Which pretty much guarantees that Miss Petrie will have to return to the States to straighten out her account. She does have credit cards, so I guess she could max them out. Abner, did you happen to notice what her limits are?"

"I did notice. I guess I should have mentioned that. Her Visa has a fifty-five-thousand-dollar credit limit. She has a platinum American Express that pretty much has no limit. She has an excellent credit history and pays off her cards in full at the end of the month. If she had to live off the cards for six months or so, she would not have a problem. What she would do after that is anyone's guess."

"It is easy to get lost in Europe," Isabelle said. The others nodded.

"We take a wait-and-see attitude on that little matter then," Annie said. "Avery will be on top of it." She then filled Charles and Fergus in on Nikki and Kathryn's plans for the afternoon.

"Are you sure that's wise?" Charles asked.

"Wise or not, that's what they're going to do. We didn't put this to a vote or even discuss it, but I'm bringing it up now, and yes, Charles, I know all about your rule of not discussing business while eating, but I don't care. Do you understand, I-don't-care?" Myra said. There wasn't much for Charles to do other than nod. Any fool could clearly interpret the glaring looks he was getting from everyone.

"I would like Jack, Harry, and Abner to go out to Amalie's house and see what they can pick up in the way of clues. I want a male eye on it. If Lincoln Moss sent anyone out there after Amalie and Rosalee, it would be men. Men are not as meticulous as women, and I mean no offense. It's just the way it is. I'll give you directions on how to get to the house," Pearl said.

"Count me out," Abner said. "I have too much going on here, and I'm on a roll. Jack and Harry can handle things without me." A second later, he was in his own zone, typing at the speed of light.

"Ah, action at last," Jack said, smacking his hands together. "I'm done eating, so let's hit the road, Harry. How long will it take us to get there, Pearl?"

"About a half hour depending on traffic."

She immediately started to write down the directions on a sheet of paper she ripped from a legal tablet. She handed it over to Jack, who quickly read through them. "Appreciate the map, Pearl. I know where this is, actually. I had a couple of witnesses who lived in that general area during my second stint as a prosecutor. Guess we'll see you when we see you. Sorry to be leaving the cleanup to all of you."

"Yeah, Kathryn and I are sorry, too. See y'all in a bit." Nikki laughed as she reached down for her shoulder bag.

"I guess that means the rest of us go back to the war room and see what else we can come up with," Myra said.

"Not so fast! Fergus and I prepared lunch. We do not do cleanup. We'll just sit here and have another glass of tea while you tidy up my kitchen."

"What about dinner?" Annie grumbled. "I didn't see any preparations under way."

"That's because we will be barbecuing. Dennis agreed to it when he arrived. Now, shoo! Let Fergus and me sit here and digest our lunch."

The parking lot was huge, and Nikki had no problem finding a parking space. The moment she cut off the engine, Kathryn looked at her, then at the eight-floor glass-and-steel building. "Guess tabloid journalism really pays. *In the Know* uses all eight floors."

"That's because it's a political-scandal rag. Everyone wants to know all the politicians' dirty little secrets. They aren't really into the Hollywood scene, like most of the tabloids, unless there's some politician involved. Think about it, Kathryn, gossip- and scandal-wise, it doesn't get any better than when one of the world's top models, who just happens to be married to Lincoln Moss, hits the gossip circuit."

Kathryn got out of the car and waited for Nikki to lock it. She hopped around for a few minutes, aware that Nikki was watching her. "Yeah, it hurts. No sense lying about it. Now that the dampness is lifting, and the sun is out, it's not aching as bad. Before you can ask, I don't know what I'm going to do. Between you and me, Nikki, I think I'm allergic to this damn titanium bar they put in my leg. They say no. It's my leg, but I'm seriously considering having it taken out and letting the leg heal on its own. So I walk with a limp for the rest of my life, so what. I always thought I was tough, but the pain is really getting to me. The therapy just aggravates the whole deal. I'm fed up. Okay, enough of my whining. Let's go see what the dude who runs this paper can tell us."

Nikki linked her arm with Kathryn's as a show of moral support. "It goes without saying, Kathryn, that if there's anything I can do, and I know I speak for the others, just ask. You have to ask, Kathryn. Can you do that?"

Kathryn looked at her old friend. "Maybe before the answer would have been no, but not now. Now I know when to ask, and I won't have any trouble doing it. I'm done with all the 'why me' pity parties I've been having. C'mon, let's see what *In the Know* has to say for itself."

The two women walked across the parking lot to a wide stone walkway boarded with low evergreen ground cover and colorful flowers. "Maintenance must cost a fortune," Nikki said, looking around. Kathryn nodded. "And this building had to cost beaucoup bucks. I think I read it was built twelve years ago. Looks brand-new. No one told us who actually owns this rag, do you realize that?"

"Well now that you mention it, yeah. Probably one of the other tabloids, and this is just a spin-off to throw everyone off."

Nikki held the door for Kathryn, and they walked into a wonderland of a grotto of waterfalls and live trees and every flower known to man. Soft music was being piped in from somewhere, soothing sounds along with the waterfall. Probably to soothe the minds of those here to rat out others.

Groups of people were sitting everywhere, chatting, taking notes, or just relaxing. In the center was a circular desk made out of colored stone that was so eye-catching both women gasped as they looked around to see all the mini-rainbows reflected on the walls from the overhead lighting.

The woman behind the desk looked up and smiled. She was not beautiful; nor was she homely. She was pleasant-looking. Her hair was done nicely, her makeup was flaw-less, and she was dressed conservatively. She wore Sarah Palin glasses. "Can I help you?"

"I hope so." Nikki smiled in return. "We'd like to see Mr. Goodwin, and no, we do not have an appointment, but it is important. We're here to claim our prize."

The woman whose name tag said she was Pamela Warren said, "And what prize would that be?"

"The one about the model," Kathryn said.

"Oh, I see. Please, have a seat, and I'll see if Mr. Goodwin is free."

The girls didn't bother to take a seat; instead, they walked around looking at all the marble and statues as well as trying to get a fix on all the people in the lobby. Nikki whirled around in time to see Pamela Warren motion for them to return to the desk.

"Mr. Goodwin says he can give you ten minutes because he's late now for another appointment. Will that work for you, ladies?" She beamed a high-wattage smile that pretty much said it better be okay because there were no other options.

"Sure," Kathryn drawled. "I know how to talk fast. The really big question is how long it will take Mr. Goodwin to write out the check. That might eat into the time frame." Pamela Warren didn't smile at this snappy comeback. Instead, she said, "Someone will be here momentarily to escort you to Mr. Goodwin's office."

Warren was as good as her word. A spiffy young man in a Savile Row suit, with messy hair that was all the fashion and manicured nails, appeared from a hidden doorway and motioned them to follow him. He had a fussy walk and kept waving his hands as he led the way down a well-lit corridor with framed pictures of various front pages of past editions of *In the Know.* When he reached the last door at the end of the hallway, he knocked softly. Then he opened

75

the door and stepped aside. The door swished shut on well-oiled hinges.

It was a white-and-black office with white furniture, black carpeting with not a speck of lint, glass-topped tables, and overhead lighting. A black vase held two dozen beautiful white roses and was centered in the middle of the glass-topped coffee table. The desk at the end of the room was a slab of glass on stainless-steel columns. Not a comfortable room at all, but then, as Nikki said later, maybe that was the point.

Joel Goodwin got up and walked around the glass desk. He introduced himself, as did his visitors. He motioned for them to take a seat in two low-slung, furry-looking, black chairs that faced his desk. He sat back down and leaned forward. "Miss Warren said you're here to claim the prize. If you're referring to the prize for information on the model whose picture we ran in the current edition, I'm sorry to tell you that was a big mistake on our part. We're retracting it all in next week's edition. As much as I hate to admit it, we were scammed. I am, however, authorized to give you a free year's subscription to the paper if you fill out this form," he said, sliding two single sheets of paper across his shiny see-through desk.

"Well, that's not fair. What do you mean

you were scammed? A paper like yours! I was counting on taking a vacation with that money," Kathryn snarled. Nikki worked her face into an expression of disgust.

"We even brought our proof, and we came all the way from Delaware, and we didn't come this far for a free subscription to your paper. We acted in good faith, so you need to pay us," Nikki said.

"It wasn't a valid story, ladies. Like I said, we were scammed, and we're going to be making a sincere apology in the next edition."

"Who said you were scammed? How did you find that out? How do we know you aren't lying to us because you just don't want to pay us? Don't go thinking we're stupid, Mr. Goodwin. We can go to the Attorney General and a real paper like the *Post* and tell them all about this. This is fraud! We want our money," Kathryn snarled again.

Goodwin worked his fingers under his collar, and the girls could see he was starting to sweat despite the fact that the room was ice-cold.

"Look, ladies, I'm sorry, but I can't help you. We pulled the story. Because there is no story. I can't help you. How about a two-year subscription?"

Nikki laughed. "Nope! How did you find out you were scammed? You must have thought you had a story last week when you put that model's name on the front page. Tell us what changed, and maybe we'll let you off the hook. I said maybe," Nikki said, menace ringing in her voice.

Goodwin sighed. These two were trouble, he could smell it. Common sense told him to up the free subscription to five years and get them out of the office as quickly as possible, but one look at the tall, mouthy one, and he knew that wasn't going to work.

"Look, two days ago, right after the picture ran, two men from the government showed up here and told me to pull it. That's the beginning and the end of it. That's all I can tell you. How about a five-year subscription?"

Kathryn laughed in his face. She looked at Nikki, who nodded. At the same moment, both women reached into their handbags and pulled out their gold shields. They leaned halfway across the desk to make sure Goodwin could read the fine print on the infamous shields. "Talk!"

Goodwin turned pasty white. He licked at his lips and struggled to say something. "What do you people want from me? I told those two men everything I know."

"What two men? Be specific. Did they have ID?" Nikki demanded.

"Lady, men like the two who came here do not need to *show* ID. They are their own ID. Their looks, and their demeanor, said it all. They talked into their goddamn sleeves. Who does that? Secret Service, that's who. They looked like twins. Brush-cut hair, aviator glasses, Hugo Boss suits, polished shoes, and a bulge under their jackets. They were packing heat. They simply and politely asked for the file and for the name of the tipster. I gave it to them after they told me they could shut this paper down in the blink of an eye. Let me tell you something, dark glasses or not, I knew they meant it; I didn't have to see their eyes.

"Why are you here? Don't you people talk to each other? What else can I tell you?"

"Did you give them Miss Petrie's name?" Kathryn asked.

"Yes, but I called her the minute they left. She's given me some good stuff over the past few years. I figured I owed her that much. I told her to split," Goodwin said defiantly. "I didn't do anything wrong."

"You paid her sixty-six thousand dollars for the picture and whatever she told you, right?"

"Since you already know all that, why are

you asking me again? The answer is yes. The check cleared the moment we confirmed the info was legit. She was . . . is to get another sixty-six thousand dollars if we managed to get the after-surgery picture. She said she was almost positive she could get her hands on it. No, I do not have it, no, she did not get it. At least as far as I know, she did not get it. That's all I can tell you."

"You said the two men were Secret Service. Are you basing that on anything other than the fact that Secret Service agents wear sleeve mikes?"

Goodwin thought about it for a moment. He shook his head. "Just my own personal opinion. Maybe I watch too much TV. Look, everyone in this town knows that guy Lincoln Moss is married to the model on the front page. He didn't want her picture splashed all over a tabloid, so he sent the President's goons here. That's my feeling. Can I prove it? Hell no I can't. It's done, the retraction is ready to go.

"Oh, wait a minute, there is one other thing. The day after those men were here, a messenger came by with a letter. Inside was a check for sixty-six thousand dollars drawn on the Royal Bank of Scotland. Pam told me earlier the check cleared this morning."

"So, you're good with all this?" Nikki asked, the lawyer in her surfacing. "By that I mean you're okay with someone's dictating to you what you print in your paper. Aren't you up on your First Amendment rights, and all that freedom-of-the-press stuff, Mr. Goodwin?"

"I think I value peace of mind and nights that I can sleep and not worry about someone out there possibly, I say possibly, trying to do me harm. In the scheme of things, that model, and did she or didn't she have plastic surgery, mean nothing to me compared to my own well-being. Call me selfish. I don't care. Does that answer your question about First Amendment rights and freedom of the press?"

Nikki and Kathryn stared at Goodwin with cold, unblinking eyes. Nikki toyed with the gold shield she was holding in her hand. Seeing what she was doing, Kathryn spit on hers and then proceeded to shine the shield on her pant leg.

"You have nothing to do with those two guys, do you?" Goodwin asked nervously.

"That would be correct," Nikki said.

"Does that mean you're ah . . . legal and they aren't?"

"That would be correct," Nikki lied.

"Well, in that case, I guess I might as well

turn over what I kept, which is a copy of everything. I'm not a complete fool. But, I want a receipt. No receipt, no nothing."

Nikki waved her shield in the air. Kathryn dropped hers on the desk. It landed with a solid *thunk.* They waited until Goodwin pressed a buzzer on his desk and spoke into it. "Pam, bring me that file I had you put in the safe the other day."

"How many copies did you make?" Kathryn asked.

"Just one. I'm not lying. You can have it, but you have to sign off on it."

Kathryn laughed, and so did Nikki.

"How about we just take you with us, and you can explain all of this to some other very important people. Oh, my goodness, will you look at the time? We've overstayed our ten minutes. What's it going to be, Mr. Goodwin?"

Pam Warren entered the office and placed a manila folder in front of her boss. She scurried out quickly and closed the door quietly behind her.

Goodwin inched the file closer to Nikki, using a pencil. He didn't touch it at all.

Nikki stuffed the file in her carry bag. "We'll be in touch, Mr. Goodwin. Now, should you hear from anyone else, call this number." She handed him a card with

Abner Tookus's burn-phone number, which was untraceable. "We can see ourselves out."

Neither woman spoke until they were outside. "That was almost too easy," Kathryn said.

"Yeah, it was." Nikki grinned. "Sometimes it just works out that way."

CHAPTER 5

Harry Wong brought the Ducati to a full stop. Both he and Jack hopped off and looked around. Two nondescript Hondas sat side by side in the driveway. Both were locked. One was black and the other a silver gray. They looked clean and well maintained.

It appeared to be a quiet neighborhood even in mid-July, when people were usually outdoors talking to neighbors or working in their yards. No one was about that either man could see. "Maybe it's a working-class neighborhood. It's a cul-de-sac, not that that means anything, but I like the area. Look, Harry, they even have sidewalks, and the maple trees are old. They look like big old beach umbrellas, and they shade the second floors of all the houses on the block. I counted the houses, there are nine. Four on each side and the one in the middle. I'd say they were built in the fifties, what do you think, Harry?"

"The picture windows would seem to indicate that time period. Sixteen hundred square feet would be my guess. What we call starter homes today. You have the key Pearl gave you, right?"

"Right here in my hot little hand. Let's not stand around here too long so as not to arouse suspicion. I'm thinking these two ladies didn't get much company, and two guys on a hot-rod motorcycle might raise some red flags."

Harry mumbled something that sounded like, "Then pick up your feet and move."

The door opened silently. The moment they were inside, Jack turned around and shot the dead bolt. There was no need to turn on any lights. The bright summer sunshine coming through the huge picture window lit up the entire room. The sheer curtains couldn't contain the sunlight.

The living room was simply furnished. Four club chairs that swiveled, no sofa. Two lamps and a small coffee table with a few gardening magazines and a bowl of hard candy stood in front of two of the chairs. A twenty-inch television hung on the wall, directly in line with two of the club chairs. The room was painted a soft dove gray, and the matching area carpet was also gray, with a few splashes of a design that looked like a fern frond. Plain, simple. Neat and tidy. No sign of trash or dust.

A small, narrow, circular stairway was tucked into the farthest corner. "Toss you for it," Jack said. "Heads you take the second floor, tails I take it. Call it, Harry."

"Heads!"

Jack flipped the coin. He laughed. "It's all yours, pal. Don't miss anything. Women are tricky, we both know that. Look for unlikely hiding places. I'm not saying either one of those women hid anything, but it is a possibility."

Jack walked through the living room and out to the kitchen, which was small and compact. Like the living room, the kitchen was sparkling clean. All kitchens, at least in his opinion, had their own distinct smell. Nikki's kitchen always smelled like pumpkin-pie spice. The kitchen at Pinewood smelled like vanilla, cinnamon, and sometimes garlic. This kitchen smelled like apple pie.

Jack stood perfectly still as he tried to get a fix on the room and the two women who had lived here for a short period of time. Even with the few personal touches, like the fern hanging in the dinette window, red crockery on the kitchen counter, and red-

and-green tartan-plaid place mats, there was no sense of permanence. At least he wasn't feeling any. The words *temporary* and *stopover* came to mind.

The square table was set into a breakfast nook that overlooked the backyard and a tiny porch. Thrift-store furniture, he decided. Not ugly, not pretty. Serviceable. The cushions on the chairs matched the place mats. A small bowl with green plants sat in the middle of the table. The soil was just starting to dry out around the edges, an indication the women hadn't been gone that long. Jack took a cup from the hook under the cabinet and watered the plant. He dried off the cup and replaced it.

The floor was covered in what looked like new linoleum, which was clean and waxed. Braided rugs that looked to be handmade were by the sink and stove. The cabinets were painted white, with bright red knobs. So in a way the women had tried to personalize at least the kitchen to some extent. Nikki would have picked up on that right away.

A small ten-inch television sat on the counter next to a toaster oven. In the corner, there was a red bowl with a green plant. It looked to be thriving with the light from under the counter. He poked his finger into the soil. It was nice and moist. Nikki would know about that, too. He made a mental note. The only other thing on the counter was a small red dish with two sets of keys.

Forty minutes later, Jack pulled out one of the chairs and sat down. He'd gone through the contents of all the cabinets, even dumping out the cereal boxes, flour, and sugar cans. He found nothing. There was food in the refrigerator — yogurt, eggs, milk, a loaf of bread, some apples, two lemons and two limes, and two cucumbers. There were two bottles of unopened wine on the refrigerator door along with six bottles of Corona beer and a six-pack of bottled water. The freezer contained two packages of frozen chopped meat, a whole chicken, and one package of pork chops along with a frozen strawberry-rhubarb pie.

The tiny laundry room boasted a stackable washer and dryer and held nothing but a load of towels waiting to be folded. He had the crazy urge to fold them, but he ignored the urge. The overhead cabinet contained two bottles of detergent, some dryer sheets, and a gallon of Clorox, along with six one-hundred-watt lightbulbs, the old kind.

Jack looked up to see Harry standing in

the doorway. "This was a bust. I didn't find a thing. How about you?"

"Just these phones. They were on the dresser. It's just one big room up there, like a loft. Twin beds, twin dressers. Not a lot of clothes, just enough. Same with the shoes. Some boots, and yes, I checked inside them all. Nothing. No excess of anything. One change of bedding. Six towels in the linen closet. Tissue, bathroom stuff. Nothing out of the ordinary. Nothing under the sink. No tub, just a shower. I'd say the two women are very frugal. No sign of jewelry or anything fancy. I can almost guarantee, Jack, that no one but us has been here. If there was someone before us, then it was a woman who knew how to put everything back exactly like she found it. That's my opinion, for whatever it's worth."

"Same here," Jack groused. "At least you found the phones. The car keys are here on the counter. I guess we should check the cars before we leave and take the keys with us."

"This is a nice kitchen. Yoko would like it. She likes the color red. Do you think we should water the fern hanging in the window?"

"Why?" Jack asked. "I already watered the plant on the table."

"So it doesn't die. Pearl is going to be moving someone else in here in short order. Don't disturb yourself, Jack, I'll do it."

"Harry! You know what we didn't find? Their purses. Every woman has a purse or a fanny pack. I didn't find any down here. How about upstairs?"

"No. I looked, too."

"Makes sense, I guess. A woman never leaves the house without her purse. Take Maggie. She carries her whole life in that backpack of hers. It isn't exactly a purse but close to it. Nikki would never leave the house without her purse."

"You're right," Harry said. "Yoko wears a fanny pack because she likes to have her hands free."

"I guess we should check out the backyard. And that little porch. They might have buried something, but I'm not about to start digging up the yard. Jeez, there must be a thousand flowers out here. Those women must have loved gardening."

"Jack, you know what else we didn't find in the house? Trash. There was none upstairs. How about in the kitchen?"

"No. There is a garbage disposal. No other trash anywhere. Maybe outside in the can. We'll check it when we leave. I saw it when we got here. There's a little fence around it.

To hide it, I guess. The girls are going to be really disappointed that we came up dry," Jack said.

"We should leave, Jack. We've been here close to two hours. I'll check the cars, you do the trash."

While Harry poked around inside the two cars and the trunks, Jack flipped the lid on the trash can. He stared down into the can. A lone grocery-store bag sat on the bottom and was tied in a knot. He tilted the can and reached in for the bag and undid the knot. Candy wrappers, an empty apple-strudel box, and a copy of *In the Know* were the only things in the bag. He retied the knot and joined Harry in the driveway. He shook his head to indicate he had found nothing in either car.

Jack slapped at his forehead. "The mail, Harry! We didn't check the mailbox!"

Harry raced to the end of the driveway and opened the mailbox. He shook his head to indicate there was no mail.

Jack pointed to the grocery bag in his hands. "They saw the tabloid. It's here in the bag. That's why they left. They were afraid possibly the neighbors or others would see it. I'm thinking they got out just in time."

Harry gunned the Ducati, backed up, then

hit the throttle. They flew out of the cul-de-sac like the Devil himself was on their heels.

Dinner over and the kitchen and terrace restored to normal, the gang headed back to the war room and took their places at the table.

"I have an idea if anyone wants to hear it," Maggie said.

"Of course we want to hear it, dear. Tell us what it is," Myra said as she settled herself more comfortably in her chair at the head of the table.

Maggie took a deep breath, then let it out with a loud *swoosh.* "Here it is. You all know the *Post* does a Man of the Year contest every year. We usually gear up for nominations around September and pick the leading entry at the end of December. Why can't we start a little early under some pretext or other like this year there are so many nominations we need to start early so we can investigate the nominees. We can start by putting little announcements in the paper daily, then hit it full force a week later. Our lead nominee, of course, will be Lincoln Moss! What do you think, guys?"

"I love it!" Annie bellowed. "It's perfect! You deserve a raise for that, Maggie!"

Maggie turned beet red as all the others

congratulated her, saying it was the perfect way to get to the oh-so-private Mr. Lincoln Moss.

"Any other suggestions, plans, strategies?" Myra asked.

Dennis held up his hand as though he were back in grade school. "Jason Woods!"

"What about him, kid?" Jack asked.

"Don't we need to know more about him? We think, don't we, that he is the one who spirited the two women to safety? Jack, you said after you and Harry went through the house that it was both of your opinions that the women skedaddled on their own. Meaning that Lincoln Moss did not find and snatch his wife." Jack nodded. "Then we need to find out all there is to find out about Jason Woods and the best place to do that is . . . drumroll please . . . *Facebook!* Young people, especially college students, *live* on Facebook. All they do is tweet and twitter and blog and text. I am confident we can find out everything there is to know about that young man within an hour. There is no reason to think this guy is any different. With both their cars still in the driveway, how did they get away, and don't tell me they walked. Someone had to pick them up and take them somewhere, and my guess is

Jason Woods is the one who drove them away."

"He's absolutely right," Abner muttered as he tapped furiously, which just proved to everyone what he had said all along, he could do two things at once.

"Do it, kid!" Jack said. Dennis grinned, his thumbs tapping away almost as fast as Abner's busy fingers.

"We are making progress here," Alexis said happily as she winked at Espinosa. "So far, Isabelle, Yoko, and I are the only ones without an assignment. With the exception of Myra and Annie," she added hastily. "Charles, what can we do?"

"What would you ladies like to do?" Charles said, turning the question right back at Alexis.

Charles pretended to think, then finally said, "This might be a good time for you girls to put pen to paper where Pearl is concerned. She doesn't have to go anywhere to get her files since they're all in her head. I think once we see everything there is to see as to how her underground works, names, profiles, we'll be better equipped to go down that road. All in favor say aye!" The room burst into sound.

Pearl turned white, made a move to get up until she saw Kathryn's hand poised

94

midway to the tabletop. Her eyes filled as she settled back down on her chair.

"You have to give it all up right now, Pearl," Myra said gently. "It goes without saying that all of us here will take your secrets and those of your people to our graves."

"If you don't, Pearl, I will shoot you myself, and you know what a good shot I am," Annie said, her eyes sparking dangerously.

Pearl nodded, her face miserable, tears puddling in her eyes. "It all started the day I found out my son-in-law was abusing my daughter and their child. I was still a sitting justice on the Supreme Court at the time. I knew . . ."

Two hours later, the group sat back in their chairs and stared at Pearl. Not with anger or frustration but with *admiration bordering on awe.* No one said a word. Only because none of the people in the room knew what to say. It was Kathryn who got up, walked around to where Pearl was sitting, and held out her hand. "I honest to God don't know of another person in this whole world who could have done what you've done, Pearl. Please, I'd be more than honored to shake your hand. I think we all now understand where you are truly coming from." Instead, Pearl reached up and hugged Kathryn so tight, she squealed.

"Don't you feel better now, Pearl, since you shared all of that? We can help. We *will* help," Myra said. Pearl nodded, but she still looked miserable.

"It's getting late. I say we call it a night and pick up tomorrow morning where we're leaving off right now," Annie suggested.

"Who's staying over?" Charles asked.

It turned out that everyone elected to return to their respective homes with the promise of reconvening at eleven the following morning.

When the last car left the driveway, Charles turned to Myra and kissed her on the cheek. "It was a good day, wasn't it?"

"It was, Charles. I had no idea Pearl's underground was as involved and as extensive as it is. I understand the secrecy, but I also understand that if she were to keep on the way she's been going, mistakes would be made, and those mistakes could have a domino effect. Now that we all have her back, the chances of that happening are just about zip. Do you agree, Charles?"

"I do. So, what would you like to do now, dear? A nightcap? The eleven o'clock news? A last walk with the dogs? Maybe a midnight snack?"

"Oh, Charles, that's all so boring. Why don't we throw caution to the winds and race each other up the stairs. I have it on a good authority, from a dear old friend of mine, that ripping off one's partner's clothes with one's teeth is very exciting!"

Charles was at the top of the steps gnashing his teeth before Myra could even catch her breath.

CHAPTER 6

Jason Woods was a hard worker. His supervisor at the Home Builders Depot wished he had six more employees like Jason Woods. A dozen would be even better. He watched Jason now as he unloaded hundred-pound bags of peat moss like they were five-pound bags of sugar. He wasn't smiling today, which was odd. In fact, he looked angry. He wondered if he should talk to him, but he hated getting personal with his help. Better to leave well enough alone, he decided. He was going to miss him when he left in August to return to college even though he said that he would work weekends if his schedule permitted. He moved off to check on another delivery of topsoil.

Jason knew that his boss was watching him. He must be giving off bad vibes or something. How could he not? He'd just allowed himself to become embroiled in what he was beginning to think of as a nasty domestic mess, but his gut was telling him it was something way worse than domestic violence.

The tall, well-built young man swiped at the sweat dripping down his face. Damn, it was hot. But, then again, it was mid-July. He looked at his watch. Four more hours till quitting time. Home to shower, change, grab something to eat, then make the two-hour ride to his family's cabin, where he'd stashed the two women.

Jason almost jumped out of his skin when he felt a hard push to his shoulder. He whirled around expecting to see law enforcement but instead saw the laughing face of Emily Appleton's friend, Stacey Copeland. "Hey, Jason!"

Jason removed his Redskins ball cap and swiped at his soaking-wet head. "Hey yourself! Things boring in the paint department, and you had the urge to smell peat moss and manure?" He laughed, but even to his own ears it sounded phony and forced. *And who are those two women standing by the wilted petunias? They're staring at me and trying to pretend they aren't.* His heart kicked up a beat.

"Something like that," Stacey said. "Hey, what's up with Emily? She hasn't been in for four days, and she hasn't called in either.

She isn't answering her cell phone. Since you two are you know . . . kind of an item, I thought maybe you might know what's going on. Do you?" she asked bluntly.

Jason swallowed hard. He shook his head. "I haven't seen her. I tried calling yesterday, but the call went to voice mail. And we're not an item, we're just friends," he lied. *Who is that young guy checking out the clay pot planters? He looks familiar.* He almost missed the look the two women shot his way and the young guy's almost imperceptible nod. The muscles in his stomach tied themselves into a knot. They were together, he was sure of it. And they were checking him out. Shit, shit, shit! He could feel the panic starting to build in his stomach inch its way up to his chest, causing him to gasp for breath. He broke out into a cold sweat.

"Can you take a break, Jason? I'm on mine. Let's go get a cold soda or something. I'm worried about Emily."

Not half as worried as I am, Jason wanted to say, but he didn't. Instead, he waved to his supervisor and said he was taking his break. He followed Stacey to the back of the store to the employee kitchen or what they called the break room, where he popped two bottles of cola and offered Stacey one. He gulped at his, his mind racing a hundred miles a minute. What to say, what not to say, how to look, how not to look. *Stop sweating,* he cautioned himself. Like that was possible.

Stacey Copeland eyeballed her friend, concern etched on her face. "You look funny, Jason, is anything wrong? By the way, I've been meaning to ask, did you register yet for fall classes? I was thinking of going over to CU after I got off work. Want a ride?"

"I'm okay. Haven't been sleeping well these past few nights. Our A/C is out," he lied with a straight face. "I'm working till four. That's if I hold out that long. My stomach is kicking up. I might leave in a little while. I need the hours, but if I'm going to be puking my guts out, I'm no good to anyone here."

Stacey gave him a look that said she wasn't buying anything he'd said. "Hey, Jason, this is me. We've been friends since our first day at CU. You can talk to me. I even got you this job. If something is wrong, maybe I can help. C'mon, Jason, open up."

"You sound just like my mother does. I told you, nothing is wrong. I'm not feeling a hundred percent, so ease up, okay?"

"Sure, no problem. You'd tell me if Emily dumped you, right?"

"Emily did not dump me," Jason said through clenched teeth. "I told you, we're just friends."

"Ha-ha, yourself, Jason. That's not what Emily told me. She told me you two are more than best buds. A lot more," she fibbed, hoping to get a rise out of Jason. "Don't you dare hurt my friend, Jason. If you do, you'll have to deal with me. I'm going out to her house before I go to CU and see what's wrong. Put that in your pipe and smoke it, pal.

"Just for the record, Jason, I hate it that you're lying to me. I know when you're lying because your left ear turns red, and it's red as a beet right now. So there!"

Jason watched as the tall redhead stomped out of the kitchen and back to the paint department. He finished his Coke and threw it in the trash bin. He hated it that he'd lied to Stacey. But in the scheme of things, what other choice did he have at the moment? None. He felt like crap.

Back at the loading platform, Jason eyed the bales and bales of peat moss that still had to be unloaded. Out of the corner of his eye, he could see the two women who had been eyeing the wilted petunias. They were on to the last of the flats of Gerbera daisies, which looked just as sorry as the petunias. The young guy had moved from the clay pots to the retractable hoses.

They were on to him. He could feel it, sense it in every pore of his body.

Jason swiped at his forehead again and walked over to where his boss was talking to a customer. He waited until the customer walked away. "Mr. Quincy, I'm afraid I have some kind of stomach bug. I have to leave. I'm sorry if I'm leaving you shorthanded, but I'm about to pass out here."

"Sure, Jason, go on home. Take off tomorrow if you're not better. We can manage. Take care of yourself. Don't forget to punch out."

"Thanks, Mr. Quincy. I appreciate it."

There was no way to get out of the gardening department without passing the two women and the guy checking out the hoses. Where did he screw up? What had he done wrong? Were they following him? How in the hell did they find him to begin with? He didn't have to pretend to be sick. He *was* sick now. He had to call the girls, but he'd given them his cell phone since they were afraid to use their own. He hadn't had time to get a new one. Well, shit, there was a phone in the kitchen. He could call his cell from there. Whoever was following him didn't have access to the kitchen. He could punch out and leave by the back entrance that a lot of the employees used. He had to act normal, do things the way he always did them. Shit, shit, shit. This spook stuff was not something he was good at. And from where he was standing, it didn't look like he'd get any better at it anytime soon.

Jason looked around to make sure the kitchen was empty. It was. He quickly called his cell. Emily picked up on the first ring. He spoke quickly, explaining about Stacey's seeking him out, the three strange people in the gardening department, and finally explaining that he was leaving.

"But I don't understand," Emily said, panic ringing in her voice. "How did you come under their radar? Think, Jason!"

"That's all I've been doing, Emily. I guess I screwed up somehow. I'm sorry. Look, I'm going home to change and shower. I'll leave right away and come pick you up and take you somewhere else. Don't make any calls on that phone. They can triangulate or something to find out the pings. I'm not up on all that stuff, but I do know they can track cell-phone usage. I probably shouldn't have called you now either. Sit tight, okay?"

Jason was standing under a steaming shower when the answer to his question rocked him back on his heels. Facebook! Of course. His whole life was on Facebook. He'd even bragged about his new friend Emily. Thank God he hadn't told Emily about that little indiscretion. He'd even posted a picture of her. How could he have been so stupid? Maybe because he was starting to think of Emily Appleton as a little sister who needed help and who wasn't really Emily Appleton at all but someone named Rosalee Muno. He didn't even want to think about Patricia Olsen and who she was married to.

Jason was shaking like a leaf in a rainstorm when he stepped out of the shower.

He had to be smart now. Really smart. If they, whoever *they* were, found him at Home Builders Depot, then they knew where he lived. They had probably followed him home and were waiting outside somewhere to follow him when he left. Smart. Think smart, he cautioned himself. How was he going to get out of the apartment without anyone's seeing him? His two roommates were still sleeping since they worked the night shift at one of the big hotels. That meant their vehicles were in their assigned parking spaces. He could take one of their cars and leave his for them. They were good enough friends that they wouldn't squawk, especially if he left a ten spot for gas. He quickly scribbled a note, left his keys on the counter, and pocketed Joe Cramer's keys. He left a ten-dollar bill on the counter, scribbling another short note asking both roommates not to talk to anyone if they came around asking questions. It was all he could think of to do.

Now he had to figure out how he was going to get out unnoticed. He lived on the third floor. He looked out at the small balcony, then across at the one next door. He was in good shape. He should be able to hop over, then jump down and hit the ground running. Unless they had people stationed around the back. He peered out the sliding doors but didn't see anything out of the ordinary. He shrugged. It wasn't like he had any other options at the moment. It simply came down to go or not to go.

Poised on the mini-balcony, Jason closed his eyes. Man, he was so not ready for this. Before he could wallow in his own self-pity, he took a flying leap and landed perfectly. He took a deep breath and moved on to the next and then the next until he was four units away from his own. Then, before he could think twice, he dropped to the second-floor balcony, then the first, and finally landed on solid ground.

He'd lived in the apartment complex going on four years, so he knew the property like the back of his hand. He raced across and between cars until he found Joe's Saturn. He unlocked it and sat there a moment, trying to catch his breath. When he had his breathing finally under control, he drove away, around the Dumpster, and out to the service road. Finally, he turned onto the highway. He drove, literally holding his breath as he kept his eyes glued to the rearview mirror. As far as he could tell, no one was following him, but he was the first to admit he didn't know what to look for. The same car following him for miles, he supposed.

Jason drove aimlessly for a while, through villages, through neighborhoods, then out to the main artery and, finally, to the Beltway. He was reasonably sure no one was following him. He drove for almost an hour before he hit a small mini shopping mall, where he stopped at a drugstore to buy two TracFones. He paid cash.

Jason's next stop was an ATM machine. Even he knew he could be tracked for making a withdrawal, but if he was going on the run, he needed money. He hated that he was taking his tuition money, but at the moment, he couldn't think of any other way to get money quickly. Four stops later he had over a thousand dollars in his pocket. Then he backtracked all the way to his apartment parking area, where he plugged in the TracFone, programmed it, and then blocked the number so he could call his cell again to give the women an update. He was getting pretty good at this spy stuff, he decided.

Jason set out again, this time going in the opposite direction. As far as he was concerned, he'd done all he could. Now all he had to do was let his mind wander to his Facebook page and all the silly nonsensical things he'd posted, like the stupid oaf that he was. It was true what his elders had been preaching: Once it was out there, it was there for the whole world to see, and the whole world as he knew it was seeing it in all its glory, his whole life story. Stupid, stupid, stupid!

Two hours later, Jason barreled up to the cabin and stopped on a dime, the brakes squealing and protesting. He was out the door before the engine stopped sputtering. The women looked at him, and he could read the panic on their faces. "C'mon, get your gear, we're outta here. Shake it, ladies." The women didn't need to be told twice. They had their canvas bags over their shoulders and were at the car within seconds.

"I need to reset the generator and shut down the pump and lock up. Did you wipe everything down that you touched, and I mean everything? Ten minutes tops."

"We did just what you said," Rosalee called to his retreating back.

"Good!" Jason bellowed in return.

"Whose car is this?" Amalie asked.

"I have no clue, but if I had to take a guess, I'd say it probably belongs to one of Jason's roommates. He switched up so it would be harder to follow him. God, Amalie, what happened? I thought we were safe."

"I'll tell you what happened. It's our own fault. Mine actually. You just did what I told you to do. We never should have bolted. When we didn't call in the way we were supposed to, 001 saw the red flag."

"The lady that runs the underground railroad. Is that what she's called? You never said she was 001. Why can't we just call her now and meet them somewhere so they can place us someplace safe?"

"It doesn't work that way, Rosy. Didn't you pay attention when we first got there when they told us what the rules were? They said as long as we obeyed the rules and did what they said, we would be safe. To deviate or break the rules meant they were done with us. No second chances. I blew it because I panicked when I saw that tabloid. Now we're dependent on Jason. He's now in as much jeopardy as we are, and it's all my fault."

"Do you think they know about Jason?"

Amalie looked at Rosalee and grimaced. "Total disclosure, remember. We told our handler about Jason the first time you met him and how you were friends. By now, they know everything there is to know about him. That's not a bad thing, Rosalee. What's bad is Jason is in harm's way just the way we are. Lincoln has sources 001 wishes she had. It's just a matter of time before he finds us."

Jason sprinted back to the car, his breathing ragged. "You guys ready to split this place?"

"Yes and no," Amalie said quietly. "Where are you going to take us? Listen, Jason, I'm sorry you got involved in this. Maybe you should just take us to a bus depot, and we'll take the next bus to wherever it's going and hope for the best."

"Now you know I'm not going to do any such thing. I have an idea if you girls don't mind camping out until we can make some sense of what is going on."

"What do you mean by camping out?" Rosalee asked nervously.

"The whole nine yards. Tents, sleeping bags, camp stove, kerosene lanterns. If you're okay with it, we'll stop at the next mall we see and buy what we need. I know a place that I think is safe. When I was a little kid and belonged to the Boy Scouts, we used to go camping. No one goes to that campground anymore. I read somewhere not too long ago that the Scouts shut it down and opted for more modern campgrounds. I felt sad because I had some good times there. I think it will be safe for a little while. No wild animals or anything like that. The downside is I won't be able to stay with you. I have to get back and get into the same routine. Are you following me here?"

"And then what?" Amalie asked.

Jason took his eyes off the road to look across at Amalie, who was sitting in the front passenger seat. "Then I don't know is my answer. We have to play it by ear. We'll get enough food to last you a good while in case I can't get to you for a few days. I can't think of any other way. Do either one of you have a better idea?" Both women shook their heads.

"Then I guess that's our plan." Jason

looked over at Amalie again, and asked, "In your opinion, how long do you think it will take your husband to find you?"

Amalie shivered as though she was chilled to the bone. "With his money and his resources, not long at all. He never gives up. Never."

That is not exactly what I wanted to hear, Jason thought. What was that old saying his mother was so fond of quoting? Oh, yeah, when life gives you lemons, make lemonade. Like that was really going to work. He decided right then that he was scared out of his wits. He wished now that he'd read more spy novels instead of the science-fiction novels he was addicted to.

If only . . .

CHAPTER 7

Kathryn Lucas bit into her bacon, egg, cheese, and onion burrito and watched the world go by as she sat in the parking lot of a Taco Bell. She'd slept late, barreled out of bed, showered, and headed straight to the fast-food shop before heading out to the farm. She was going to be late, but that was okay. The world wouldn't come to an end. She munched contentedly as she watched a steady stream of people going about their early-morning business. She was so into her own zone that she almost missed the tall imposing figure heading up the walkway to the *In the Know* building. How ironic that she was sitting here across the street. When she'd pulled in, she thought the area looked familiar, but she hadn't put it together immediately. Her phone was in her hand a moment later, her burrito forgotten. She quickly thumbed a text to Nikki and scooted out of the car. She was across the highway

113

in seconds and in the building just as she saw Lincoln Moss get into the elevator.

Kathryn waited for the next elevator to *ping.* It did just as a return text buzzed on her phone. She stepped in and looked at the message at the same time. *Do what you have to do. See you at the farm.* Well, damn, that could mean anything. She grinned at what she imagined she could do to Mr. Joel Goodwin. She supposed she could flirt with Lincoln Moss. Ha!

The elevator door opened, and she was staring across the room at Pam Warren, who looked like she was going to black out any minute. Kathryn smiled, showing all her perfect teeth. The smile said, *gotcha.* Because she had excellent vision, she could see Warren about to hit a key on her console that would undoubtedly alert Mr. Joel Goodwin to her presence. She wagged her index finger back and forth and shook her head. Pam Warren sat back on her swivel chair as she placed her hands flat on her desk.

Kathryn continued to smile as she advanced to the counter. She did love to intimidate people. She leaned forward, and said softly, "This is what you're going to do, Miss Warren. You can now press that little button and you will say, 'Mr. Goodwin,

Miss Goldshield is here, and she doesn't have much time. She's returning the packet you gave her yesterday but says you must sign for it in person.' "

Kathryn tilted her head so that she could hear Goodwin's response, which was almost immediate. "Show her into the conference room. I'll be there in a moment."

"Promptness is such a virtue," Kathryn said lightly as she tripped behind Pam Warren. "Having said that, the other virtue I admire most is silence. I know who that man is in there with your boss. Now, sweet cheeks, if you were a betting woman, who would you be betting on right now?"

"Ah . . . ah . . . you. Would . . . um . . . you care for coffee or tea? Anything?"

"Coffee would be lovely. Black." Kathryn thought about the delectable breakfast she'd left behind in her car. It would be cold when she got back. Oh, well, she'd just order another one. She grinned at how fast Warren made it out of the room. Within a second, Joel Goodwin was in the room. He looked ill. He closed the door, then he locked it.

"Why are you here? I gave you everything yesterday. I thought we were done. Do you know who is in my office right now?"

"Well, yeah," Kathryn drawled. "Why do you think I'm here? Do you want to see that gold shield again? Just so you know, Mr. Goodwin, it trumps Lincoln Moss."

The little man wrung his hands. "I think there's something you didn't tell us yesterday, Mr. Goodwin. I'm sure you just happened to forget, so I'm very generously giving you another chance," Kathryn said so softly, Goodwin had to strain to hear the words.

"All right, all right. I sent Jane Petrie a text to warn her. I'm in the newspaper business, and I have to protect my sources. You know how that works."

"Actually, I do know how that works. What does he want?"

There was no sense pretending he didn't know who the *he* was that Kathryn just mentioned, so he didn't bother. "The same thing you want. I already told him I had no further information. He was just telling me what he could have done to me when Pam buzzed me that you were here. I don't mind telling you that he made my hair stand on end. Everyone in this town knows how powerful he is. He is a very intimidating man. But . . . but you scare me more, lady, agent, whoever you are."

Kathryn let loose with a chuckle. "You are a wise man, Mr. Goodwin. What did Mr. Moss threaten you with?"

116

Goodwin tugged at his collar. "For starters, he said a full-blown tax audit. Then he said he could shut down this paper in a nanosecond. Then he said he could have my kids expelled from their schools, then he started on how he could ruin my wife's reputation. How's that for intimidation?"

Until now, they had been standing. Kathryn looked at Goodwin, and said, "Sit." He sat. "Is there a phone in here with a speaker?" Goodwin nodded and pointed. "I want you to listen very carefully to this call. Can you do that?" Goodwin nodded again. Kathryn pressed in the digits and waited.

"Federal Bureau of Investigation."

"Well, good morning, Allison. I'd like to speak to Director Sparrow ASAP. You know who this is, right?"

"Yes, ma'am. Hold please for Director Sparrow."

"Good morning, Director. Nice day, isn't it."

"Couldn't be better. What can I do for you on this bright summer day?"

"I'm having a bit of a problem at the moment. The same problem we spoke about a few days ago when my partner and I briefed you. I am right now, this minute, in the conference room of *In the Know* talking to Mr. Joel Goodwin, who has been really

117

helpful. He has been very cooperative, so please remember that. I'd like to keep it that way. There is a gentleman in his office named Lincoln Moss, who is threatening the very cooperative Mr. Goodwin. He is promising a full-blown tax audit, closing down the paper, ruining his wife's reputation, and having his kids thrown out of their respective schools. I'd like you to personally assure Mr. Goodwin that none of that will happen, so he will continue to cooperate with us. Can you do that, Mr. Director?"

"Of course. Mr. Goodwin, can you hear me?" Not waiting for a response, Sparrow kept speaking. "I want to assure you that you have the full weight of the Bureau behind you. Just do what our agent tells you, and you are golden. Thanks for the heads-up, Agent."

"My pleasure, Mr. Director," Kathryn said as she ended the call.

Kathryn reached for the coffee cup that had suddenly materialized. She drank it in two long swallows. "You happy now, Mr. Goodwin?" He nodded. The color was coming back to his cheeks.

Pam Warren poked her head in the door, and said, "Mr. Moss said to . . . ah . . . tell you if you aren't in your office in two seconds, he will make a call to the IRS. He

118

also called you a . . . pipsqueak."

Goodwin took a deep breath and squared his shoulders. "Tell Mr. Moss the pipsqueak said to sit on a pointy stick and twirl around. I'll get there when I get there, or he can leave anytime he wants since he didn't have an appointment in the first place. Tell him to make his call if that will make his day. Make sure you give him the message verbatim."

Pam Warren looked like she would rather go two rounds with a two-headed cobra than tell that to Lincoln Moss. She swallowed hard and left to deliver Goodwin's message.

"Okay, Mr. Goodwin, we're on the same page here. Just so you know, Mr. Moss will follow through because he is a bully. So I'm going to call Director Sparrow again when I get out to my car and have him alert Mr. Sangelli at the IRS. Now what do you have for me?"

"Jane Petrie's cell-phone number and the *pensione* where she's staying in France."

"Good! Good! I do love your spirit of cooperation. I think we're done here. I'll be in touch. Just don't take any sudden trips, Mr. Goodwin. If you do, we *will* find you. Don't let that ego-driven bastard in your office scare or intimidate you. He puts his pants on the same way you do." In spite of himself, Goodwin laughed out loud. "Now, is there a way to get out of here without Moss's seeing me?"

Goodwin pointed to the door at the end of the room. "It will put you in a side hall, take the steps to the end of the hall, and you'll come out at the parking lot. Is that where you're parked?"

"No, I'm parked across the street in the Taco Bell lot."

Goodwin thought that was funny, too. He laughed again. "I get it, that's where your stakeout is. Smart."

Goodwin waited a full five minutes after Kathryn left before he felt ready to return to his office. He sucked in his stomach, straightened up, and marched down the hall to his private office. Now that he had the FBI watching his back, he felt like he was King of the Walk. He blasted into his office like he owned it, which he did. "Are we done here, Mr. Moss, or do you plan to threaten me some more?"

Moss narrowed his eyes. Something had happened while the man was out of the room. He hated it when he didn't have all the facts at his fingertips. And this guy was suddenly too cocky. Before he'd left the room, he'd been in a world of stress.

"We're done. For now." The implied threat that there was more to come was there. He turned on his heel and left the office, his fingers hitting the number three on his speed dial, the Director of the IRS, Aaron Sangelli.

"Aaron, Lincoln Moss here. How's it going?"

"This is the IRS, Lincoln, how do you think it's going? What can I do for you on this humid hot day in the middle of summer?"

Was it his imagination, or did Sangelli's voice have an edge to it? He got right to the point. "I'd like you to schedule a full-blown audit for one Joel Goodwin. He owns that political tabloid called *In the Know.* And the tabloid, too. ASAP. I'd like you to send out the notice to both Goodwin and the paper no later than tomorrow. I'll owe you one for this, Aaron." The silence on the other end of the phone brought Moss to full attention. He felt a distinctive flutter in his stomach.

"Sorry, Lincoln, no can do. I just got a personal call from the Director of the FBI, and he said there will be no audit of Mr. Goodwin or his paper. He also was kind enough to alert me to the fact that you, as in you, Lincoln Moss, do not tell the IRS what to do, when to do it, or how to do it. He mentioned you by name, Lincoln, and I've been around this town long enough to know the man was loaded for bear. So, do you want to rethink that request? Look, if it's that important to you, you have the ear of POTUS. If you want its getting out to the media, that is. Think carefully, Lincoln. And this conversation never happened."

"What the hell! When did the director call you?"

"About six minutes before you did. Listen, Lincoln, I'm late for a meeting. Let's get together next week for a round of golf. This is not the best place to be discussing any of this."

"Yeah, sure." Moss broke the connection and stood still. Who the hell was it in the conference room back at the paper that had the kind of juice to call off the IRS? Who?

Kathryn literally flew into the kitchen at Pinewood, forty minutes late. Lady and the pups greeted her with enthusiasm. She stopped for a few moments to tussle with the dogs before she headed for the war room, where she whooped her pleasure as she waved the slip of paper with Jane Petrie's information.

"Nice going, Kathryn!" Jack said. "There's

a lot to be said for being at the right place at the right time. C'mon, tell us everything."

Kathryn was like a runaway train as she recounted word for word what went down at *In the Know*. "Do you believe that guy? And do you believe all those threats?"

"He is the President's best friend as well as his cousin from sandbox days. He's run roughshod over a lot of important people in this town. It's time he got his come-uppance," Annie said.

"And we're just the people who can do it," Isabelle said, clapping her hands.

"I need two people to go to Paris! Who wants the gig?" Annie asked. Every hand in the room shot upward. "Oh! Well, I guess we're going to have to draw straws. Who speaks French well enough to get by?" Every hand but Jack's went down.

"Okay, Jack, you're it! Pick a partner. I'll call to get the plane ready. You leave *now*. Time is of the essence. Myra, call Mr. Sparrow to alert the authorities in Paris and have them pick up Miss Petrie and keep her safe till Jack gets there. On your return, bring the young lady here. You're still sitting here, Jack. Move!"

"C'mon, Harry, let's go. See ya, honey," Jack said, as he blew a kiss in Nikki's direction. Harry did the same thing to Yoko, who giggled at the look on his face. Everyone in the room knew that Harry was petrified about flying and fretted for days when he and Yoko were scheduled to fly to China.

"What's next on our agenda?" Myra queried.

"Well, I did my bit," Kathryn said.

"I'd like to go to Home Builders Depot to stake out Jason Woods. Follow him and possibly even confront him. I think I can get him to talk," Dennis said.

"Don't anyone look at me," Abner said. "I'm so deep into Lincoln Moss's business, I can't do anything else."

"Listen, Ted and I, along with Espinosa have to get back to the paper. We have a campaign going, and we need to give it some final tweaks. Our Man of the Year contest will hit the paper first thing in the morning. We're going to be fudging a lot of it, so I'm warning you all ahead of time," Maggie said.

"That's fine, dear. Just make it work," Annie said, knowing her comment was not needed. Maggie and Ted always made sure things worked. Always.

"I'm outta here," Kathryn said. "I have three hours of therapy. If you need me, call my cell." The others nodded.

"Well, I feel like chopped liver all of a sudden," Nikki grumbled. "What do you want Alexis, Yoko, and me to do?"

"Let's go topside and make some lunch," Myra said. She looked up at the dais, where Charles and Fergus were conversing in low tones. She shrugged.

"I'm not liking this one little bit," Nikki continued to grumble, as they made their way up the steps to the main part of the house. "We're always in the thick of things. How did this happen?" she demanded.

The others looked as confused as Nikki.

"I don't know, dear," Myra said. "Once we sit outside on the terrace in the sun, I am sure we'll come up with something. I do agree that everyone has something to do but us."

"Well, I'm all for stirring up some trouble," Annie snapped. "Put your thinking caps on, girls! Go along outside, and Myra and I will bring lunch out. Tuna melts with fresh strawberries in sugar. The sweet apple tea is in the fridge. You girls can take it and the glasses, along with the ice bucket. We won't be but a few minutes. Scoot now."

Nikki lowered the retractable awning Myra had installed in the early spring. It covered the entire terrace and helped keep the potted plants from wilting. Normally, Myra or Charles lowered it early in the

125

morning and had their coffee out here while the dogs romped through the yard. They must have been busy this morning, she thought.

"Ah, that's better," Alexis said.

"So, here we are. With nothing to do. I'm all charged up, and I'm standing, or in this case sitting, still. There must be something we can dig into," Nikki continued to complain.

Alexis reached down into her oversize bag and pulled out the before and after pictures of Amalie Laurent Moss. "I've heard the fashion world describe Amalie as looking like a Botticelli angel. Personally, I wouldn't go that far, but she certainly is beautiful, there's no getting around that. The after picture is still beautiful, but something's gone from her face. I can't pinpoint it exactly. If I saw the new Amalie on the street, I am quite sure I wouldn't recognize her as Amalie. To me that means she's safe. But to her husband, now that's a whole other ball game. What do you all think?"

"I agree," Nikki said. Isabelle nodded.

"What are you all agreeing to?" Myra asked as she set a platter of sandwiches on the glass-topped table. Alexis explained. Myra nodded in agreement, as did Annie.

"What does all that mean? To us," Alexis

asked as she reached for a sandwich. She popped a cherry tomato from a side dish and chomped down.

"Not a darn thing," Nikki said.

"Maybe we should be concentrating on Lincoln Moss. If Kathryn is right, and we have no reason to think she's not, then Moss has his jockeys in a knot about now. I'm up for taking him on. I hate those high-powered Washington insiders who think they can get away with anything. Oooh, I can't wait to end this guy's career," Nikki said as she bit down into her crisp sandwich.

As an afterthought, she asked, "Do you all think it's true that he has a black book? Kind of the way J. Edgar Hoover kept all those files on everyone? I think he does. I think he has something on every single person in Knight's administration. Why else is he so powerful? Why is everyone so afraid of him? It sure explains how he practically lives at the White House, calling the shots." The others said they agreed.

"I might be able to help with that," Annie said suddenly, excitement ringing in her voice.

"Oooh, are you thinking the same thing I'm thinking, Annie? Of course you are, I can read you like an open book, and it's not a black book either." Myra laughed.

Myra turned to the girls. "I'll show you!" She ran into the house and returned with a cream-colored envelope. "This is an invitation I received three weeks ago to a gala at the Four Seasons this weekend. All you need to get in is this invitation, which you present at the door. Annie has one, too. I'm sure with very little effort Charles can come up with some extra, and we can all go. Tell me, is that brilliant or what?"

"What's it for, and how do you know Lincoln Moss will be there?" Isabelle asked.

"It's for children with disabilities, a pet project of the First Lady. I saw the guest list in the paper this morning, and Lincoln Moss's name was on it. Annie agreed to buy a table for ten. I'm not sure if the committee will send six additional invitations or exactly how that will work, so we'll have Charles work some magic just to be on the safe side."

"Oh, Myra, that's a great idea," Nikki said, as she bit into a crunchy celery stick. "We can pepper him with questions about his wife and watch him lie. I bet you five dollars he's going to want his picture taken with the Countess de Silva!"

"And of course, the countess will demur and make him work for the picture. I think it's doable. It pays to brainstorm. Now, doesn't it?" Myra laughed.

"Will you wear your tiara, Annie?" Isabelle asked. "And your cowgirl boots?"

"We can vote on my attire later, dear. Now, let's work out a plan."

CHAPTER 8

Nikki and Kathryn arrived at Pinewood at almost the same moment, Nikki riding a motor scooter across the field and Kathryn in her MINI Cooper with the top down. They looked at each other and at the exact same moment said the exact same words, "We missed something."

"I was up all night, couldn't sleep, and believe it or not, it wasn't my leg bothering me. We missed something, Nikki. Sure as shooting we did."

"I know, I know. I couldn't sleep either, and it had nothing to do with Jack's being gone. It wasn't Goodwin, I think he leveled with us yesterday. That only leaves . . ."

"Pam Warren!" Kathryn snarled. "Five bucks says that skunk Lincoln Moss got to her. We need to go there right now. Hop in, girl!"

Myra and Annie appeared in the kitchen doorway. "Where are you two going? You just got here!"

"I screwed up!" Kathryn shouted. "We're on our way to fix it! We'll be back as soon as we can get here!" In the blink of an eye, she had the MINI whipped around and was blasting out of the gate, tires smoking on the little compact car.

"What do you think that was all about?" Annie asked.

"Kathryn screwed up," Myra said, shrugging her shoulders. "The only place she went yesterday was to the tabloid paper. At least as far as I know. They said they got what they went after, so I don't have a clue what Kathryn was talking about or what she meant about screwing up. If they're going back there, then it's obvious something has happened there since yesterday and that Kathryn is involved. We'll just have to be patient and wait till they get back for the details."

"I just hate being on hold," Annie grumbled. "What are we going to do now, Myra? Everyone is out doing something, and here we sit."

"I thought we were picking out our outfits for the gala this weekend. You're the one who said we needed to knock everyone's socks off with our outfits. So, since time is

131

of the essence, we had best get back to work."

"That is so humdrum. We need to be where the action is. Think, Myra, what can we do?"

"By *do,* do you mean like visit Nellie and Elias or possibly pestering Pearl? Define the word *do,* Annie."

"That's the problem, Myra. I don't know. All the bases seem to be covered at the moment. We are at this point in time at ground zero and empty-handed. Unless you have some ideas."

"Let's have some coffee. We think better with coffee. Charles can pick our outfits. For some reason, he has good fashion sense, and no, Annie, I have never figured out the why of that."

While Myra prepared the coffee, Annie paced the confines of the kitchen. "I think we should concentrate on Lincoln Moss. Who do we know who knows him? Think, Myra. I'm sure I must know *someone.* Do you think Charles knows anyone? Or better yet, do we know anyone who knows . . . or knew his wife?"

"Off the top of my head, the answer is no. But let's run it up the flagpole and see if either one of us can salute it. There has to be someone. How much have you read up on Moss, Annie?"

"Pretty much everything. Self-made. Private person. Loves politics. Best buds with the President. POTUS, according to the political gossip, doesn't make a decision until he clears it with Moss. Moss sits in on top-secret meetings. So that has to mean he's got clearance. He's a dollar-a-year man. Which brings up the question of why the President didn't give him some high-ranking political job or, at the very least, a title. He attends all the White House functions, usually alone. I think I read somewhere that his wife only attended four functions. Because, according to Lincoln Moss, she has a career, and he wouldn't dream of interfering with her career, which keeps her in France a good many months out of the year. Oh, one other thing, he's into physical fitness. Works out, runs the Tidal Basin. Lifts weights, all that macho stuff. As the young people say today, he is buffed and ripped. I would assume that for a man in his fifties, that is about as high as you can go, compliment-wise.

"And yet he manhandled that beautiful wife of his. To the point where she had to get away from him. She gave up her career in the process. So it had to be pretty bad. That's my opinion," Annie said. "It isn't making any sense, Myra."

Myra poured coffee. "I agree. Maybe we're looking at this all wrong, Annie. The man has to have servants. Do they live on the premises? I think Abner said they do, and he has a lot of them. Maybe we could get to the cook or the housekeeper. They have to go to the market because the man has to eat. We could stake out the house and do a snatch and grab. Or if that isn't feasible, we could try to bribe them. You know money talks and poop walks as they say."

"That's a possibility. I'm sure Moss has private security. Not Secret Service. Security he pays out of pocket. So that lets that out of the equation. I say we call Avery Snowden and ask him to arrange a stakeout unless you want the two of us to sit in the bushes and wait for the housekeeper to go to the market. Ah, I see by your expression that's a no. Okay then, I'll call Avery and arrange it. He can then follow her and call us, at which point, we'll take over. You okay with that, Myra?"

Myra nodded. It hardly came under the heading of action, but if it was all they were going to get, she was all for it.

While Annie conversed with Avery Snowden, Myra let her thoughts go to Nikki and Kathryn and what they were doing to correct Kathryn's screwup.

The elevator slid open without a sound or a ping to announce its arrival. Both women stepped out and almost knocked over Joel Goodwin who groaned and muttered something that wasn't too complimentary. "Good God, ladies, what are you doing here again? You picked my brain, you drained my blood. I swear on everything holy, there is not one other thing I can tell you."

"We know that, Mr. Goodwin. We aren't here to talk to you. We're here to talk to her," Nikki said, pointing to Pam Warren, who had gone as white as the blouse she was wearing.

"Pam! What does Pam have to do with anything?" He addressed his next comment to his secretary-receptionist, who looked like she was going to black out any moment. "Pam, do you know anything?"

"I think what you should have asked her, Mr. Goodwin, is what did she tell Mr. Moss this morning about our visit here and whatever else she knows? Then I think you should ask her how much money he paid her. Then you should inform her we ran her bank account, and guess what we found?" The last comment was a lie, of course, but

135

neither Goodwin nor Pam needed to know that.

"Pam! Is this true? Did you sell me out? Why would you do such a thing? Tell these ladies it isn't true? Oh, God, it is true. I can see it on your face. Why? Tell me why you would do such a thing?"

Pam Warren started to sniffle, then outright bawl her eyes out. She reached into her desk for a wad of tissues.

"I'll tell you why, Mr. Goodwin. Lincoln Moss intimidated her for one thing. Then he flashed a wad of cash, and what woman can't use a wad of cash. She probably viewed Jane Petrie as someone doing something she wasn't supposed to do, which, of course, is true, so she figured why not. It's that simple."

"Dear God! What did you tell that monster, Pam?"

"All right, all right! I gave him Jane Petrie's address in France. And her cellphone number. He paid me a hundred thousand dollars. He only wanted to give me ten thousand. I laughed at him. I wanted more than the sixty-six thousand dollars you paid Jane Petrie. You would have paid her another sixty-six thousand if she'd supplied that after picture. You know it, Joel. He said . . . he said . . . I could have an accident. And that no one would ever know it wasn't really an accident. Everyone in this town knows how powerful Lincoln Moss is.

"Then he said he would call me at home and asked if he had the correct telephone number. I have an unlisted telephone number, and yet he somehow had it. He wanted to know who was in the conference room with you this morning. I couldn't give him names, so I just said the FBI. Then he left."

"You're fired, Pam. Clear out your desk. You just put Jane Petrie's life in danger. You do realize that, don't you?"

"Well, if I did, it's your fault, Joel. You deal with people who break the law. What she was doing was illegal. So I took his money? So what? Do you think I wanted to end up in some ditch alongside the road or worse yet, mugged and raped?"

"And do you really think you're any safer now than before you spilled your guts?" Kathryn asked.

"Now he knows what you know, and he knows who told him. I think if I were you, I'd run to ground," Kathryn said. There was not one ounce of sympathy in her voice. Pam Warren burst into tears again, all of her defiance gone.

Pam Warren looked at the faces staring at

her as she shoved her personal things into an oversize shoulder bag. Her hands were shaking so badly, she could barely pull the zipper to close the bag.

"What does this mean now?" Goodwin dithered.

Kathryn shrugged as she watched Nikki's fingers on her iPhone. She knew without asking that she was sending a text to Jack in France. "Let me ask you a question, Mr. Goodwin. Do you think Jane Petrie would have heeded your advice when you called to warn her and relocated? If so, then we can assume she's safe, at least for the moment."

"I think so. I scared her, I do know that. Where she would go I have no clue. She's gone many times to France so I have to assume she's made some friends who could, I guess, hide her out. For all I know, she could be out of France by now and be someplace where she thinks she's safe. I did tell her to read up on Lincoln Moss. If there is nothing else, ladies, I'd like to head on out and get myself a stiff drink."

"Don't expect me to give you a reference, Pam," Goodwin snarled, as his secretary headed for the elevator.

It was brutally hot as only July can be in Washington. Doubly hot in the garden

138

pavilion at the Home Builders Depot. The overhead sprinklers that dispensed a fine, cool mist on the hanging wilted plants did nothing to cool things off.

Dennis West looked around for Jason Woods and finally spotted him at the back end of the pavilion, stacking different-colored wheelbarrows. Woods, he noticed, spotted him almost immediately. He could see the young man's shoulders tighten up. Dennis chewed on his lower lip as he made the instant decision to approach and confront the young man. He didn't think twice but sprinted across the pavilion and held out his press credentials. "Got a minute, Jason?"

"Actually, I don't. My boss doesn't like it when we conduct personal business during work hours. Since you aren't a customer, that puts you into the personal category."

"I can clear it with Mr. Quincy for you. That is his name, isn't it? I just want to ask you a few questions. It concerns Rosalee Muno and Amalie Moss. Look, let's not beat around the bush here. I know you're helping them, and that's a good thing. Really it is. Those two women need all the help they can get right now. But, you see, here's the thing, you are out of your league. Lincoln Moss is not a guy you want to tangle with. Trust me on that. I represent people who can truly help."

"I don't know what you're talking about, Mr. West. You must have me mixed up with someone else."

Dennis sighed. "No, I do not have you mixed up with someone else. Please, tell me where you took those women. And here is another question for you. Do you know the FBI is also looking for those women? They are. You really do not want to mess with the feds, young man. Not because they did anything wrong but to protect them. And there is one other thing you need to tell those two women. The nurse, whose name is Jane Petrie, the one who sold the picture to *In the Know,* left the area and is now in France. The FBI is looking for her, too. The people I work for, and I'm not just referring to the *Post,* told me that Lincoln Moss might, and we are certain of this, just so you know, have people on the way to France to talk to Petrie. We believe she is in danger. She did sell that picture to the tabloid, then she hightailed it out of here. That should tell you something, Jason."

Jason felt like his insides were turning to jelly. How much could he bluff? "I don't know why you're telling me all this. I have no idea why you are fixated on me. I can't help you. Listen, I have to get back to work. I get paid by the hour. You want to stand here and watch me, that's fine. If you don't leave me alone, I'm going to alert the manager and file a complaint. I need this job, so butt out of my life, mister."

"Listen, kid, everyone knows you and Rosalee are very good friends. The neighbors told us how you went to the house to see her. The chick in the paint department introduced you to Rosalee. You're making a mistake by not talking to me. I just want to help."

"I don't need your help and I don't want it. Go help someone else. Now leave me alone."

Dennis shook his head to show his disappointment, but he did walk away. The kid would crack sooner or later. He walked out to the parking lot and reported in to Ted and Maggie, who had been whispering with their heads close together. Dennis was almost inclined to tell them to get a room.

"We need to put a tail on him. Call that guy Snowden. I think I scared him, so he's going to do something. The thing is, will he work the rest of the day or leave early? I'm thinking he knows he's being watched, so he is going to finish out the day, then try to give us the slip. He's a bundle of raw nerves.

I'm on my way to the paper now. I don't think he's going to do a thing right this moment because he's too scared. He's going to try to bluff it out. That's my opinion, for whatever it's worth."

Back in the garden pavilion, Jason was indeed a bundle of nerves. He had to play out the day and act normal. Whatever the hell normal was. He looked down at the watch on his wrist. An hour to go till lunch. Maybe he'd get a brainstorm before then. Maybe he would somehow be able to recruit Stacey Copeland. But if he did that, it would mean one more person would know about Rosalee and Amalie. Crap! Sweat dripped down and into his eyes, burning them. Talk about being between a rock and a hard place. What to do? What not to do? Whom to trust? Hell, that was easy, no one!

Soaked to the skin in his own sweat, at one minute to twelve Jason stripped off his work gloves, swiped his forehead on the sleeve of his T-shirt, and headed back to the break room. Inside, he leaned up against the door and started to shake. For one wild, crazy moment he wanted to go to the police. He squashed the idea the moment it entered his head. More sweat trickled down his face. He could smell his own stink. He wished he could dive into a pool of ice cubes. He raised his eyes and saw the intercom directly in his line of vision. Stacey! Maybe Stacey was his answer. Like he had so many choices to draw from. He marched over to the console and pressed the number nine for the paint department. Stacey herself picked up. "How can I help you today?" she said, cheer ringing in her voice.

"You can help me by hightailing it to the break room, but don't look obvious. I'm in some deep trouble, and I need your help. Can you do it?" Jason hissed into the phone.

"Oh, yes, we're open till nine. We have hundreds of colors to choose from. I'm sure you'll find one to your liking. Be right there," she hissed in return. "You're scaring me, Jason."

Five minutes later, Stacey Copeland slithered into the room. "Why do I feel like I'm in some kind of *I Spy* movie? My God, you look awful. What's wrong?"

Jason rolled a can of cold Pepsi across his forehead and around his neck. "Everything and anything is wrong. I need your help. Actually, it's Emily whose name is really Rosalee who needs your help. And her boss, too. I'm being watched. I have them in a safe place for the moment, but I can't go to them because people are . . . people want to harm them." He knew he was babbling, but he couldn't seem to stop himself.

Stacey held both her hands up, palms facing Jason. "Whoa there, Nellie. Back up and start at the beginning and tell me everything. If you want my help, you need to tell me every little thing and do not hold anything back. Deal?"

Jason nodded, the words tumbling out of his mouth at the speed of light. He ended with, "This is the only place where you and I can talk. They even know about you. The guy flat out told me the girl in the paint department introduced me to Rosalee. They're probably going to start watching you, too. That's why we have to move fast. We cannot be seen together. You understand that, right?" Stacey nodded.

Stacey brushed at her long auburn locks. She swallowed hard. "That . . . that's awful, Jason. I hate men who abuse women. Absolutely hate them. I'll do whatever I can. Don't worry about me, I can take care of myself. I take martial-arts classes."

Jason looked at his watch. Satisfied that he still had time on his lunch hour, he started to lay out his plan. "You have to go get them in your car. I'll write you a note to give them. Even though Rosalee knows you, she might not want to leave with you. The note will reassure her and once you explain, it should be okay. Pack up the gear and keep it in your car. Take them to a hotel. I'm thinking hiding in plain sight is better than skulking around and hiding. Draws too much unwanted attention. I took some money out of my tuition fund, but I made a serious dent in it when I bought the camping equipment. I'll have to take out some more tonight on my way home." He fished around in his pocket and pulled out a roll of bills. "This will have to do for now until I can get more. So, you'll do it?"

"Of course I'll go get them, but they don't need a hotel. I'm house-sitting for some people I know. I have the house till August fifteenth. That's almost a whole month. We can hide them out there. No one will know. It's a big old house that was refurbished in the Columbia Heights neighborhood. Three blocks from where I live with my roommate. It's just a hop, skip, and a jump from ritzy Adams Morgan. Actually, the more I think about it, the more I like the idea. And get this, it's less than a mile from the White House. It will be like hiding them like you said, in plain sight, so to speak." At Jason's blank look, she said, "You know that old adage, keep your friends close, your enemies closer? Same kind of thing. No one expects to find what they're looking for right under their nose. For now it is a plan. You okay with that?"

Jason continued to roll the cold Pepsi can, which wasn't so cold anymore, all over his neck and up and down his cheeks. "Yeah, yeah, I'm okay with that. I'm going to draw you a map. Whatever you do, do not call them. Do not use your phone at all. Better yet, take the batteries out till you get back. Don't call me either. This break room is the only place we can meet and talk. I appreciate your helping me, Stacey."

"Hey, what are friends for? And besides, I owe you. You introduced me to Jackson. We are becoming good friends. Almost as good as you and Rosalee." What she didn't say was she would like it a lot better if Jason and Jackson switched places, but she didn't. "Hey, you want half my sandwich. It's turkey and roast beef," Stacey said, taking her lunch bag out of the fridge.

"No thanks. I'd barf it up if I ate it. My stomach is in knots."

"Well, mine isn't, and I make good sandwiches. You need to calm down and relax. You'll give yourself a coronary." Stacey bit into her sandwich and rolled her eyes. It was all lost on poor Jason, who was busily drawing a map on a strip of paper toweling.

Stacey popped a can of Dr Pepper and took a long gulp. "How will I let you know I got them safe at the house?"

"Tomorrow morning in this break room, that's how. Soon as we report in in the morning. I will just assume you made it safe and sound. If there is a problem or something goes awry, then call this number. I just got it. Here's the number," he said, writing it on the map he was making. "Only call the number if something goes wrong. Got it?"

"Got it."

"Listen, don't follow me out. Wait at least ten minutes. I have to be back on the pavilion. Today, I hate this job. Good luck, and thanks, Stacey."

"No problem. See ya in the morning. Hey, what about food and stuff?"

"You gotta do it all for them. Make sure you stress to them they are not to leave the house."

"Okay. Okay, Jason. Please, relax, it's going to be okay. I got you covered."

CHAPTER 9

A look of disgust on his face, Jack looked over at Harry, who sported the same look of disgust. They'd arrived at Charles de Gaulle Airport, were picked up the moment they stepped outside by a man in a chauffeur's uniform who did not speak one word of English. He held up a placard with Jack's and Harry's names on it, and motioned for the two of them to follow to where he'd parked his town car.

From the airport, he'd taken them to their hotel, a private mansion owned at one time by a royal named Lord de Breluil. Annie said on arrival they should ask for Oliver, the head concierge, and to tell him the countess said hello and to do whatever they asked of him. Such as arrange car services, make dinner reservations at the Le M64 restaurant. He was helpful, but without telling the man what they were really after, they had to do the rest on their own.

The hotel was a short walk from the Champs Élysées, not that either Jack or Harry was in the mood for sightseeing.

"We've been here twelve hours and have nothing to show for our efforts other than all that rich food that is lying really heavy in my stomach," Jack grumbled. "Nikki would kill me if I told her what I ate for dinner. Yoko would string you up by your toes, Harry."

"The police were no help, and we struck out at the flat Jane Petrie rented. All we know is she registered, then checked out. She turned in her rental car just hours after she rented it. No one we talked to remembers seeing an American in the area where she'd booked her reservation except for the reservation clerk, who said when she checked out she said that she had a sudden family emergency."

"Annie and the girls are not going to like this," Harry said.

"You're right about that. Did you get the feeling when we were talking to the landlord or whatever these people call the person who owns the flat that handles the registration or whatever . . . that she wasn't being entirely truthful? She was giving off vibes that made my hair stand on end. Maybe we missed a beat and should have offered a bribe. What do you think, Harry?"

"What I think is if Petrie has been coming here several times a year and staying at the same place, she's more than likely built up some kind of rapport with the owner of the flat. I'm thinking when she left in such a hurry, she would have told the landlady not to answer any questions if someone came looking for her. She also probably told her to go ahead and rent out the flat and didn't take a refund. Petrie probably slipped her a few bucks to keep quiet, and along with being able to rent out the flat again, the woman was happy. Petrie will probably call her from time to time to check to see if anyone really is checking up on her. We can go back first thing in the morning and take another shot at her. This time, we lean a little harder and of course offer up a substantial . . . ah . . . gift for whatever knowledge she has to share. Your French is good enough to get your point across, isn't it, Jack?"

Jack was always astounded when Harry said more than two words at a time. "It's worth a try, that's for sure. Since the local police were no help, I was also thinking maybe we could get Jack Sparrow to intervene on our behalf. They have something over here called the *Direction*

Générale de la Sécurité Extérieure. It's France's top external intelligence organization. I read about it on the plane on the way over. I also remember the Attorney General's talking about them when I was a prosecutor. Sparrow has the juice to make the call and do it as one director to another, then it's one of those, I owe you, and if I'm lucky, you won't want to collect for years and years. It's all in the spirit of cooperation. I can call if you agree, Harry."

"It can't hurt. If we bomb out with the landlady tomorrow, we might as well go home unless you want to tramp these streets in the hopes of spotting Petrie. We both know she's gone to ground. Hell, she could be in Belgium for all we know. The only thing in our favor is she's traveling using her own passport. Maybe Sparrow or Abner can find out if her passport is in play. If it isn't, that means she's still here and in hiding."

Harry was right, Jack decided. "I'm dead on my feet, Harry. I hate jet lag. I'm going to call Nikki, report in, and you call Yoko. And then I'm hitting the sack. I'll send Abner a text and ask him to do what he can. If we don't hear back first thing in the morning, then we hit the streets as soon as we dress and have breakfast. I'll send

Sparrow an e-mail before we turn in. When we wake up, he might have some news for us. I'd call him now, but it's four in the morning in the States. Ditto for the text to Abner." Jack yawned to make his point that he was dead on his feet.

Harry was already punching in the country code and the area code to call Yoko, but Jack knew he heard every word he'd said. Harry never ceased to amaze him.

It was a beautiful morning, Maggie decided as she trotted along to meet Ted, Espinosa, and Dennis for breakfast to plan out the day. It was early, just barely past six fifteen, and already the sidewalks were full of people heading for their early-morning caffeine fix. Under her arm, Maggie carried a copy of the *Post.* She pretty much knew that the boys would also have a copy, but she never was one to leave things to chance.

Maggie grinned when she saw the trio already settled in a booth at the back of Casey's café, which, according to Ted, served the best bacon, cheddar, mushroom, onion, and a host of other things on top of a perfectly fried egg that was piled on top of a perfectly toasted English muffin. A plate of delectable hash browns accompanied each muffin. It was up to the customers how to fit it all in their mouths. Maggie always cut her muffin in four squares. The coffee was excellent, too, and the owners offered endless refills at no extra charge.

Maggie slid into the booth and slapped the paper down, the top folded over so that the pictures on the bottom half were front and center. "Great pictures, Espinosa," she said, reaching for her coffee cup and filling it from the carafe already on the table.

"Did anyone notify any of the nominees?" Dennis asked. "As in Lincoln Moss."

"The paper is the announcement. That's the purpose of the whole thing. We can't appear to show bias in any way. You do know that Moss was nominated twice before, but there are those in this town who actually do not like him, so he didn't win."

"Don't you mean they fear him?" Espinosa said.

"That, too," Maggie said. "You all do realize that this is all rigged. We'll figure out something later on to turn it back to the legitimate contest we've always run. This is just to get us into his house to do an interview. Along with the other nominees we have so far who have to be interviewed."

"Who's going to make the call and do the interview?" Dennis asked.

"Since it was my idea, who do you think,

Mr. West?" Maggie growled.

"Can I go with you?"

"No. You are on Jason Woods. Espinosa is going with me. Ted has other interviews to do. I seriously doubt Moss will agree to an interview, but I am going to give it my best shot. I am, if nothing else, persistent. Right now, I'm thinking Moss will be afraid some of the questions will be about his wife."

"Any news on Jack and Harry?" Ted asked as he watched the waitress approach with their breakfast.

"I was going to call Nikki but didn't want to wake her. I'll call when we finish breakfast," Maggie said as she sawed through the four-inch loaded English muffin with a serrated knife. "Tell us how it went with Jason Woods, Dennis."

"Avery Snowden's men are tailing him twenty-four/seven as of yesterday afternoon. I haven't heard a thing since I left Home Builders Depot yesterday."

"No one asked for my opinion, but I'm going to offer it up anyway. Is anyone following the girl? The one from the paint department. Seems to me if Woods is lying low, he has to have someone helping him," Espinosa said.

"In my opinion, she's the logical choice. Think about it, guys, they can meet up in

154

the break room at Home Builders Depot. No one can get in there but employees. That's where they meet up and talk about stuff. I'll go so far as to bet a week's salary." Espinosa had no takers because it made perfect sense.

"You know, Espinosa, you are absolutely right. Five bucks says that's exactly what is going on. There's your answer, kid. You stake out the girl if that's what you want to do or call Snowden to put some people on her. Around the clock," Ted said.

"I think I'd like to give it a shot. I'll have Abner hack into the employment records there and find out her hours, and I'll use a different car and tail her myself. I know how to do that. Jack gave me some great pointers when we were working out in South East last Christmas. This is really a good breakfast. I've never been here before." The others watched as Dennis downed his glass of orange juice in one long gulp.

"I'm heading out to the farm. Anyone want to go with me? I want to be the one to show Annie and Myra the actual paper. They hate reading it online," Maggie said.

"Nah, pick me up on the way back. I'm going to the paper," Espinosa said.

In the end, it was decided that Maggie would go alone, then return to plot out a plan as far as Lincoln Moss was concerned.

Maggie looked over at Dennis. "Ask Abner to get me any of Moss's private cell-phone numbers, especially the one the rumor mill says is only connected to POTUS. That should blow him out of the water right off the bat. I'm thinking he would guard that like he would Fort Knox if he owned it."

"No problem. Whose turn is it to pay?" Dennis asked.

"I'm paying," Ted said. A second later, Dennis was gone. They watched him with smiles on their faces. "He does have a bounce in his step, that's for sure. I really like that kid's dedication." Maggie and Espinosa agreed with Ted's assessment.

Outside, the threesome split up, each going their separate way with one thought paramount, how to nail Lincoln Moss to the wall.

"Here it is, ladies," Maggie said as she spread out the morning edition of the *Post* on the kitchen table. "I wanted you to see it in person because I know it's not the same as reading and seeing online. What do you think?"

Annie shrugged. "He was legitimately nominated the last two years but didn't make it. I imagine it's sticking in his craw that his cronies didn't endorse him. By the way, Abner called with his mobile number, one that only a very few people have. He also wanted to know if you want his secure, as in secure phone, issued to him by the White House. I said of course, so here they are." She handed over a sticky note with two numbers on it.

"I'm thinking he's going to go nuclear if I call the one issued by the White House. But I think I will wait until Espinosa can document his reaction to that." Maggie laughed. "How about if I make the call to his cell phone now, and you can listen in?" Maggie wiggled her eyebrows to make her point. Myra and Annie laughed out loud.

"Go for it, dear," Myra said.

Lincoln Moss sat down at a ridiculously long dining-room table that seated eighteen comfortably, twenty-two if needed. He sat at the head like the king he thought he was. The table was set perfectly for one. A delicate Bavarian lace place mat, Baccarat crystal, fine Lenox china, sterling silver utensils. A spray of orchids that he insisted be fresh every day sat in a cut-crystal vase to his left. To the right of his coffee cup sat a small crystal bell that he tapped for coffee refills or seconds if he really enjoyed whatever he was having for breakfast.

Four newspapers were to his left: the *Post,* the *Wall Street Journal,* and the *New York Times* along with a copy of *In the Know.*

Breakfast for the most part was always the same because he liked routine. Fifteen minutes to eat whatever he was having, then forty-five minutes to peruse the four papers along with a second cup of coffee. On rare occasions he dabbled with a third cup but rarely finished it.

Moss chewed his way through six gluten-free pancakes with sugar-free syrup, four strips of crisp crunchy turkey bacon with two slices of six-grain toast slathered with sugar-free strawberry jam. He looked at his watch when he touched the bell for his plate to be taken away. Fourteen minutes. He held up his index finger to indicate he wanted a refill on his coffee. His cup was filled immediately just as the housekeeper shook out the *Post* and placed it precisely in front of him on the table. He jerked back when he saw his own picture staring up at him. In his opinion, it was an unflattering picture, and he couldn't help but wonder if the people at the *Post* had chosen that particular one on purpose. Probably, the bastards. He was livid when he finished reading the write-up that said, he thought,

snidely, that maybe the third time would be the charm for Lincoln Moss. That, he decided, was a definite insult. He debated a full five minutes about calling the paper to ask them to withdraw his name but decided that might look petty on his part. Still, he seethed. If he lost again this year, the damn political machine would never let him live it down. It didn't and wouldn't matter if Gabriel Knight, President of the United States, voted for him or not. What the hell good was a vote of one?

Moss scanned the pictures again to see who he was up against. A growl shot out of his mouth. Losers, all of them. And yet he'd lose out to a loser. His anger mounted till he could barely see straight. He reached for his coffee cup and took a huge swallow that exploded out of his mouth like a gunshot. He'd forgotten to add cream, and he'd burned his mouth. "Son of a bitch!"

His cell phone rang, not the White House special one but the other. He thought about not answering it but knew in his gut that it was someone important calling to congratulate him. Besides, only a very few power brokers had the number. Without checking caller ID, he answered the phone and struggled to make his voice sound normal when he said, "Good morning, my friend."

"Uh . . . I'm sorry but this isn't one of your friends. This is Maggie Spritzer from the *Post*. I'm calling to congratulate you on behalf of all the staff here at the *Post* and to ask you if we could meet to do an interview, and, of course, to take some pictures that are a little more flattering than the one we ran today in the paper."

Moss felt his heart fluttering in his chest. He fought to take a clear deep breath. "Where did you get this phone number, Ms. Spritzer? There are very few people who know it." He didn't realize how tight he had clenched his jaw until he felt the pain ricochet down his neck.

"I'm a reporter, Mr. Moss. As you know, a reporter never reveals his or her sources. So, can we schedule an interview?"

Moss's gut instinct warned him not to make an issue of the phone number. It would be a simple matter to have it changed within the hour and notify those who had it. "I'm afraid not, Ms. Spritzer. My calendar is full for the next six weeks. Thank you for the nomination, however. Now, if you'll excuse me, I'm late for a meeting."

Maggie was, if nothing else, a dog with a bone. "Well then, perhaps you could find a few minutes on Saturday night at the First Lady's gala at the Four Seasons. The *Post* bought a table, and I understand it is right next to yours. That way, we can also interview your beautiful wife at the same time."

Who in the damn hell is this woman? Then he remembered. She'd done so many exposés along with that guy Ted something or other who was a Pulitzer Prize winner that her name was almost a household word. He felt his stomach tighten. "I'm afraid that won't be possible either. I never do interviews, especially at social occasions. I think the First Lady might frown on that."

"Well then, is there any truth to the rumor that your wife had facial surgery to alter her appearance and that no one has seen her in five years?"

Lincoln Moss broke the connection. He was blind with fury, the veins in his neck twice their normal size. He could feel the blood rushing through his body. He knew he'd just screwed up, but he didn't give a good rat's ass. He dropped his head between his knees and struggled to take deep breaths.

Moss looked at the beautiful orchids, the crystal, his delicate china, and the Bavarian lace place mat that was handmade. With one sweep of his arm, he sent the whole mess sailing across the room. He got up, didn't look back, and strode out of the room. His destination — the White House.

Moss was less than a block from the White House when the fine hairs on the back of his neck started to move. He was never a superstitious person, but he had learned a long time ago to pay attention to his gut instincts. And right now, his gut was telling him *not* to go to the White House. Because . . . because . . . the President had not spoken to him today. The first time that had happened since Gabe took office six years ago. It had to mean something. But what?

By the same token, he hadn't called Gabe either. Gabe should have called him by now. Regardless of how busy the man was, he always managed to call, even if he did it when he was taking a bathroom break. And he should have called to congratulate him on that Man of the Year crap if nothing else to tease him about maybe the third time would be the charm.

Without thinking, Moss made a left turn and swept right by the White House.

Tomorrow was another day.

CHAPTER 10

Jack Emery felt like he'd been hit by a train even though he was up and walking around. He realized he felt more like a zombie than anything else, and that included a train wreck. For some reason, he never bounced back like other people did when he flew through time zones and had to adapt to a different climate and time change. He looked over at Harry, who himself looked like he was zoned out on another planet. He did, however, appear peaceful as he sat in a corner of the suite and meditated. Jack knew better than to invade his space, so he sat down and leaned his head back, praying he didn't fall asleep again. He just knew in his gut that Harry had slept through the night like a baby. Harry could lean against the wall and grab a catnap.

At precisely eight o'clock Paris time, Harry untangled himself and stood up. "I'm ready to go."

"About time," Jack snarled. Harry ignored him.

Outside in the early-morning air, Jack sniffed. He was smelling some kind of flowers, a pleasant scent. Perfumed air. He had to remember that phrase so he could share it with Nikki when he got home. Paris had perfumed air. Well, they were masters at perfumes and cosmetics in France, so why shouldn't the air be perfumed? Who the hell cared anyway? He hated it when he got cranky like this.

Jack watched while Harry commandeered a cab that was just pulling to the curb. He beat the uniformed bellman by a hair and opened the cab door himself. "I don't need someone to open a car door, I can do it myself. Nor do I feel the need to tip someone twenty bucks for the pleasure. Don't go giving me that when in Rome do as the Romans do. How the hell do you know the Romans tipped twenty bucks for a chariot ride?" Harry rattled on before Jack could open his mouth.

"I have an idea, Harry. Get back out of the cab and kill the guy so we can be on our way." Harry actually laughed out loud as Jack spieled off the address they wanted to be taken to.

By the time they reached the complex

where Jane Petrie had planned to spend her vacation, Jack's headache was almost gone, and he was starting to feel human again. "How do you think we should play this, Harry? Good guy, bad guy, all muscle and gold shields from the git-go, or flat-out threaten with something or other?"

"Well, Annie and Myra always say, and Charles backs them up, that you get more flies with honey than vinegar."

"We tried honey yesterday, and she bamboozled us. What's even worse, we fell for it. Today is pure vinegar. I say we go with two bad guys flexing their muscles as they whip out their gold shields. Last resort, we pony up with a wad of euros."

"That works for me," Harry said agreeably. "The good thing is the lady speaks excellent English, so you won't have to torture her with your pidgin French."

Jack looked around to get his bearings when he stepped out of the cab, Harry right behind him. "I think this is the main entrance we went in yesterday, but we came from another direction. Left side is vacation rentals, right side for long-term rentals. Is that how you remember it, Harry?"

"Yeah. Let's go."

"Now who's being surly?" Jack called over his shoulder.

Jack opened the door. A bell tinkled overhead. He could smell French roast coffee. Why the hell not, they were in France, after all. The lady behind the desk had her coffee cup almost to her mouth when she looked up and saw Harry and Jack. Instead of drinking it, she used both hands to set the cup in front of her. Her face looked pinched, her eyes wary as she waited for them to say something.

Jack took the initiative. He reached for his gold shield and held it up. "You lied to us yesterday, mademoiselle. Yesterday, you told us you didn't know where Ms. Petrie went. We've come to find out that you do indeed know. In fact, we're told you arranged for the transfer. True or false?"

"I did no such thing," the woman whose breast pin said she was Vivian François replied in a jittery-sounding voice. While her mouth said one thing, her eyes were saying something totally different.

Jack extended the gold shield. "This gives us the authority to turn you over to Interpol, Scotland Yard, your very own DGSE, and the American CIA or MI6." When François didn't look impressed, Jack smiled, and said, "Or how about those cuties at Mossad?" That got her attention. "One phone call, and an agent will be here within twenty

166

minutes." While Vivian François considered her options, Harry held up his shield, his face full of menace.

"This is what I suggest, mademoiselle. We are going to forget we were here yesterday and forget that you lied to us. We are going to ask you again for your cooperation, and for that cooperation, we will be leaving this behind when we leave." Jack pulled out the wad of euros that represented five hundred American dollars. He held the euros in one hand, his cell in the other. "I have every agency that I just mentioned on speed dial. Mossad is number one. Now, where is Ms. Petrie?"

François started to wring her hands. "I can tell you where I sent her. I cannot tell you if she is still there. She said she would call me, but she has not done so. She did not tell me what trouble she was in, but she did appear to be frightened. I sent her to a friend who . . . how do you say in English, rents rooms by the day? Ah, yes, boardinghouse with meals included, no?"

"Boardinghouse, yes," Jack said. "Where? Write it down. How long will it take us to get there?" Bingo!

François drew a crude map. "There is no point in explaining since you do not know the area, monsieur. Just give this map to the cab driver. Forty-five minutes by cab if you leave now."

"Has anyone else been here looking for Ms. Petrie?"

François hesitated. Harry advanced a step and held out the gold shield at eye level. "I think so, yes. My night clerk left me a message that two men came in a little after ten o'clock last evening and asked the same questions you asked. He told them to come back this morning because he knew nothing. The man is . . . how do you say . . . slow. That is why he works at night. Nothing goes on at night."

"I do not want to frighten you, mademoiselle, but this would be a very good time for you to go somewhere else. For a day or so. Those men do not carry gold shields, and they are not nice like we are. We mean you no harm. I cannot say the same for them. Do you understand what I just said?"

"I understand perfectly. I will post a sign on the door. What is it you Americans say on your signs? Gone Fishing!"

In spite of himself, Jack laughed. Harry grinned.

Jack held out the wad of euros. "Does this buy your silence, mademoiselle?"

Vivian François didn't have to think twice

168

about her answer. "Yes, monsieur, it buys my silence. Now if you would be so good as to leave, I need to close down."

The moment the door closed behind Jack and Harry, the blinds inside were pulled. A second after that, a single white sheet of paper was Scotch-Taped to the door. In big bold letters it said, GONE FISHING. Jack clapped Harry on the back just as a cab pulled to the curb. They climbed in, handed over the map, and settled back for the forty-five-minute drive. Both Jack and Harry passed the time by sending texts Stateside with a real-time update on what was happening in France.

"We just might get out of here today, Harry, if we can do the snatch and grab. Call the pilot and put him on alert."

Jack finished with his last text and pulled up the morning edition of the *Post,* and scrolled down. *Good going, Maggie,* he thought. *Everything's in play now.* He smiled to himself and suddenly realized his throbbing head was still quiet. He actually felt peaceful. He closed his eyes and allowed his thoughts to run amuck.

Back in the States, Dennis West patrolled the Home Builders Depot parking lot, looking like a lost soul who had lost his wheels.

For the most part, he stayed close to the garden center since Stacey Copeland came into work early and would have a choice front parking space. Abner had confirmed that her hours were six-thirty to two o'clock. She was off weekends, and management did its best to work with the students who worked part-time to control their hours. He now had her home address and the make and model of her car. At the moment, he was parked one row over and three cars behind her silver Ford Taurus. Since he already had Copeland's address, all he needed was to see her get into her car, and he could drive out to Columbia Heights where she lived and mosey around on his own. This way he didn't have to worry about her spotting her tail. He continued to look around, but he couldn't detect any of Snowden's operatives. If they were even here. If they were, they were damn good at what they did. Then he caught Copeland out of the corner of his eye. Tall for a girl. Lanky, actually. She looked to be in good shape. She wore jeans and a T-shirt with the Home Builders Depot logo on the back. She yanked at a baseball cap that was smashed into her back pocket, clamped it down on her curly head, then got into her car. She very casually looked around before she pulled her sunglasses off the visor and put them on. She backed out of her parking space carefully, her head going to the right, then left, then back right again. Clearly to Dennis, she was looking to see if anyone was paying attention to her.

Dennis gave her a good five-minute head start because he wanted to see if anyone appeared to be following her. When he deemed the coast clear, he changed gears and left the parking lot. He'd already programmed her address into the GPS. For all he knew, he might even get to where she lived before Copeland did. He wished he'd taken a dry run while he waited so he had an idea of the area. Well, too late now. He settled down for the drive, glad that traffic wasn't heavy.

Thirty-seven minutes later, after two drive-bys, Dennis pulled into a private driveway with a FOR SALE sign on the lawn. If the house was empty, and it appeared to be with nothing on any of the windows, he was good to go. Parking as he did at an angle, he had a clear view of the four-apartment building complex where Stacey Copeland lived through his side-view mirror.

Dennis felt comfortable enough to know he had a story to offer if anyone asked him why he was parked so long in the driveway.

"I'm waiting for the Realtor, who said he was delayed." Period, end of story.

Three hours later, Dennis realized that wasn't the end of the story. Stacey Copeland had not returned to her apartment. He knew he hadn't screwed up, but he checked with Abner again to make sure he had the right address. He did. Maybe she went shopping. Women did like to shop. But for three hours! Especially after a workday.

Dennis opened the car door, got out, and stretched. He was soaked with perspiration and itched all over; plus, he had to use the bathroom. Leave or not to leave? His bladder finally won out, so he got back in the car and headed for the nearest gas station. The A/C on full blast felt so good, he swooned.

Twenty minutes later he was back in the neighborhood driving up one street and down another searching for something to make sense of his even being out here. He had just turned left onto a nicely tree-shaded street when he spotted Copeland's silver Taurus parked in the driveway of a small brick house with a well-landscaped yard. He checked the license plate to be sure it was the right silver Taurus. The numbers matched perfectly.

Copeland must be visiting a friend, he

finally decided. Women did that all the time. For all he knew, she could be there for hours. Women did like to yack and jabber and tend to forget the time. Espinosa had told him that once. Now what should he do? He called Ted to ask for advice.

"Stay with it, kid. You might be onto something. For all you know, she might have those two women stashed inside that house. Wait till it gets dark, then check it out on foot. In the meantime, call the address in to Abner and see if he can find out who owns the house. You know what, now that I think about it, it's starting to make a lot of sense. It just so happens I know that neighborhood, and it's only about a mile from the White House. Hiding out in plain sight. Figures, because that's exactly what I would do if I were her, hide out in plain sight. Works every time. Good work, kid, keep me posted. Hey, one other thing, kid, don't get caught."

Dennis snorted. Like that was going to happen. His thumbs worked frantically as he sent off a text to Abner. The only thing left now to do was go back to the empty house and park in the driveway again. It hit him then. Copeland's car was the only one in the driveway at the new location. And there were no actual garage doors attached to the house. The owners must have converted the garage to usable living space. Details, details, details. He patted himself on the back for being so observant.

Chapter 11

Dennis knew he was in trouble the moment he heard the tap on the car window as a flashlight momentarily blinded him. A cop! Busted! Oh, jeez. He needed to think quick and fast. He lowered the window, blinked, seeing stars for a moment. "What's up, Officer?" he managed to croak as he tried to shield his eyes from the bright light.

The officer appeared to be middle-aged and wore an expression that he wasn't about to put up with any crap. Dennis ran with his story he concocted on the fly. "I guess someone called to say I've been sitting here all day, huh? It's true, Officer, except for a couple of bathroom breaks. Here's the deal. I paid a Realtor who represents this property a deposit of five thousand dollars to buy this house. I came to find out he took down payments from two other people. I told him if he didn't meet me here to return my money, I was going to the police. I'm getting married next month, and my fiancée loves this house. We saved for five years to come up with the down payment, and I'm not leaving till he gives me back the money. First, he said he'd be here by four, then he sent a text saying he was delayed and would be here by seven. Then at seven he sent another one swearing he would be no later than ten, and he has my check with him. What would you do, Officer? I gotta tell you, right now I'm more afraid of going home and telling my fiancée I don't have the check than I am afraid of you." This was all said with a straight face on his part. It looked to him like the cop was buying it.

The cop looked at Dennis's earnest face and relented. "Several neighbors called to say you were sitting here all day. Okay, I'll cut you some slack and let you stay, but you better be out of here by ten o'clock. I'll be back to check on you on my rounds."

"I didn't do anything wrong," Dennis grumbled. "I didn't even get out to walk around. So, what you're saying is if that skunk doesn't show up by ten, I have to leave. Is that what you're saying?"

"Pretty much, son. You need to take it up with the real-estate board. I wish you good luck."

Dennis pressed the button to raise the

window before he collapsed against the seat. That, he congratulated himself, was an Academy Award moment. He looked down at his watch: 9:11. It was fully dark now. He'd originally planned to make his move at nine-thirty, to check out the house on foot the way Ted suggested. When he saw Stacey Copeland arrive back at her apartment building a few minutes past eight, he made the decision to go at nine-thirty.

With the cop now wise to him and the fact that he was patrolling the neighborhood, Dennis realized he needed to relocate or go home. The third possibility was to call in reinforcements. He decided to go with the third option, and quickly punched in Myra's cell-phone number. She clicked on after the first ring. He quickly repeated the night's events and waited for a response, which was for him to go to the gas station and wait for Myra and Annie.

Dennis pressed the starter button and turned on his headlights. He sighed. He wasn't sure if he was disappointed or delighted. He'd done all the legwork, and now, if the two ladies didn't want him in at the finish, assuming he was right and Amalie Moss and Rosalee Muno were in the house, he was going to be one very unhappy camper. He was almost certain that Myra and Annie would want him at the finish line. *Who else would they get to skulk around the backyard and peer into windows? Yours truly, that's who.*

Dennis made it to the gas station without running into the cop who'd checked him out. He felt grateful. If he was allowed to go with Myra and Annie, he'd leave his car at the gas station and drive with them.

Even if Annie drove like hell, he knew it would be thirty minutes before they joined him at the twenty-four-hour gas station and convenience store. He decided to use the restroom for the fourth time that day. He splashed cold water on his face and toweled off with scratchy brown paper towels. He washed his hands and combed his hair. Satisfied that he looked as good as possible, he marched into the convenience-store section of the gas station and bought a cold iced tea, some Twinkies, and chips.

The night was hot and humid, typical weather for Washington in July. He dumped everything in the car and decided to limber up, so he jogged in place for a good ten minutes. He was sweating profusely when he climbed back in the car and turned on the air-conditioning, knowing full well he was going to catch a cold but not really caring.

The iced tea was gone in two long gulps. The Twinkies and chips took less than ten minutes since he hadn't eaten anything all day and was now starved. He was glad Harry wasn't around to see what he was eating. Harry was into seeds, grain, and that shitty green tea that he mainlined. "Sometimes," he muttered to himself, "you just gotta do what you gotta do."

With nothing else to do to occupy his time, Dennis sent texts to everyone advising them of what was going on. To Jack he texted, *How about an update on what's going on with you over there in gay Pareee.*

When there were no incoming texts, Dennis turned his phone off and waited. The wait was short. It was only seven minutes later that he saw Annie blasting her way through the parking lot. She skidded to a stop next to his car, her tires practically smoking.

Dennis hopped out of his car, locked it, and literally dove into the backseat of Annie's fancy-dancy car and came face-to-face with Myra's dog Lady. Lady barked at her space being invaded. Perfect! He should have thought of Lady himself. Nothing like a lady walking a dog or two ladies walking a dog. He felt stupid but only for a minute. He hugged the gorgeous golden retriever.

Even before Dennis could close the door, Annie had the car in reverse and was barreling back across the lot. "What's the plan, young man?" Myra asked.

Dennis gave Annie directions. "Well, first I think we should do a couple of drive-bys to get you two familiar with the neighborhood. Which, by the way, is actually very nice. I think we should park a few streets over and walk to the house, at which point I'll check out the yard, front and back. There are a lot of bushes, but I also think it's a good idea that you brought Lady with you. No one pays attention to dog walkers."

Two drive-bys later, Dennis pointed to a small copse of evergreens at the entrance to a cul-de-sac. "Pull in here and park. Don't worry, I know exactly where we are. I can get us in and out of here in a flash if necessary. We're going to walk now like we belong here. Everybody good with that?"

Everybody, meaning Myra and Annie, said they were good with that, so they took off walking down the street. They encountered no one, but they did hear muted voices coming from various front porches. Voices they ignored.

"What's the address?" Annie hissed.

"Sixty-six Nightingale Lane," Dennis hissed in return. "It's just around the corner, two houses in. There's a big old sycamore tree right by the driveway, where you can have Lady pretend to do her business. I'll go around back. There are lights on inside. No outside lights, that's a good thing. No strange dogs barking either, which is also good.

"While I'm checking out the back, you two ladies decide how you want to handle this. Do we blast in? Do we identify ourselves and ring the bell? What? Personally, I'm all for blasting in. They'll bolt for sure if we give them notice. Make up your mind real quick," Dennis said, "because I won't be gone long."

"The youngster has a point, Myra. What do you think?"

"What I think, Annie, is who is going to be doing the blasting? Does that mean Dennis is going to kick in the back door, which probably leads to the kitchen? The women will undoubtedly run out the front door unless one of us is waiting by the front door. That's what I would do if I was in their position. Do you have your gun in your purse?"

"I do. Never leave home without it, you know that, Myra."

"I know. I know. I was just making conversation. I'm just a little bit nervous.

And Lady is getting jittery."

"The only reason Lady is jittery is because she's picking up on your nervousness. Think, Myra. When was the last time we failed at anything? Never, that's when. So lighten up and go with the flow here. Damn, it's humid. My clothes are plastered to my body, and we've only been here less than ten minutes. Supposed to rain tonight, too, and all day tomorrow. This whole thing started on a rainy day, remember, Myra, we were getting our nails done when Pearl hit the shop like a tornado?"

Myra had her mouth open to speak when Dennis appeared out of the darkness. The women backed up so they were closer to the young reporter. "All the blinds are pulled except on the kitchen window. No blind or curtain there. There's food on the table, groceries, staples actually, that haven't been put away yet. I got right up under the window and looked in. I could see light coming from another room, so I guess they have the television on. I couldn't tell for certain which room it is. The house is small, five rooms off a short hallway would be my guess. That has to mean the front door opens into the living room. So, how do you want to do this? I could try to pick the lock, but I might make noise. They're going to spook real easy; I think we all know that. Or, I can kick in the door. It's just your regulation kitchen door, four panes of glass on the top and wood on the bottom half. Standard lock. The front door is probably solid. If I kick in the door, they're automatically going to run for the front door."

"I've got it covered," Annie said, pointing to her purse.

"Okay, then. Myra, you come with me. Leave the dog with Annie. Dogs, even gentle ones like Lady, are always a deterrent. We're good here?"

"We are good," Annie said as she reached out for Lady's leash. She moved into position as Myra and Dennis ran around the back just as a few drops of rain splattered on Annie's cheeks. Rain was good right now. Anyone meandering about outside would head indoors. She waited, her hand in her purse.

Annie heard the crash minutes later. Lady threw her head back and howled. Annie heard the snick of the front door's being unlocked. Her hand was out of her purse in the blink of an eye. She was on the steps that led to the front porch within a few seconds, the gun pointed straight ahead. "Go back into the house, ladies. No one is going to hurt you. We are here to help you.

Just so you know, 9643 and 9644, people you trust sent us here."

As she advanced across the porch Annie could see that Dennis had his hand clamped around the wrist of a young girl, and Myra had her hand on Amalie Moss's arm.

"Guard, Lady," Myra said as she let go of Amalie Moss's arm. She turned on a lamp in the living room. She looked over at Annie, who was still holding her gun in her hand, pointed at the two women.

"Do not believe what they tell you about golden retrievers being gentle and everyone's friend. Lady will rip out your throat if you make a move we don't like." It was a lie, but it sounded good even to Myra's ears.

Annie looked over at Dennis. "You need to go get the car and bring it here. We'll drop you off at your car on the way out. While you do that, we will explain to these ladies that they are as safe with us as they would be in their mothers' arms."

There were only two words to describe Muno and Moss as they huddled together on the chocolate-brown sofa: *defeated* and *terrified*. "How did you find us?" Amalie Moss demanded bravely.

Myra sniffed. "Just chalk it up to dogged detective work. I want to reassure you that you are safe with us. We know who you are, Rosalee Muno and Amalie Moss. You, Mrs. Moss, are married to Lincoln Moss. You were given safe passage in the underground railroad operated by a dear friend of ours. Your ID numbers were 9643 and 9644. We know all about the picture that was in the tabloid. We are currently in the process of locating the woman who sold you out for money. She was a nurse at the clinic where you had your facial surgery. We will deal with her separately. For now, we just want you to know you are safe."

"I'll never be safe from *him*," Amalie whimpered.

"I guarantee your safety," Myra said gently. "You need to trust us. Can you do that?"

Muno's head bobbed up and down as she started to cry. "I'm sorry, Amalie, I can't do this anymore. We have to trust someone. I believe these people. I really do, Amalie. I want to see my family again. All we succeeded in doing was getting Jason and Stacey in trouble. That lunatic husband of yours is going to go after them. We're lucky these people found us first. I'm going with them. What you do is up to you."

Amalie put her arm around the young girl. "You're right. I can't do this anymore either.

I just want a life again." She looked Annie dead in the eye, and said, "We won't give you any more trouble. I promise."

"Do you have any belongings?" Myra asked. Amalie and Rosalee both shook their heads from side to side.

"As soon as our partner gets here, we're going to take you someplace that you will truly be safe. You have to trust us and give us your word you won't try to cut and run. If you can't do that, then we're going to have to tie you up," Myra said.

Rosalee Muno's eyes opened wide all of a sudden. "Are you . . . I think I know . . . you are, aren't you?" Annie didn't think it was possible, but the young girl's eyes opened even wider when she smiled at her. "You are! I knew it! Amalie, they're the Vigilantes. She's right, we're safe with these people."

"Who are the Vigilantes, Rosy?"

Rosalee laughed out loud. "Good people who make our world a better place to live. I'll explain later when things are a little more calm." Amalie nodded, and the look of relief on her face was a joy to see.

"Ma'am, can we leave a note for Stacey?" Rosalee asked.

"I'm sorry, no, you can't. We'll get word to both Stacey and Jason that you're safe.

It's for their own safety in case anyone is watching them. Please, just trust us." Once again, the women's heads bobbed up and down.

"I can see the headlights in the driveway. Come along, ladies. Let's get into the car quickly," Annie said.

"What about the back door?" Myra asked. "At the very least, we have to leave some money for the repairs. Get the women in the car, and I'll see what I can do."

Myra inspected the damage to the back door and winced. All she could do was push the kitchen table and chairs up against the door. She looked up to see Dennis watching her.

"Let me do that, Myra. Annie said to give you this," he said, as he handed her five crisp hundred-dollar bills. "She thinks that will cover the damage." Within five minutes, the back door was as secure as he could make it.

Myra fanned out the bills on the kitchen counter and set a cup on them so they wouldn't move.

"The front door is self-locking. By the way, it's pouring rain outside, and I did not see a soul on the roads driving here," Dennis said. "I think we're going to get out of here clean as a whistle. After you drop

187

me off at the gas station, do you want me to follow you out to the farm, or should I go home?"

"You've had a very stressful day, young man. Go home, take a good hot shower, and fall into bed. Come out to the farm tomorrow unless you're needed at the paper. It goes without saying, Dennis, Annie and I are proud of you. You came through for us and saved these women. I don't know why I say this, but my feeling is we were just one small step ahead of *someone* and got to those women in the nick of time. All thanks to you."

Dennis felt a ring of heat around his neck. He wasn't good at accepting compliments. "I just ran with it, Myra. Any one of you would have done the same thing. Time to go," he said, looking around.

"I think our fingerprints are all over the place," Myra said.

Dennis laughed. "With that gold shield in your back pocket, fingerprints are the least of your problems. Besides, Abner told me he was going to make sure he erased all of our prints on Aphis. Never sweat the small stuff is what he says."

"Then that's good enough for me. Let's go home now."

CHAPTER 12

It was a starless night with a hint of rain in the air as Jack and Harry made their way on foot through what appeared to be a working-class neighborhood. "Reminds me of Baltimore, with the rows of brownstones," Jack said. Harry just shrugged.

There was a bit of anxiousness in Jack's voice when he asked, "Do you think she's going to put up a fight?"

"Well, Jack, take a minute and think about it. If you were in her shoes, what would you do? Then take that thought a step further and ask yourself who exactly is she afraid of? Does she even know about *us*? Is she smart enough to be afraid of Lincoln Moss? Goodwin warned her, so that lets him out of the fear category. So why'd she run?"

It was Jack's turn to shrug. "If I had to hazard a guess, I'd say that the day the picture hit the tabloid, she realized what she'd done and instantly regretted it. According to Goodwin, the two of them had an arrangement. People rat other people out all the time, even their friends, for money, and nothing ever happens to them. The worst thing that happens is they lose a few friends. How do you think all those tabloids get the goods on those movie stars? Cash for scandal. Whatever . . . here we are. Let's just hope this doesn't go down badly."

Off in the distance, a dog barked, then another bark answered the lonely call. The light drizzle of rain that was falling when they started out was now a full rainstorm, coming down steadily. The street took on an eerie feeling, with the drizzle dripping past the yellow light emanating from the lampposts. Both men shivered in their wet clothes even though it was a warm evening.

Jack and Harry, aware of the time, marched up the nine brick steps that led them to a narrow sheltered slab of concrete with an equally narrow overhang. Jack punched the doorbell. A bonging sound could be heard inside. Both men watched through the oval glass in the center of the door as a heavyset woman waddled to the door. Outside, a light came on, illuminating them. Jack held up his gold shield. Harry was a little slower on the draw, but he finally got his out of his pocket. The door opened.

The first words out of Jack's mouth were, "Do you speak English, mademoiselle?"

"Yes." She waited, her eyes never leaving the gold shields.

"Vivian François sent us," Jack said. It wasn't really a lie, he thought. It was the right thing to say. Some of the tension left the woman's shoulders.

"How can I help you gentlemen."

"By taking us to wherever Ms. Petrie is right at this moment."

"Ah, yes, Mademoiselle Petrie. I sensed she was trouble. I did not want to have her here, but Vivian is a very old and dear friend. She begged me. You understand this, no?"

Jack said nothing. He waited. Harry transferred his weight from one foot to the other. "I do not want any trouble. I operate a respectable rooming house. Follow me, and I will take you to Mademoiselle Petrie. You will not be returning here again, will you?"

"Absolutely not," Jack said truthfully. He looked down to see a fat tabby cat rubbing against his ankles.

"That is Fefe. She loves it when we have guests, always hoping for a catnip treat. It is the second door on the left. I will leave you now, so you can conduct your business. We are finished, no?"

"We are finished, yes," Jack said. He watched as the woman bent down to pick up the fat cat. Both he and Harry waited until she was at the bottom of the steps before they knocked on the door.

Jack looked over at Harry, and whispered, "Show time. Hold up that shield. I'm thinking that should be enough to scare the crap out of her."

Jack knocked softly on the door but loud enough for the occupant to hear and not disturb the other guests on the floor.

"Yes, who is it?" came a muffled response. Jack and Harry remained silent. He rapped again, this time a tad harder. Petrie repeated her response. Jack knocked a third time and mumbled something. The door opened a crack, Harry pushed it, and the woman on the other side was pushed backward.

A ripe curse split the air. Jack closed the door as Harry clamped his hand over Jane Petrie's mouth.

Jack leaned in close so he could whisper in Petrie's ear. "Stop the caterwauling. We are not going to hurt you. Unless . . . listen to me . . . you don't shut up. If you don't shut up, we will slice off your ears." He was rewarded with instant silence. "That's better. Now listen to me very carefully. We want

192

you to pack your things. Do it quickly. We are taking you back to the States with us."

"No, no! You can't make me go back there. I have dual citizenship. My mother was French. You can't make me go with you."

Jack whipped out a small, wicked-looking switchblade from his key ring and brandished it in the air. "What part of 'we are taking you back to the States with us' didn't you understand? You caused some very nice people a lot of trouble. You'll have to answer for that, not to us but to the people you harmed. Now, do what I say and pack your stuff. Or, leave it. The choice is yours."

Jack nodded to Harry to call the pilot to tell him they were on the way. "Then go downstairs and have the lady call us a taxi."

Jack watched as Petrie pulled a Gucci suitcase out from under the bed. He continued to watch as she threw her belongings in any old way, her toiletries on top of the mess. She closed the suitcase, locked it, and stared defiantly at Jack.

"Give me your passport," Jack said.

"I will do no such thing." Jack waved the switchblade in front of her. She swallowed hard but remained defiant.

"Last chance," Jack said, advancing on her.

"I want a lawyer! I have rights!"

"I bet you do. Want a lawyer that is. You have no rights. I just took them away. Now, hand over the passport, or you're going to be minus an ear."

One look at Jack's determined expression, and Petrie backed up a step and groped on the unmade bed for her purse. With one eye on Jack and the other on her purse, she fumbled until she found the passport. She handed it over, her hands shaking.

Jack looked down at the blue cover on the passport — American. "Now give me your French passport. What? You thought I was stupid. Well, shame on you. C'mon, hand it over."

Petrie knew then that she was beaten. She fumbled some more in the oversize purse that could have passed for an overnight bag or a backpack and finally withdrew her rouge-colored French passport. She handed that over, too.

Jack skimmed through it as well as the American one. Many stamps on both. Well, Miss Jane Petrie's traveling days were coming to a close. He jammed both passports into his jacket pocket and pulled the zipper to assure they remained safe and sound.

"Let's go. You get to carry your own suitcase. Try anything funny, and you'll regret it. My colleague is waiting at the bottom of the steps, so be fair warned. Do not talk, do not scream, just act normal. One peep out of you, and, like I said, you will regret it. And if you think for one minute that the taxi driver is going to help you, you're wrong. What's it going to be, lady? Decide now."

"Okay, okay," Petrie said through clenched teeth.

"Good choice. This might be a good time to tell you that Lincoln Moss has people tracking you down. So far tonight, we are one step ahead of them. If you're smart, you'll want to keep it that way." Petrie nodded.

Seventy minutes later, Jack and Harry ushered Jane Petrie up the portable steps to Anna de Silva's Gulfstream. Harry carried the Gucci bag and stored it beside the stewardess's jump seat.

Ten minutes later, they were wheels up and headed back to the good old United States.

While Petrie sulked and cried, Jack and Harry were busy sending texts. Their ETA was sunup.

Mission accomplished.

■ ■ ■ ■

It was raining the proverbial cats and dogs when Dennis West parked his car in the Home Builders Depot parking lot to wait for Jason Woods. He really wanted to be with Maggie, Ted, and Espinosa at the airport to greet Jack, Harry, and their guest. He'd spent a sleepless night worrying about Jason and Stacey. He had to put their minds at ease and warn them once again to be careful. Their peace of mind won out, and here he was. He didn't even know if Jason or Stacey knew that the two women were gone. The only way they could know, he thought, was if Stacey stopped by the house before work. He seriously doubted that had happened because mornings were hectic, traffic was a bear, and she knew when she left last evening that the women were safe and secure. Possibly she might take a run by on her lunch hour to check on them, but he didn't really see that happening either.

Dennis looked down at his watch; it was twenty-five minutes past seven. Both employees should be arriving right about *now*. He looked up and saw Jason Woods climbing out of a pickup truck he didn't recognize. Dennis was out of the car in a flash, not caring if he got soaked or not. Jason himself was wearing a Home Builders Depot slicker.

"Jason, hold up. Please, this is important. I need to talk to you. It's about Rosalee."

Jason stopped in midstride and whirled around. "Mister, I am getting sick and tired of your harassing me. I've had enough. Beat it."

"I wish it were that simple. I thought you might like to know that after your friend Stacey secured the two women, they left. I just wanted to tell you they are as safe as if they were in their mothers' wombs. I wish I could tell you more, but right now, I can't. If you will just be patient for a little while longer and not go off half-cocked, Rosalee will be back in your life. Do you understand what I just said?"

"Yeah, yeah, I heard you. Just who the hell are you anyway, mister, aside from being a pain in my ass?"

"In time, I'll be happy to answer any and all questions, but this is not the time. In the meantime, I need to give you some money to pay for all the camping equipment you bought for the women. We left five hundred dollars on the kitchen counter to repair the back door. I'm sorry to say I had to kick it in. The element of surprise, you know. You might want to get on that as soon as possible. I did stack up the table and chairs, so the door wouldn't blow open."

"What . . . what the hell did you do? I mean, why would you do that?"

"Weren't you listening to me? I kicked it in. I really didn't want to do that, but we had to go with the element of surprise. And we didn't want the women scooting out the front door. I didn't have any other choice, Jason. The bottom line here is, Rosalee and Amalie are safe, and Lincoln Moss will never get to them, not in a million years. If it's any consolation to you, they both wanted to leave a note for you and Stacey. Unfortunately, we could not allow that. That's why I'm here, to put your mind at rest."

Jason Woods swiped at the rain pelting his face. "I repeat, just who the hell are you people? Why should I trust you?"

"Maybe because I'm the only game in town? Does that work for you? Look, I didn't have to come here to tell you all this. I could be home sleeping in a nice warm bed instead of standing here in the pouring rain. In case you haven't noticed, I'm soaking wet, and these shoes I'm standing in cost five hundred bucks."

Jason stared at Dennis for a long minute.

Whatever he saw in his expression seemed to satisfy him, at least for the moment. "So, how long?"

"I don't know, Jason. My best guess would be no more than two weeks. Possibly as soon as this weekend. There are a lot of things in play right now. Just trust me. Can you do that?"

Jason nodded. "What about Stacey? She stuck her neck out on all of this. Is she safe?" Jason realized something then to his own chagrin. He was more worried about Stacey than he was about Rosalee. Why was that?

"I want to say yes, but again, I don't know. For now, my best advice would be for both of you to stick together. Don't go anywhere alone."

"You're scaring the shit out of me, mister."

"Good, that will keep you on your toes. Listen, I gotta go now." Dennis held out a roll of bills. "Take it, you're going to need it for your tuition. Sell the camping gear and keep the money. I'll be in touch."

Jason watched Dennis walk away in his sopping-wet five-hundred-dollar shoes. What kind of jerk paid five hundred dollars for shoes? He looked down at his beat-up Nikes. Hell, he didn't even own a pair of leather shoes. He realized as he walked across the lot to the garden pavilion that he didn't feel bad. He didn't feel good, either. He headed for the break room to wait for Stacey. Five hundred dollars for a pair of shoes. Sheez.

Maggie, Ted, Espinosa, Jack, and Harry formed a cordon around Jane Petrie as they led her to the *Post* van. Maggie gave her a shove, and she sprawled across the seat. "I want a lawyer! Do you hear me, I want a damn lawyer! You kidnapped me! Kidnapping is against the law!"

"And what you did isn't against the law?" Maggie shot back. "Buckle up and shut up, or I'll pull out your teeth with my bare hands."

"You're terrorists! This is terrorism! You're holding me against my will," Petrie screamed shrilly.

"Will someone shut her up so I can concentrate on my driving," Ted said.

Harry leaned over, and before Petrie could take a deep breath, she was out cold, thanks to Harry's thumb finding and pressing oh so lightly on just the right spot below her left ear.

"How long will she be out, Harry?" Jack asked.

Harry shrugged. "An hour, maybe a little more."

"Good, because the next step would have been to put a bag over her head so she doesn't see where we're going. I suppose if we went with the bag deal, it might be construed as terrorism. Not that any of us cares."

"Talk to us, Jack. Tell us everything. And don't leave anything out," Ted said.

Jack rattled away nonstop, Harry filling in the blanks.

Jack ended up with, "This chick doesn't think she did anything wrong. She thinks of herself as an entrepreneur. Survival of the fittest, that kind of thing. The funny thing is, she's scared, but I don't think she knows exactly what she's scared of. My personal opinion is of losing her money. Not that Moss is gunning for her. Or us, for that matter."

"Hey, I got an incoming text from Dennis, guys," Maggie said. "Oooh, he locked it down, the ladies are safe now out at Pinewood. And he's just left Home Builders Depot. He says the two kids are okay. He's on his way to Pinewood. We're lookin' good, people." Maggie chortled. "Two down, meaning Petrie and the ladies, one to go, meaning Lincoln Moss."

"How's the contest going?" Harry asked.

"We have six serious contenders of which Moss is one. And we have nineteen applicants who can't even pass the sniff test."

"Any news on the First Lady's shindig on Saturday?" Harry asked.

"Not that I know of. I'm sure Myra and Annie will give us an update when we get to the farm. Three days away. I'm actually looking forward to getting all gussied up and dancing the night away. Half of Hollywood's music people are performing."

"With whom?" Ted asked sourly.

"Why, Mr. Robinson, with whoever asks me." Maggie giggled. She just loved jerking Ted's chain.

"Yeah, well, guess who's covering that shindig? Yours truly, and Espinosa will be snapping away all night, so be warned. Everyone in this town will be there, and I do mean everyone. Should be interesting."

"What about us?" Jack shot back. "Is it just the girls, or do we get to go, too? I hate those damn things, but if Moss is going to be there, then I want to be there, too."

"That, my friend, you have to take up with Myra and Annie. All I know is that Annie bought a table. I'm not sure if they seat eight or ten. At fifty grand a pop, that's as in per person, that's a lot of bread to shell out," Ted called over his back. "Another thing. Security will be tighter than a duck's ass. Secret Service all over the place."

Jack laughed, then Harry laughed. "We got into the White House once, or did you forget that, Mr. Reporter." Jack guffawed. "Even with all those tight-duck-ass Secret Service agents milling around."

"Oh, yeahhhh, I did forget about that. So, guess that means we'll see you there whatever Annie and Myra say. By the way, did I tell you that the kid bought a table under the Welmed name?"

"Dennis bought a table!" Maggie shrieked. "I swear, that kid never ceases to amaze me. Plus, he's a damn good reporter. Wow! Well, Jack, your problem, along with the rest of the guys', is now solved. You will be at Dennis's table partaking of rubber chicken, cold, baked potatoes, limp salad, and coffee that tastes like it came out of someone's rain boots. I'm pulling your leg here. We posted the menu in the *Post* yesterday. Because this affair is a children's benefit, so is the menu. You wanna hear it?"

Jack wasn't sure if he did or not. "Go for it?"

"Pizza. You know, the kind you make at home with toasted English muffins; SpaghettiOs, the ones with the little meatballs;

sloppy joes, the President's personal favorite sandwich in the whole world; weenies; apple juice; and your choice, oh happy days, Pop-Tarts or Little Debbie chocolate cupcakes. I, for one, can't wait," Maggie said, giggling.

"All that for fifty grand a pop. And I bet the First Lady got it all donated," Jack grumbled.

"Yep."

"Okay, folks, we are here at the farm. Who's going to carry in Sleeping Beauty? I'm thinking the ladies will want her stashed in the cell next to the war room," Ted said.

After a five-minute discussion, it was decided Espinosa would carry in Jane Petrie, aka Sleeping Beauty, and Ted would carry in her Gucci suitcase.

Harry ran to the kitchen door and opened it. Maggie yelled, "We're home." There was no response to her happy greeting.

CHAPTER 13

Yoko and Nikki sat on stools outside the cell where Jane Petrie slept on a hard cot. They were whispering to each other as they watched the sleeping woman. "Harry said she should be awake by now. I think she's faking it!" Yoko hissed behind her hand.

"Hmmmm, I think you're right. Hold on a minute, I think I know a way to find out." Nikki was off her stool and running down the tunnel. She returned a few minutes later with a whistle around her neck and a set of bells she'd removed from the ceiling beams that held up the dungeon tunnels. "Okay, watch this! On the count of three, yell 'FIRE!' at the top of your lungs!" Yoko did as Nikki had instructed, joined by Nikki, who also clanged the bells, making an earsplitting sound that reverberated throughout the tunnel at the same time that they shouted, "FIRE!" Both women stepped back, overcome with the sound, but their eyes remained on Jane Petrie, who bounded off the cot like she was jet-propelled.

Nikki and Yoko waited for sound in the tunnel where the cell was located to stop reverberating and return to normal. "Playing possum, eh?" Yoko said quietly.

Jane Petrie gripped the bars on her cell and screamed for a lawyer. "Where is this place? What am I doing here? I want a lawyer! You kidnapped me! That's against the law."

"So is ruining other people's lives. How many notches do you have on that sleazy belt you wear?" Nikki demanded.

"I don't know what you're talking about. I want a lawyer! I have rights!"

"No, you don't. Have rights, that is," Yoko said. "We took them all away. The lawyer hasn't been born yet who would take you on as a client. You're a terrorist, pure and simple."

Petrie's indignation was almost comical. "I am not a terrorist. I'm French and American. What do you want from me anyway?"

"What do you think we want?" Nikki asked.

"I don't have a clue. I want a lawyer. How many times do I have to ask for one? This will not go well for you when it all comes out. I'm a citizen, I have rights."

"Will you please sing a different song. Get it through your head. There will be no lawyer. Period. Now, tell us what we want to know, and maybe we'll let you go," Yoko said.

"Yeah, like I'm really going to believe that. Put it in writing and notarize it, then maybe we can talk."

Nikki narrowed her eyes as she stared at the young nurse. She was a pretty thing, creamy complexion, healthy, shiny hair down to her shoulders, clear blue eyes, and a nice trim figure, proof that she worked out. She didn't know how she knew but she suspected the young woman got by on her looks. "You're a disgrace to the nursing profession."

Petrie tried rattling the bars of her prison cell. When nothing happened, she kicked at them, then howled in pain as she hopped around on her uninjured foot. "See what you made me do! You're the terrorists here, not me, and for your information, I'm a damn fine nurse. I have repeat patients. I'm hungry, and I have to go to the bathroom."

Yoko pointed to the small sink and toilet in the corner of the cell. "Tell that all to someone who cares! C'mon, Nikki, we have better things to do than spend time down

207

here with *her.*"

"What! What! You're leaving me here! I hear rats scratching on the walls. Rats carry rabies. I want a lawyer!"

"Make friends with them, one rat to another, and maybe they won't bother you," Nikki called over her shoulder as she followed Yoko out to the tunnel, then down another tunnel to the war room.

Nikki flopped down on a chair at the big round table. "What are we supposed to do with her? I don't even understand why we're bothering with her, do you?"

Yoko shrugged. "She knows about Mrs. Moss and who she is. I don't think the others are sure if she has a picture of Mrs. Moss after the surgery or not. She might have one and is holding on to it for just the right moment to up the ante from that tabloid guy. That's just my opinion. Then there is the question of how many other people's lives she's ruined doing the same thing. I wonder what they'll do with her."

Nikki looked at her watch. It was almost noon. Jack should be waking up about now. She led the way to the moss-covered steps that would take them up to the main part of the Pinewood farmhouse.

"I'm kind of looking forward to seeing and

talking to Mrs. Moss. How about you, Nikki?"

"Myra said both women were very nice. She said they were kind and gentle but scared out of their wits. I guess if I were married to a wife-beating control freak like Lincoln Moss, I would be scared out of my wits, too."

Yoko laughed. "No you wouldn't. First of all, you would never have let what happened to Mrs. Moss happen to you. Nor would I. Therein lies the difference. Sad to say, some women just do not have it in them to fight back. I could understand if there were children involved, but the Mosses had no children. Why didn't she just walk out and ask for help?"

"Because of who she's married to. I assume she thought, because he probably drilled it into her head, that she couldn't run without being caught because he would find her with all his contacts and who he is. Fear is a terrible thing, Yoko."

"It's also a powerful motivator to get out from under. Maybe we'll never know."

"Where is everyone?" Nikki said, looking around the kitchen. "Look outside, Yoko. Are they on the terrace?"

Yoko laughed. "I see my dear sweet husband sitting next to your dear sweet husband. I guess they got a few hours' sleep. They appear to be drinking lemonade. Shall we join them and let them wait on us hand and foot?"

Nikki giggled. "Absolutely!"

The dogs appeared out of nowhere and bounded up the steps to the terrace, where they stopped and waited, panting, for belly tickles and treats. Behind them were Myra, Annie, and their two new guests, Amalie Moss and Rosalee Muno.

"We were just walking around the property," Myra said. "Let me introduce you to our new guests." Heads nodded, hands were shaken, and everyone sat down while Jack poured lemonade into frosty glasses. "We're just going to socialize for the moment until all the others get here. We don't want our guests to have to repeat their story over and over again. How is our . . . um . . . other guest doing?"

Nikki laughed out loud. "She wants a lawyer. She called us terrorists. If there's a way to dig herself out of that cell, she'll probably find it."

"Is that the young woman who is responsible for putting my picture in that tabloid?" Amalie Moss asked. Everyone at the table nodded. The sudden silence was interrupted by the arrival of Alexis and Isabelle, followed by Ted, Maggie, Dennis, and Espinosa.

"Where is Abner?" Jack said, stretching his neck to see past a flowering hibiscus on the terrace.

"Abner is in his lair chasing down Mr. Moss's money trail. He said he's onto something and will be out later and wanted to know what was for dinner. Charles said he's making Cornish game hens with chestnut dressing. He also said we are dining out here on the terrace by candlelight," Annie said.

The gang clapped their hands in approval, even their two new guests.

Myra disappeared into the house, followed by Annie, to fetch more lemonade and some sweet apple tea. Charles was already at the stove along with Fergus, starting preparations for their dinner.

"Do you two want to sit in on our meeting, or will you trust us to give you all the details later?" Myra asked.

"Later will be fine. Do you want some munchies to go with the tea and lemonade?"

"Darling, that would be perfect. What do you have in mind?" Myra smiled.

"Pretzels and chips." Charles laughed.

"That'll work," Annie said, poking Fergus playfully on the arm. He looked at her adoringly. Annie wiggled her eyebrows at him. Fergus looked like he was going to melt.

"Why do you tease that man like that?" Myra whispered.

"To keep him on his toes. You should try it, Myra. The outcome is always spectacular."

"Hmnnn, spectacular, you say?"

"Uh-huh." Annie giggled as she held the door for Myra.

Fresh drinks were poured and everyone settled down.

"Okay," Kathryn, the last to arrive, said. "The gang's all here, so let's get started. Oh, what about . . ."

"*She'll* be by later to abide by our guests' decision. No names, please," Myra said.

Kathryn winced. "Ooops, sorry about that." Mentioning Pearl by name was definitely a no-no. She'd almost unwittingly blown Pearl's cover.

Myra looked over at a nervous Amalie Moss and nodded.

The beautiful model looked around the table and saw only friendly faces. She swallowed hard, then bit down on her full lower lip. "I was very young when I met Lincoln Moss. I had been modeling about a year and was starting to get some really good recognition and really good press. Clients were asking for me. I was very flattered. But I had very wise parents. Simple, humble people who did not allow me to get caught up in the fast lane. I did not party. I didn't drink or do drugs that are so rampant in the industry. I went home at night and had dinner with my parents and my siblings. I was able to contribute to my parents to make life easier for them. I was glad to do it because I love them all dearly.

"I met Lincoln Moss at a wrap luncheon party for a photo shoot. I didn't know it at the time, but he owned *La Natural.*

"Lincoln swept me off my feet. Remember now, I was young and impressionable. He wined and dined me, gave me expensive gifts, flowers, chocolates, champagne. He had a yacht and a private plane. My parents liked him because he was so charming. He brought gifts for my family, fawned over my mother, praised my father for raising such a beautiful daughter. They bought into it all just as I did, I'm sorry to say.

"The courtship, if that's what you want to call it, lasted for about eleven months. The day I agreed to become the face of *La Natural,* which by then I knew he had owned for three years, he asked me to marry him. Of course, I said yes because I was in love. My parents approved.

"My first mistake was assuming we would live in France. I was wrong. As soon as we returned from our honeymoon on some exotic island, Lincoln made plans for us to return to America. I was devastated. I had already agreed to become the face of *La Natural*. This massive ad campaign was all worked out. All the photo shoots were done in Washington, D.C. The props they used were French. No one, he said, would ever know the difference, and as far as I know, that never came up. For all intents and purposes everything was done in France, Paris to be precise, while it all took place in a rented studio on K Street, all except for the outdoor shots.

"By then he had had all the products repackaged and tripled and quadrupled the price of everything. *La Natural* was suddenly the most expensive cosmetic in the universe. And there I was touting all those crappy products and saying I used them and that's why I was so beautiful. It was all a lie, of course. The products were no better than those purchased by teenagers in a drugstore. The ad campaign was a horror. He worked me like a dog under those hot lights for eighteen hours a day. One day I collapsed because he monitored my food intake and would weigh me each morning. If I gained an ounce, he slapped me. If I gained five ounces, he punched me. Where it didn't show."

Amalie pointed to Rosalee. "Rosy was my maid. It was up to her to bring me ice packs, tape up my ribs, and, of course, to count my calories. She hated doing it, but she was as afraid of Lincoln as I was. He made so much money, he didn't know what to do with it. I know for a fact that after Gabriel Knight became President, Lincoln would take bushel baskets of *La Natural* to the White House and hand them out to the female staff. He would tell them his beautiful wife sent them. Mr. Charm himself. Beautiful packaging will do it every time. Place an astronomical price tag on the product, and you can't go wrong. At least that's what Lincoln said. He was right, and the company took off like a rocket."

"Why didn't you leave?" Maggie asked.

Rosalee spoke up. "Because he said he would kill her and make it look like an accident. By that point, we finally realized how powerful he was. I stayed because I was afraid for her. I think if it wasn't for me, he would have crippled or killed her. He said Amalie *belonged* to him. There was always security around. When she went to get her hair done or her nails, there was always security. She was never alone. At times I would be with her but not always. To answer your question, it was impossible."

Isabelle leaned forward. "I realize this is a personal question, but what kind of . . . um . . . intimate life did you have?"

Amalie laughed out loud, a bitter sound of misery. She raised her head defiantly, and said, "I could count the times we had sex on one hand. It worked once, on our honeymoon; four other times he said it was my fault that it didn't. For all I know, the man prefers other men. Or maybe he is just so into himself that having sex with another person would be demeaning. All I do know is that the day I said I would like to have children, he beat me to within an inch of my life. Rosalee thought I was going to die. She called her mother to ask what to do for me. I survived because of her."

"What was the final straw?" Alexis asked.

Amalie Moss drew a deep breath, and said, "I told him if he didn't let me go, so I could return to my family, I was going to tell the whole world what a fraud he was, that I did not use *La Natural,* and how he had done nothing more than repackage the same junk the company was selling when it almost went broke, mounted a splashy ad campaign even before I was involved, and tripled the price. And the new product the chemists were working on, something he said would make Botox obsolete, would all be lost. He had some scheme to use my mother and me with the new product. I was so furious, I then threw in the President and said that Gabriel would be a laughingstock because of him. I never saw the blow. The next thing I remember is waking up in bed in a world of pain. Rosalee was sitting by the bed crying.

"Rosalee is the one who got me away. I know in my heart I would be dead by now if it weren't for her."

"How did you do it?" Kathryn asked.

"I had a cousin who had been helped by some women who run an underground railroad several years ago. I called my mother and between her, two of my sisters, and many cousins, we came up with a plan. When Amalie was recovered enough to go out, we went shopping at Neiman Marcus. We, of course, had six security people with us at all times. Fortunately for us, they were all men. Lincoln Moss does not like women for some reason. Maybe Amalie is right about that.

"Anyway, we went into the dressing room looking like ourselves and came out looking like two old ladies. My cousins were waiting for us. They entered the dressing room looking like we looked when we walked out. Moss's security saw them enter before we did, so they weren't paying attention when we left in our new disguises. We headed for the nearest door, and that's the end of the story until that picture appeared in the tabloid."

"Lincoln wants . . . expects to step into Gabriel Knight's shoes when his term of office is over. He's spent these years currying favor, making a name for himself so that when his time comes, as he put it, he'll win the party's nomination by a landslide. As we all know, Lincoln Moss is a handsome man albeit an evil one. He turns on the charisma like a faucet. He said it would be Camelot all over again with me, his beautiful wife, as the First Lady. It was sickening to listen to him. And, of course, there is his little black book of secrets, which he guards with his life. Are you sure I'm safe with you people?" Amalie asked anxiously.

"Safe as you can possibly be," Myra said. "What about your family? What do they think?"

Amalie snorted. "He allowed me to call home once a month, and he wrote out a script for me to read. As far as they know, I am happily married and love, just love, living in America. Lincoln constantly sent gifts and flowers to them. I hate to admit it, but my family has become a little shallow since meeting him. They love the freebies and the attention he showers on them."

"Understandable to a point," Maggie said sourly.

"Now what happens?" Rosalee and Amalie asked at the same moment.

"Now what happens is we all put our heads together and see how we can make Saturday evening work for us," Myra said. She looked around the glass-topped table, and said, "We're open to any and all suggestions."

Amalie raised her hand, albeit hesitantly. "What is happening Saturday evening?"

"A rather big event at the Four Seasons. The First Lady's pet project for children with disabilities. It's pretty much A-list only. Heavy hitters. Each table seats either eight or ten people. Each individual chair costs fifty thousand dollars. Annie bought a table for ten, and so did Dennis. That means we can take twenty people into the gala. Our people. I'm sure your . . . Lincoln Moss will be there, and I am just as sure he bought a table. He is, after all, the President's best bud," Annie said.

"How are we going to make that work for

us? We only have three days to come up with a plan. Bear in mind there will be as many Secret Service agents as there are guests," Maggie said. "By the way, I've called Moss a dozen times to get an interview for his nomination for Man of the Year. So far, he has not returned any of my calls. I'm not giving up, and I am not above camping out in his driveway."

"Attagirl," Alexis said.

A frown on her face, Nikki looked around the table. "Like Maggie said, three days is really only seventy-two hours. Whatever we come up with better be foolproof."

"The Secret Service doesn't protect Lincoln Moss," Dennis said. "That means he's fair game."

"True. But despite what Annie said, we cannot be certain that he's going to attend," Isabelle said.

Myra chewed on her lower lip for a second as she tried to gather her thoughts. "I have an idea. At best it is risky, and the decision will be up to Amalie.

"What if Maggie makes one more call to Mr. Moss and mentions that Amalie is going to attend. She can say she somehow got a copy of the RSVP list. Reporters get that kind of information all the time from their sources. And they never divulge those sources. Now, having said that, we can either take Amalie with us as she looks now, or Alexis can . . . ah . . . return her to her original appearance with that magic red bag of her tricks."

Before anyone could comment on Myra's idea, Kathryn said, "How's this for a shocker! We have Jack Sparrow escort her, in whichever persona she goes as, if she's willing."

"Oh, wow!" Dennis shouted. "That has to be the best idea ever!"

"It is daring," Annie admitted.

All eyes turned to Amalie and Rosalee. Both women were white as the T-shirts they were wearing. "I . . . I . . . what if he tries to . . . take me with him. I'm not sure I can be in the same room he's in. I think I'd black out."

"We'll do it!" Rosalee said forcefully. "I will be right at your side, Amalie. Who is Jack Sparrow? Can I bring Jason Woods as my partner?"

"Of course you can, dear. And Jack Sparrow is the Director of the FBI. I know for a fact that he despises Lincoln Moss," Annie said. "Oh, and before I forget, the gala is black tie. That means I get to wear my tiara."

Jack laughed. "And where will you be

packing your heat, Annie?"

"Inside my blue garter!" Annie shot back.

Harry laughed so hard, Yoko had to pound his back.

"Be serious, people. Don't worry, Amalie, we will all be there to protect you. You have my word that nothing bad is going to happen to you. Between now and then, you have to psych yourself up to attending, then leave the rest up to us. You're a strong woman, you can do this. I know you can," Myra said.

Amalie drew a deep breath. "Okay. Okay, I'll do it. Will it be over then?"

No one said yes or no.

"Alexis, can you make it happen where Amalie is concerned?" Nikki asked.

"Absolutely."

That was all the group needed to hear. The conversation turned to jewels and the designer outfits that were on order, thanks to Annie and her special "in" with Vera Wang and Donna Karan.

Bored out of their minds, the boys left the terrace and entered the kitchen, where they informed Charles and Fergus what was going on.

"It occurs to me that Jack Sparrow is single. Shortly, if I am not mistaken, Amalie Moss will be single. Just out of curiosity,

222

was that my wife's idea?" Charles asked.

The boys busied themselves rooting around inside the fridge for cold beer.

"Aha, just what I thought," Charles said, smacking his wooden spoon down on the countertop. When the handle flew off, he didn't bother to look surprised. Fergus, on the other hand, laughed out loud.

CHAPTER 14

Maggie struggled with the text she was attempting to send to Lincoln Moss. She was on her fourth try after deleting the first three. She looked over at Ted. "I can't seem to get it just right for some reason. For starters, he's going to go nuclear that I even have his oh-so-very-private-number-that-no-one-else-in-the-world-has. Except . . . drumroll please, Amalie and the President of the United States. And he doesn't even know that Amalie has the number. Rosalee got it one day when he left his phone behind. I guess because she's young, she knows how all that stuff works. Both women said the number is seared in their brain because they thought maybe someday they might need it. Guess this is the someday in question."

"Short, curt, and to the point, that's the best way," Ted said. "Say what you have to say and move on."

"When he asks where you got his private

number, tell him the same thing you did when you called his other semiprivate number, that a reporter never divulges his or her sources. He has to respect that. He's been around Washington long enough to know how that works," Dennis said.

"I say we go to his house and camp out in his driveway," Espinosa said. "I'm real good at candid shots. I'll catch the bastard in the act when he starts to shake his fist at you."

"We have to be professional about this. Simply sending a text to do a short interview for the Man of the Year contest isn't going to cut it. He'll just blow it off and make noise about my having the number. I want to ask him why Amalie is going to the First Lady's gala with the Director of the FBI instead of him. But I'm not sure I want to put that in a text. I'm not even sure it's a good idea to tip our hand. Like Espinosa says, we want to capture his face on film when I throw that at him, if, and it is a big if, I follow through." Maggie flapped her arms in the air like a bird as she tried to figure out what she should do.

"We don't even know if Sparrow will agree to any of this. You could be putting the cart before the horse," Ted snorted.

"We do now," Maggie said, looking down at an incoming text from Annie confirming the director's date for the gala. "Annie can charm the bees out of the trees, as we all know. She really has a special rapport with Sparrow. I think we all knew he would agree. I also think Annie is going to try playing matchmaker. Sparrow is single. Amalie will be single *soon.*"

Maggie flapped her arms some more. "Maybe I should just go with my original thought, which was to casually mention that Amalie is on the guest list and responded that she will attend. My gut is telling me to throw him the bone and see if he bites down on it. Of course, he is going to want to know how I came by that information, so once again I will have to refer to reporter's privilege. Then I think he'll probably just shoot the four of us. Any of you have any ideas?" She flapped her arms again to show she was confused and needed to make a decision.

The boys looked at Maggie but didn't offer an opinion because they knew her well enough to know that if her gut was talking to her, that's what she would listen to, not them, no matter how much sense they made.

Espinosa shuffled from one foot to the other. "You guys do know that Lincoln Moss hates Jack Sparrow, right? When the

President, at his advisers' urging, nominated Sparrow, Moss opposed it. Because Sparrow had been in the federal pen on a trumped-up charge. Moss said it wouldn't look good and would taint the President. There was more to it than that, and we all know, as did Moss, that Sparrow got a clean bill of health on that trumped-up charge. The feds paid him handsomely for the time he spent in prison, too. I think I read somewhere, and not in the *Post,* that it was the only time Gabriel Knight vetoed a suggestion from his old buddy Lincoln Moss. You guys have to remember that, don't you?"

"Vaguely," Ted said. "I know we didn't think it was newsworthy enough to write about. Even back then, the *Post* was anti-Moss."

"I don't remember it at all," Dennis said.

"Me either," Maggie said. "Okay, I pulled up his address on Glenbrook Road. It's in the Wesley Heights area. Ah, here's a picture. Looks like a mansion to me, and I'd estimate at the time of purchase maybe five or six million. No clue what the value is today. Pricey will do it for now, and would we really expect anything less when it comes to Lincoln Moss? He's got some well-heeled political neighbors, too. The power elite as they say."

"Dennis, do a Google Earth on the property so we can get a look at it. We need to know if he has electronic gates and maybe a guardhouse, that kind of thing. I'm thinking we can bluff our way to the gate even if there is a guard. They, whoever *they* turn out to be, won't want to antagonize the press. That would be us. Especially when we tell them it's about the Man of the Year contest. Hell, even the gardener will be impressed with that," Ted said. "I've heard Moss has some serious security at his home. If I remember correctly, the security is made up of retired Secret Service."

"And he pays triple what they would earn elsewhere in the private sector," Dennis chirped up. "Amalie told me that. I also think she knows a lot of stuff that she hasn't told us. My opinion is that we have barely scratched the surface where Moss is concerned."

"I think you're right, kid," Ted said.

"So, what are we doing here? Do we have a game plan or not?" Espinosa asked.

Maggie nibbled on her thumb as she contemplated her next move. She hated it when she was indecisive. Just take the bull by the horns and wrestle it to the ground. Whatever happens happens. End of story.

"We're going out to Glenbrook Road. Ted, get the van. We'll meet you out front. Dennis, send Annie and Myra a text telling them what we're doing. Espinosa, you got all your gear?" He nodded. "Then I think we're good to go."

"Did you send the text, Maggie?" Dennis asked.

"Nope. I'm going to wait till we pull into his driveway. From the looks of the Google display, he can see his driveway all the way to the road from every front window of his mansion. Wonder who uses that pool, tennis court, and that mini putting green."

"Amalie said it's all just for show. She said they did a whole spread in *Architectural Digest.* Everything about Lincoln Moss is for show. She said his motto is, 'Hey, look at me!' "

"That's downright sick. I can't wait till we get our hands on that miserable cretin."

Dennis swallowed hard at the look on Maggie's face. He almost felt sorry for Lincoln Moss. Almost.

Forty minutes later, with Ted driving at breakneck speed, the group arrived at the Glenbrook Road address. Ted let out a loud whoop, and said, "Okay, I know exactly where we are now. Two doors down on the left is where that female senator lived. You remember, Maggie, the one who loved to entertain all those virile young Georgetown students on the taxpayer's dime. See that Tudor, that was where she lived. Now that was a scandal to end all scandals." A quick glance in the rearview mirror told Ted Dennis was about to ask a hundred questions since the scandal was before his time. "Later, kid, we're here. Now what, Maggie? I don't see any guards or security."

"That's because you haven't pulled into the driveway, Ted. I think there is a structure, according to the Google map, right up there at the end and under that weeping cherry tree. At least I think it's a weeping cherry tree. I'm not into foliage of any kind. Slow down and pull up, then stop. Let's see if anyone comes around to talk to us."

Ted did as instructed. He let his breath out in a loud *swoosh.* He lowered the window and waited. As one they all almost jumped out of their skin when a man appeared from the rear and leaned into the van window. "You people have an appointment with Mr. Moss or are you lost?"

The moment the shock of seeing the man or guard come up from the rear wore off, Maggie summed him up. Six-four, aviator glasses, brush cut, deeply tanned, probably around midforties or closer to the fifty mark. Trim, muscular, like he had a daily workout routine. He was dressed in pressed khakis and a white button-down dress shirt open at the throat, with the sleeves rolled up to his mid-arm. Pleasant voice that at the moment sounded more curious than anything else. His name tag said his name was Paul Prentice. And, she decided, he smelled good, like some earthy woodsy glen. Her final consensus was a very nice package indeed.

Maggie leaned closer to the window and flashed her credentials. "I just this moment sent Mr. Moss a text. We just want to take a few pictures and ask a few questions about his nomination for our Man of the Year award. Would it be too much trouble for you to call him for us? He doesn't seem to be responding to my text."

"We don't actually have to go inside those security gates, sir. We can do the interview right here if Mr. Moss is agreeable. We already did all our other interviews, and Mr. Moss is the last one. We can't go to press without his comments," Ted said.

Dennis leaned forward, "That's not quite true, Ted. We could make up something or just say Mr. Moss flat-out refused. The thing is, Mr. Moss might not like what we print."

Dennis flashed his credentials to prove he truly belonged with the group.

"Wait here. Please stay in the van. I'll go up to the house and see if Mr. Moss is available. I won't be long. I have to tell you, though, that I've never known Mr. Moss to see anyone without an appointment, so be fair warned."

"We understand. We know how busy a man like Mr. Moss is," Ted said, tongue-in-cheek.

"The guy got the drop on us. We must be slipping," Espinosa groused. "I got some good pictures of him, and he didn't even know what I was doing."

"He did not get the drop on us," Maggie seethed. "What he did was sneak up on us in that golf cart he was driving. Golf carts do not make noise. So far, so good. If Moss doesn't come down here, then I say we run the picture of the guard with whatever caption we can come up with." She looked down at her phone. Still no returning text from Lincoln Moss.

They waited, the minutes ticking by.

Fifteen minutes later, Ted said, "This sucks. I say we leave. The guy obviously is not coming. Why give him the satisfaction of sitting here cooling our heels? Let's take a vote."

It was three to one to leave. Maggie wanted to stay.

"Let's give him five more minutes," Maggie said.

Exactly five minutes later, Ted said, "Okay, we're outta here." He was backing up the van when the monster iron gates opened slowly to allow the golf cart carrying Lincoln Moss, with Paul Prentice doing the driving, to emerge.

Everyone hopped out of the van and stood silently, watching to see if Moss would get out of the golf cart to shake hands. He did not. What he said was, "Make it quick, folks, I'm right in the middle of mixing some cement for some planters I'm building."

Maggie was appalled at Moss's attire. He looked like the hired help next to Paul Prentice. He wore ragged, cut-off shorts, a dirty, sweat-stained T-shirt, and a baseball cap. Just one of the guys. He looked sopping wet from his own sweat. He was also as deeply tanned as Prentice was.

"It looks like you have the lead this year in our Man of the Year contest. How do you feel about that, sir?" Maggie asked.

"Humbled. Appreciative. I'm sure there are others out there more worthy of the honor than I am."

Maggie mulled over the response and

knew it was a crock. She forced a smile, and said, "That is so generous of you. All of the nominees are top-notch. In other words, you are in excellent company. Do you object to a few pictures?"

Moss showed genuine surprise at the question. For a moment, he looked confused but recovered quickly. "Well, if you don't mind the way I'm dressed, then I guess I don't mind either." He hopped out of the golf cart and stood with his hands jammed into the pockets of his ragged shorts.

"We caught the Director of Homeland Security building a tree house for his grandson. His attire was similar to yours, sir," Ted said. "We also captured Congressman Doolittle in a Speedo at the YMCA teaching a class of tadpoles how to swim."

Moss quirked an eyebrow, tilted his head, and offered up a smile for Espinosa.

Maggie fixed her gaze on Moss, and said, "They say clothes make the man, but I think that's a myth. What designer tux will you be wearing for the gala Saturday night? And our readers will want to know what that gorgeous wife of yours will be wearing. Care to share that with us?"

Moss's smile was gone in a nanosecond, replaced with an ugly look in his eyes. He looked to Maggie's eyes like he was going to explode, but he got himself under control. "I'm not sure I will be attending, Miss Spritzer. My wife is in France, and I don't like to attend these sorts of functions without her. However, I did sponsor a table. Now, if that's all, I need to get back to my cement. Oh, all of my tuxedos are by Hugo Boss." Moss slid back onto the seat of the golf cart, and said, "Go!"

"Mr. Moss! Mr. Moss! Wait a minute! Please. I don't think I got my wires crossed, but I have it on good authority that Mrs. Moss sent her RSVP confirming she was attending the gala. Ooops. Oooh, I hope I just didn't give away a surprise. If I did, I am so sorry. Your wife must be planning on surprising you. That makes sense, right? Please don't give me away," Maggie pleaded.

Whatever the little group was expecting as a response was lost on them as Moss's back was to them when Maggie let the cat out of the bag. Their only hope was that Espinosa had managed somehow to capture some kind of reaction.

"Okay, you dropped the bomb. We need to get out of here. Anyone pick up on anything?" Ted asked as he straightened out the van and switched gears.

"I think it's safe to say the guy was pissed

to the teeth. Of all the things in the world you could have said to him, that just never entered his mind. I think about now he is going nuts, and that cement he was talking about is going to turn into a rock," Espinosa said out of the corner of his mouth as he scanned the digital pictures he'd snapped one after the other, hoping for at least one good shot. "Aha! Got the schmuck. Look at this. He looks like he saw a ghost and ran into a brick wall at the same time. Oh, this is good. You got to him, Maggie. I bet he starts calling you in short order. You might want to turn off your phone so his calls go to voice mail. Unless, of course, you want to undergo a third degree. Also, don't be surprised if he shows up in person at your house or at the paper. I think you need to lie low," Espinosa warned her.

Maggie turned off her phone and patted herself on the back. "Hey, did anyone notice that Moss didn't ask where I got his super-duper private phone number?" When there was no response from her colleagues she laughed.

Some days things just worked out right.

CHAPTER 15

Myra toyed with the spoon in her teacup, watching out of the corner of her eye as Annie stared out the kitchen window at the young people on the terrace. "You're up to something, I can tell. You might as well tell me now, so I don't have to pester you all day. Besides, I know you're dying to tell me, so spit it out, Countess." While Myra's tone was playful, Annie recognized the ring of steel in the words. She needed to share.

"Well . . . um . . . I spoke to Avery Snowden yesterday and he sort of . . . kind of . . . mentioned that the young man, Jason Woods, the one who helped our guests, has had a tough time of it, working a backbreaking job and going to school. He's paying for his education himself. He has bills. A lot of them. He is also taking night classes during the summer. His other friend, Stacey, is . . . um . . . in more or less the same position young Jason is in. And with all that going on, he still found time and energy to help Rosalee and Amalie. Not to mention digging into his tuition money to help them."

"So you paid for the balance of their education. Anonymously, of course, knowing you. That's wonderful, Annie. So why is a good deed like that bothering you?"

"Well because . . . because young Jason's heart belongs to his friend Stacey, who works in the paint department, not our guest Rosalee. Jason considers Rosalee a friend, nothing more. No one is sure what Rosalee's feelings are. One of Avery's people, a female operative, wormed her way into the break room at Home Builders and posed as a new hire. Girls talk, you know how it is. The whole thing is actually a comedy of errors. Jason introduced Stacey to a guy named Jackson. They date. Stacey introduced Jason to Rosalee. They just hung out because Rosalee couldn't really date when they were on the run. The thing is, both Stacey and Jason have a 'thing' as the young people say today, for each other, but for some strange reason, neither one will admit it. It's not like the company has a policy where employees can't date each other."

"Uh-huh," Myra said, wondering where

all this was going.

"You see, the thing is, Myra, Rosalee wants to invite Jason to the gala Saturday evening. I don't know if it's just because she doesn't want to show up without a partner or if she actually cares for Jason or cares for him on another level."

"And this is *your* problem, why?"

"Well, now that you ask, Miss Smart-Ass Rutledge Martin Sutcliff, I had Dennis all picked out for Rosalee. They would be perfect together. And don't tell me you disagree either because I won't believe you. It's like Amalie is going to be so perfect for Jack Sparrow. They just don't know it yet. I need to work on that," Annie fretted.

"You're meddling, Annie."

"I am. I admit it. I need help, Myra."

Myra clapped her hands. "I thought you'd never ask. Sit down and let's plot out a . . . whatever it is we can do."

Outside on the terrace, Dennis finally managed to snag a seat next to Rosalee when Kathryn got up to stretch her legs. He grinned at the pretty young girl and made some inane comment that made her laugh. "Tell me about yourself, Rosalee. You know, before you went to work for Amalie. Where are you from? About your family, your friends. I like to know about people we

help. Are you 'a thing' with Jason Woods?"
There, he'd asked the question that had
been bugging him since he set eyes on the
dark-haired girl.

"Jason and I are just friends. I was and
am grateful for his friendship. Once we went
into the railroad program, neither Amalie
nor I could have friendships. By that I mean
meaningful friendships.

"I come from a very large family. I have
seven sisters and four brothers. My mom
never worked outside the home, how could
she? My papa has a lawn-maintenance
company. My brothers all work with him.
None of us went to college; we had to work,
but that doesn't mean any of us is dumb.
We all read, we all study things that are
important to us. My brothers could probably be horticulturists. They, along with my
papa, know more about trees, plants, and
growing than men with degrees. And they
stand behind their work. If something dies,
they replace it at no cost. My mom could
be a fabulous cook in a big, five-star
restaurant. Four of my sisters are married
with children. There are still three teenagers
at home. We all give money to our parents
to help out. That's why I took the job with
Amalie because the pay was so good and
for the health insurance Mr. Moss provided.

I have seventy-six cousins and many uncles and aunts. Twice a year, we have a reunion, Christmas and Labor Day. I've missed so many of them, and that makes me sad because I have a wonderful family.

"When things got really, really bad for Amalie I asked my family for help. And here we are. They didn't ask any questions. Family never asks questions, they just help."

Dennis digested all of this, wishing he belonged to that big, wonderful, loving family. "So what are you going to do when this is over? Will you feel safe going back to your family?"

"Of course I will feel safe. All of my family is very protective of each other. I guess I'll have to look for a job. Does that answer your questions?"

Well it did and it didn't. "I was thinking, Rosalee, if you change your mind and don't ask Jason to the gala on Saturday, would you consider going with me?"

Rosalee looked at Dennis's beet-red face and laughed. "Are you asking me for a date, Dennis, because if you are, the answer is yes, I would love to go to the party with you. No, I have not asked Jason. Even if I did, he would feel obligated to go, and I know him well enough to know he would not be comfortable at such an affair. I don't even know if I will be comfortable."

"You would! Really! Wow! This might be a good time to tell you I can't dance. I have two left feet," Dennis confessed, his face even redder if that was possible.

Rosalee laughed out loud. Dennis loved the sound, knowing there hadn't been much laughter in her life these past few years. "That's okay, I can't dance either. No time to do things like that growing up. And then, when school was over, I had to get a job. I always thought maybe I could teach myself. Amalie said she would teach me back in the beginning but . . . well, it just never happened. I understand you can fake it on the dance floor if you just shuffle your feet and sway to the music. I read that in a magazine. I think that might work. We could shuffle together, and maybe no one will notice." Rosalee giggled.

I like this girl, Dennis thought to himself. *Eat your heart out, Jason Woods,* he thought smugly. *Your loss is my gain.* He was instantly sorry for his uncharitable thought but not sorry enough that it bothered him. He convinced himself it was a guy thing, and all was fair in love and war.

"It's definite then, we have a date for Saturday night?"

Rosalee smiled. "It's definite, Dennis, we

have a date for Saturday night. I want to be a nurse!" Rosalee blurted. "When I leave here, I'm going to look into it. I realized when I was taking care of Amalie, or nursing her through her . . . you know, that I want to help people. I have to save up the money for the tuition first, though, so it might take me a while."

"I only have eighty-eight dollars in the bank, or I'd loan it to you," Dennis said craftily as he watched Rosalee's reaction.

"I have two hundred sixteen dollars. I'm frugal. I know how to pinch pennies. I learned that from my parents. And the other thing they taught us all is only buy what you can afford. Sometimes, I wish I had a credit card, and I could just shoot the moon. I don't like debt."

"Yeah, yeah, credit cards are good for emergencies but sometimes just knowing you have one and you can use it for something frivolous can get you into a lot of trouble."

"That's what my papa said. He's never wrong. Oh, well, maybe someday I'll get one. Right now, that isn't important."

Dennis felt like he'd been hit with a bolt of lightning. This was meant to happen. He wanted to shout out his good news. Who should he tell first, Ted, his idol at the paper, or Harry who he considered a big brother?

Dennis was saved from a decision when Rosalee asked him to tell her about himself. He made quick work on the tale of his life, ending with, "I'm just a reporter. I love gathering news and sharing it. Someday, I hope to be as good as Ted and Maggie." He purposely did not divulge his inheritance or how very, very wealthy he actually was. That was for another time. Then again, maybe never. Only time would tell.

"I've read some of your stuff in the papers. That was all Amalie and I had in the way of leisure activities while we were in the . . . ah . . . program — reading. You have a way with words. I think you must love your job to write so convincingly. What's it like, Dennis, going to work at a job you really and truly love? I liked my job with Amalie. I didn't like her husband, and I certainly didn't love that big old mansion they lived in either. It was cold and . . . I don't know the word. Help me out here, Dennis, your command of the English language is better than mine."

Dennis flushed and basked in Rosalee's praise. He did love his job, he loved it with his whole being, and he loved the people he worked with and the people who were now his *other* family. "I think what you want to say is there was no warmth or sense of family in the structure where you worked and lived for a while. You could live in a run-down shack, but if there's love and warmth, the condition of the building really doesn't matter."

"Yes, yes, exactly. My mother's house is full to overflowing. There is stuff everywhere. Mind you, it is not dirty; you could eat off my mother's floors. My family lives in the house. A house takes on the personality of the people who live in it. My family laughs and sings and cooks and cleans. It's how we live. I so miss that. Growing up, we had triple-decker bunk beds, two sets to each bedroom. And, somehow, we still had plenty of room."

Dennis could feel himself blushing, but for the first time, he didn't care if anyone saw his red cheeks and ears or not.

And in that moment in time, on a beautiful summer day in July at 1:07 in the afternoon, Dennis West fell in love with a dark-haired, dark-eyed, rosy-cheeked girl named Rosalee Muno.

Rosalee stared across the table at her new friend and the look on his face. She thought it was endearing. At that precise moment, at 1:08 on a beautiful summer day in July, one minute after Dennis West fell in love with her, Rosalee Muno fell in love with the sandy-haired, blue-eyed, blushing reporter named Dennis West. The realization was so startling she didn't know what to do, so she just smiled. And kept on smiling.

Dennis grinned. Life was suddenly looking really good. Oh, yeahhhh.

From the kitchen window, Myra poked Annie on the shoulder and laughed. "I think, if I'm not mistaken, those two figured it out themselves. I think those two young people just fell in love with each other. Think about it, Annie. We always say over and over that everything happens for a reason. That God works in mysterious ways. I guess this was His plan for those two young people. Everyone was at the right place at exactly the right time for those two to meet. Yes, there was a tragedy but it wasn't deadly. People, meaning Pearl and ultimately us, were there to help. Rosalee was placed there to help Amalie, then here we are bringing up the rear to create a happy ending. Tell me, my dear friend, is there not something magical about what we do."

"Spot on, Myra, spot on. Now we need to move on to Director Sparrow and Amalie."

"You never give up, do you, Annie?"

"Well, Myra, my dear soul sister, if I did

give up, where would that leave you?"

Annie's voice was so intense, so serious, Myra felt lightheaded. "How's this for a response, Annie? I don't ever want to find out, so keep on doing what you're doing, and I'm right at your side, your BFF."

Annie laughed. "Come along, BFF, and let's join the party on the terrace."

Amalie Moss watched the two women whom she now thought of as her saviors walk up the steps to the terrace. She didn't know how she knew but she knew that somehow, some way, these two women were going to change the rest of her life. A calm settled over her, knowing that with them watching over her, she was truly, truly safe for the first time since the day she had met Lincoln Moss. She knew in her heart she would never question either woman, she would simply accept what was in store for her and follow the path laid out for her by all these wonderful people.

Their plans to talk woman to woman, friend to friend, with Amalie were cut short when both their cell phones buzzed at the same time. Annie looked at Myra, and Myra looked at Annie, then at the girls. "Abner needs us. Keep Amalie company while we see what needs to be done."

"I hope it's to discuss the tapioca banana

pie I asked Fergus to make for dinner,"
Kathryn said, smacking her lips.

"We'll ask, dear," Myra called over her
shoulder. To Annie she said, "I don't think
Charles has ever made a tapioca banana pie
before."

"That's why Fergus is making it." Annie
laughed. "He makes the best pies in the
whole world. The crust just melts in your
mouth. What do you think Abner wants?
It's not like him to summon us to the war
room. As in you and me specifically."

"I guess we'll find out when we get there.
I don't think we should worry until we hear
what he has to say."

"I always worry, Myra, you know that. The
minute I get a feeling something is not quite
right, my worry button kicks on. I think I
was born to worry." To prove her point, Annie jabbed at the rosette carved into the
mantel that would open the secret door that
led to the dungeons and the war room
under the house.

"Is there a problem, Abner?" both women
asked breathlessly as they bolted into the
war room.

"Depends. Take a look at this," Abner
said, holding out a stack of printouts.

"What is it?" Myra asked.

"Everything you ever wanted to know

about the company called *La Natural* that Lincoln Moss took from virtual bankruptcy and turned into a billion-dollar juggernaut."

"Oh my," was all Myra could think of to say. "I really don't understand all of this, can you just tell us, you know, a summary?"

"The short answer is the company is going down the drain. The decline started, I guess you could say, when Amalie lit out. I've been at this for the last two days, and I finally have it all together. He bought this run-of-the-mill company that as near as I can figure out, catered to cosmetics that teenage girls bought in drugstores. In other words, cheap stuff. He hired some top marketing guns and some wizard chemists, and suddenly the company is right up there, marketing-wise, with Chanel and La Prairie. He had it all repackaged, put in new machinery, renamed the company, and hired and married Amalie Laurent, a gorgeous French model who was starting to make a name for herself in the modeling world to be the new face of *La Natural.* He then quadrupled the price of the brand to go with the packaging and suddenly the whole world stood in line to buy the products he was producing. The only thing he *didn't* do was change the actual product. It was the same product all those teenage girls were buying in drugstores.

"And when he married Amalie, and it was like Princess Diana all over again. The ad campaign he initiated with Amalie as the face of the company took off like a rocket. The ads were everywhere, TV, radio, billboards, magazines, the whole nine yards. He did not overlook one angle promotion-wise. The whole world wanted to look like Amalie Laurent Moss. You know the French. They called the couple the Princess and the Frog."

"And then . . ." Annie said.

"And then he screwed up," Abner said gleefully. He tried to . . . I don't know how to explain this . . . he used old footage of some of the video Amalie had shot for promotions and dubbed in her person. Does that make sense? The new shoots were crude, and the media picked up on it. He pulled in his horns right away, then went with all stills. The other big companies started taking shots at him and his company while they redoubled their own advertising budgets with fresh talent."

"So, the company couldn't survive without Amalie is what you're saying. It started go-ing downhill when she left, and Moss couldn't get the company back on track," Myra said.

Abner clapped his hands together. "I hate that bastard. I got into his financials, and the man made billions, that's with a *B*. The company now isn't worth the packaging. He's also taken some political hits here in town. Doesn't matter if he's the President's best bud or not. To be honest, though, a lot of it is jealousy. I mean, get real, the guy could walk in and out of the White House at any time of the day or night, whereas the others have to make an appointment and go through all that Secret Service rigmarole. Moss just acted like he owned the joint. Hey, you heard all the rumors, read all the write-ups about the guy. It was all true. Not sure now, though. Then there are all those whispers about a little black book. It's like where there's smoke, there's fire. He has a file, or so the whispers go, on every politician and advisor in the administration. Who knows if it's true or not, but you have to ask yourself how those whispers started in the first place.

"Things started going south when the industry got wind of the dubbed-photo campaigns. And then the gossip started. Where was Amalie? Why wasn't she seen in person? Moss's response when the French asked was she was in America adjusting to her new home. When the American media asked, she was in Paris doing a photo shoot. That got real old real quick. When I went through his financials, I saw that he spared no expense to find her. He went through private detective agencies like I go through Diet Pepsi. Which says a lot for Pearl and her underground railroad. Moss had the best of the best, and they couldn't find her. Which, by the way, leads me to another question. What are you guys going to do about your . . . um . . . guest back there in the dungeon? She's been screaming and hollering like a banshee for hours now."

"Let her. Maybe if we're lucky, she'll lose her voice entirely. But to answer your question, we haven't decided yet what to do with her," Annie said briskly. "Anything else you think we should know?"

"One other thing. In his desperate bid to bring the company back up to snuff, Moss circulated a rumor. At least I think it's a rumor because I can't find any data to back it up. He's saying his chemists at *La Natural* have developed something that is so revolutionary it will put Botox and all those other . . . things ladies use to fill in their cracks, I mean wrinkles, out of business. Whatever. That got him a couple of spikes in the media and the trades. He also alluded to the fact that Amalie would endorse the product by saying that when she feels she might need a little extra help with the fine lines and wrinkles, she will definitely use the product."

"Well, now, that's downright cheeky on his part, wouldn't you say so, Myra?"

"I would, Annie. Amalie did say something about that earlier. But how would she know unless it was something in the works before she left Moss? Maybe the guy plans ahead."

"Anything else, Abner?"

"I think that about covers it for now. Is there anything else you want me to dig into?"

"Not at the moment. Are you coming topside, or are you staying down here?" Myra asked.

Abner looked at the oversize watch on his wrist. "I still have some stuff I want to go through. I'm not real happy with some of the accounts I've gone through. The guy is tricky; he hides stuff like a pack rat. I'll find it, though, it just takes time. I assume you want me to earmark enough money to last Amalie and her friend Rosalee, not to mention both sets of parents, their lifetime, right?"

"Yes, of course. Amalie and Rosalee deserve a rich payday for all they've been put through by that man. Be generous,

Abner," Myra said.

Abner laughed as he rubbed his hands together. "There's nothing I love more than giving away other people's money. Even with *La Natural* tanking, the man has a vast fortune."

"Not for long." Myra and Annie laughed as they made their way to the main part of the house.

Back outside on the terrace, the women noticed that Maggie and the boys had just arrived. Chatter was at an all-time high as Maggie regaled everyone with their visit to Lincoln Moss's estate. They all tried to ignore the tenseness in Amalie's shoulders and her white face. Nikki reached out, and clasped her hand, and squeezed it. Yoko stroked her shoulder with one of her tiny hands. Amalie calmed almost instantly, and she even smiled.

Maggie finally wound down after she gave a description of what Lincoln Moss was wearing. "And the best part, ladies and gentlemen, is this. He didn't even ask where I got his oh-so-private cell-phone number. How cool is that?"

"Where *did* you get it?" Isabelle asked.

"At first Abner got it somehow. But then I also got it from Rosalee. She said one day he left his cell phone behind, and I guess she knows how to figure things like that out. She told Amalie, and they both memorized the number. And then they gave it to me. If they're right, it's the phone Moss and the President use. And it is the same number Abner gave me.

"No one else calls on it. And, supposedly, no one else has the number. I've been expecting him to call ever since we left the estate, but so far he hasn't," Maggie said.

"That's because," Amalie said, "right now, he's in a rage, with no one to take that rage out on. Don't think for one minute he isn't aware that you now have his number. I can tell you, without a shadow of a doubt, he is on a rampage, busting up furniture, banging holes in the walls, smashing windows, and God alone knows what else. Lincoln has a hair-trigger temper. The only person he never vents on is the President. Never.

"In the beginning, when I first met Lincoln Moss, he had as we French say, a certain *je ne sais quoi* that I and my friends found irresistible.

"That went by the wayside very quickly, and over time, I learned to watch for the little things that would set him off. Rosalee learned, too, in case I missed it. Sometimes we would hide for hours in the pool house or the toolshed until he was done wrecking the house. If he wrecked the house, I was safe. If I was available, then I became the wreckage."

"Good Lord, what a way to have to live," Kathryn said, her eyes moist.

"I know you all wonder why I put up with it, why I didn't leave sooner. I wanted to. It was all I dreamed about, but I couldn't. I was watched constantly. And then there is the fear factor. Until you experience real fear, you have no idea what it's like. I was afraid he would kill me. All I could think about was my family and what kind of story he'd come up with if he did kill me."

"We're not judging you, Amalie," Yoko said as she remembered what her own mother had gone through at the hands of a man just like Lincoln Moss. "We can all relate to what you went through, and we are all dedicated to making sure your life going forward is all you want it to be and more. In time, you'll be able to say, and even believe, that Lincoln Moss was just someone you had the misfortune to have in your life at one point."

Amalie swiped at her eyes. What wonderful people these women were. And the men, too. Right now, she felt like the luckiest woman walking the planet.

Suddenly, Maggie let loose with a warlike

whoop of sound. "He's calling! Mr. Lincoln Moss himself is calling! Everyone, quiet! I'll put him on speaker, so you can all hear!"

Maggie pressed the TALK button, and said, "Maggie Spritzer!"

The voice was ice-cold. Maggie envisioned icicles hanging from Moss's nose. The voice was nothing like the one she'd heard earlier out at the estate.

"Miss Spritzer, this is Lincoln Moss. We met a short while ago out in my driveway. You called me. I have a question for you. Where did you get the number you called me on?"

"Reporter's secret, Mr. Moss," Maggie said lightly. "A reporter never divulges his or her sources. Just out of curiosity, is there something I should or shouldn't know about that particular number?"

"Of course not, that's silly. I always thought a private number was a private number. Only two people in the whole world have this particular number, myself and one other person. So you should be able to understand my concern. And now you have it. That makes three people who now have the number. Four people if you count the person who gave you the number. That is unacceptable."

"That's right. I guess. I count four also.

And your point is?"

"Again, where did you get the number?" There was no more patience in the voice.

"Again, Mr. Moss," Maggie said, parroting Moss, "a good reporter never divulges his or her sources."

"Here's the thing, Miss Spritzer, this phone number is private for a very good reason, a reason I cannot divulge to you in the interests of national security, so now please tell me where you got this number."

"I'm sorry, sir, I can't give you that information. What I can do is give you my personal word that I will not divulge that particular number to anyone else. A reporter's word is sacrosanct, in case you don't know that."

"That isn't good enough for me. I'll give you till nine o'clock tomorrow morning to call me with your source. If you don't, I'll make sure you go on every terrorist list that Homeland Security has, then I'll initiate a full-blown tax audit for your entire life. And just so you know, I have the juice to follow through."

Maggie's eyes popped wide. "Did you just threaten me, Mr. Moss? I think you did. And just for the record, the *Post* has some juice of its own. There is nothing more powerful than the written word. You want

258

to take me and the *Post* on, go for it. I am sure that our readership will be very happy to know exactly what you just did, threaten me with being put on a terrorist watch list and having the IRS audit my tax returns for the rest of my life. And how do you think President Knight will respond to your threatening to use agencies of the United States government to harass a *Washington Post* reporter, Mr. Moss?"

When there was no answer, Maggie realized she was talking to dead air. "That s.o.b. just threatened me. And he hung up on me! Did you record all that, Ted?"

"I did. That guy is one hell of a whack job, that's for sure."

"I told you," Amalie muttered. "He's worse than the Devil himself."

"Yes you did tell us that, dear. And we did listen," Myra assured her.

All eyes were on Amalie when she made the sign of the cross because, as she said, that's what you do when the Devil comes out to play.

CHAPTER 16

Lincoln Moss looked around at the destruction he had wrought in the master bedroom. He blinked. It looked like a war zone. Worse yet, he could see his reflection in a long glass shard of mirror that was still attached to the huge walk-in closet that housed all of his wife's belongings. He looked worse than the room. His face was red and mottled, his hair was standing on end, and his eyes spewed hatred. Even he could see that he was out of control. He clenched and unclenched his fists as he tromped through splinters and broken glass and mirrors. What the hell was wrong with him? How could he let some smarmy reporter get the best of him? Did he really threaten to put her on a terrorist list and threaten an all-out IRS audit? Damn straight he did. Like he really had the juice to do that. He'd been put in his place the last time he'd tried that.

Moss massaged his throbbing temples.

Did he really want to go up against the awesome *Post* and their team of investigative reporters? Not in this lifetime he didn't. Well, maybe he'd take a stab at it if Amalie were still under his thumb, but she wasn't. She was out there somewhere, and his gut was telling him the smarmy reporter knew exactly where she was. He continued to massage his temples, which were pounding so hard, he wondered if he was going to have a stroke. He needed to calm down and come up with a plan, and he needed to do it immediately, before more damage could be done.

Moss's thoughts took him to the upcoming gala the First Lady was hosting in a few days. It was the last place he wanted to go. But at the moment, he could not see a way to get out of it. And then to hear that Amalie was going to attend. That news was like a silver bullet right through the heart. Maybe it was all a rumor initiated by that snippy reporter. Reporters did crap like that all the time in hopes of getting a rise out of whomever they were targeting.

On top of all that, the President had been silent. He hadn't called once in the last two days. By the same token, Moss had not called the President either. A waiting game. Who was going to blink first? Maybe it was

261

time to get out of Dodge. He had the wherewithal to go anywhere in the world he chose and live out his days in luxury. If he wanted to. The question was, did he?

Now that he was calming down, he started to think clearly. Maybe he could make things right, call Spritzer, and apologize. He could always get a new cell-phone number. In the whole of his life, with one glaring exception, he'd never apologized to anyone. Only when Gabe had proved right about the purchase of *La Natural* did Lincoln apologize for doubting him. Other than that, the reason he never apologized was because he was never wrong.

So, why start now? Spritzer was right, there was nothing more powerful than the written word, and the one thing any politician learned from the git-go was that you never made an enemy of the press. As in never, ever. And he'd done just that in a fit of rage.

Moss leaned over and pressed the button on the intercom. "Send someone up here to clean this mess. And when you're done, put some flowers in here. I'll move into one of the guest rooms until things are returned to normal."

Flowers! He'd send Spritzer some flowers. Women liked flowers. That should make things right.

Moss stomped his way out of the room, down the hall to one of the many guest rooms, where he headed for the shower. He stepped in the moment the water rushed out of the twenty-seven pulsing jets, still wearing his grungy clothes and Timberland boots. There were more ways than one to skin a cat, and he knew them all, he assured himself, as he peeled off his filthy, sweat-stained clothes.

The First Lady, also known as Emily Helen Knight of the United States, paced the family quarters as she waited for her husband to join her for lunch. He was an hour late, which was nothing new. When his press secretary called her midmorning to say the President wanted to have lunch in their private quarters, she hadn't been the least surprised. Gabe needed to talk. Or he *wanted* her to talk. As in, share the latest White House gossip. She wondered what it was this time. Probably something to do with Lincoln Moss, she decided.

Emily Knight picked up her pace as she walked from one room to the other. She was a plain, pleasant woman who was often compared to a young Bess Truman. At first, she'd been insulted, then flattered. Bess

263

Truman was a kind, gentle woman who did not let her position influence or take away from the real person she was. Lincoln Moss didn't like her. He'd made that abundantly clear the day Gabe introduced her to his best friend in the whole world. He thought Gabe could do better than a farm girl from Kansas. But Gabe had defied Lincoln and proposed, and she'd accepted. They had had a wonderful marriage until they moved here to 1600 Pennsylvania Avenue. Wonderful as long as she stayed out of Lincoln Moss's sight. It was still wonderful in many ways when Lincoln Moss wasn't in the picture, even living here at 1600 Pennsylvania Avenue, the most famous address in the world.

Emily was aware of all the gossip, the insider backbiting, and the downright nastiness that went on within these hallowed walls. There were those who said Gabe couldn't tie his shoes unless Lincoln showed him how to do it. It wasn't true, but still they said it. In many ways, it was Gabe's fault that he allowed Lincoln to overpower and overshadow him. Then there were the whispers about Moss's little black book, the book everyone feared, even Gabe, if the whispers were true. Personally, she believed it and wouldn't put it past Lincoln Moss to blackmail anyone who crossed his path. She'd learned the hard way not to interfere in any way in the relationship between her husband and Lincoln Moss. Every night, she prayed for insight and the hope that someday she would come to understand that particular friendship.

Emily looked down at her watch, a small gold face on a gold-plated expansion band. It had been her parents' gift to her when she graduated from high school. She treasured it like no other piece of jewelry in her velvet-lined jewel case. To this day, it still worked, and she was never without it. Oh, she had fancy watches, one from Tiffany and a gold Rolex, but they were too ostentatious for her. You could take the girl out of Kansas, but you couldn't take Kansas out of the girl. She was who she was, it was that simple.

Gabe was now ninety minutes late. She had a meeting at 3:15 with the caterers, one that she absolutely had to attend. She wondered what would happen if she didn't attend, then decided she really didn't care one way or the other. Right now, her husband needed to talk to her, and that was all that was important.

She didn't hear him until he was right behind her. She loved it when he nuzzled her neck like he was doing right now. "Sorry, Em. I tried to be on time, but one thing led to another." She nodded in understanding. "What's for lunch?"

"What you asked for, sloppy joes with sour-cream cucumbers. We have to eat fast, I have a meeting at three-fifteen."

"Well, it's just going to have to wait, just like my three-fifteen is going to have to wait. We are having lunch. Together. And we are not going to eat fast, either. And then we are going to have dessert. I'm up for a glass of wine. How about you?"

Emily nodded. Whatever this little luncheon was about, it must be serious. Gabe never drank wine at lunch; nor did she. Well, there was a first time for everything.

Husband and wife sat down at the kitchen table that Gabe insisted they use when they were in their private residence. They waited while the steward served them, then quietly withdrew.

"We could probably push this along if you'd get right to the point, Gabe. I know you love my company, but I sense that something is troubling you. Let's hear it," Emily said as she bit into her sloppy sandwich. Why Gabe loved these messy sandwiches was beyond her.

"Now this is what I call a good sandwich," the President said, wolfing down the oozing sandwich. "C'mon, Em, admit you like them, too."

Soft brown eyes stared across the table at her husband. Sometimes it was hard to remember Gabe was the President of the United States. Like right now, he was just the guy she was lucky enough to marry. "They are tasty. I admit it. Now, are you happy?"

"As a pig in a mudslide. So, Em, here is my problem. I need to know what the gossip is. You're the only one I can ask. I know your staff hears it all and tells you because that's what women do. Now, mind you, I'm not judging," Gabe said, his eyes twinkling.

"Are you asking for a certain type of gossip about a certain individual or just gossip in general?"

Gabe reached for a second sandwich as he rolled his eyes. "You and I agreed never to play games with each other, Em. What have you heard?"

The First Lady got a little testy at that moment. "Sometimes, I don't understand you, Gabriel. One minute, Lincoln Moss's name is never to pass my lips, and you tell me not to listen to gossip. And then you turn around and ask me what the gossip is.

I think you need to tell me what is going on. And before you can ask, yes, he did buy a whole table for ten for the gala Saturday night. However, he did not return his personal RSVP."

Emily had called him Gabriel. When his wife addressed him by his given name, the President knew he was in some serious hot water. He plucked at a crisp chunk of cucumber and popped it into his mouth. He waited to see if she would elaborate. When she simply looked at him and did what he did, popped a wedge of cucumber into her mouth, he knew he had both feet in the hot water.

The President polished off the wine in his glass and poured another. He looked over at his wife, who shook her head. "Let's hear it."

"Listen to me, Gabe. No matter what I say, you are going to take it personal. As in there is no love lost between Lincoln and me. I don't like the man, I never did. Actually, Gabriel, I detest him. Just so you know, there were many times when I almost gave you an ultimatum, him or me. The reason I didn't was because, in my heart of hearts, I believed you would have chosen Lincoln. There, I finally said it out loud. Who would you have chosen if that came to pass, Gabriel?"

Gabe brought the wineglass to his lips as he tried to imagine his life with either Emily or Lincoln missing. His hesitation did not go unnoticed by his wife. "I would have chosen you, Emily." He wondered if his response was really true, and he could see that his wife was wondering the very same thing. His stomach churned, and now he wished he'd passed on the second sloppy joe sandwich.

Emily just stared sadly at her husband. "Since we're being honest with each other, I think it's easy for you to say that now. Back then, had I given you the ultimatum, I think we both know you would have anguished over your decision. That's water under the bridge now, as they say, Gabriel. You need to cut Lincoln Moss loose before it's too late. By too late, I mean that your top people are going to resign. It would seem, if the gossip is true, that little black book everyone whispers about actually exists. That's the gossip you want to hear. Am I right?"

Gabe swallowed hard. "When you say my top people, who are you referring to exactly, and why hasn't anyone said anything to me?"

"Because . . . Gabriel, you refuse to listen to anyone except Lincoln. It's your own fault. But to answer your question, your chief of staff, your National Security Advisor, and the Director of Homeland Security. The latest rumor seems to be that the Director of the CIA is so fed up with Moss, he's one hair away of stepping down. The only one who has been silent is the Director of the FBI, Jack Sparrow."

Gabriel Knight chewed on his bottom lip. He felt lower than a snake's belly. "I haven't heard from Lincoln in two days."

"And this surprises you . . . why?" Emily snorted.

Gabe winced at his wife's sarcasm. "It was my turn to call him. I didn't. Mainly because my chief of staff, Geoff, made a few stinging comments, and I took them to heart. The truth is, I called him out on it, and he let loose. I really thought about firing him on the spot, but I didn't. He's a good man, and he is loyal to me."

"You always said you couldn't trust anyone but Lincoln. Are you saying now that all of that trust is changing? Why? What is going on, Gabe?"

"Morale, for want of a better word. Everyone is surly, no one wants to take responsibility for making decisions only to be countermanded by Lincoln. And, yes, I let that happen. I also rescinded his pass. Now he has to do what everyone else does, make an appointment or stay away. While I did not call him, he has not called me, either."

"Oh, Gabe, don't you see what he's doing? He's showing you he's in control, and you will call him when you need him. He's not going to blink if that's what you're thinking. He never did belong at your early-morning briefings. That's what started all the resentment toward him. You must know that," Emily said.

What he knew was that his wife was now calling him Gabe and not Gabriel. If nothing else, he was grateful for that. He nodded. "Okay, what's the rest of it?"

"It's just gossip, Gabe. Hurtful gossip. I even hate repeating it. But part of me believes it because it makes sense, at least to me. All gossip has a seed of truth to it, we both know that."

"Just tell me, Em. Let's get it all out right now."

"Well, the secretive looks and whispers started when that picture of Lincoln's wife appeared in the tabloid. Some of the secretaries actually had the paper. I hate to admit this, but after they left, I took it out of the trash and read it. Things like that always grow legs, and the story can become so outlandish it's like it came from another planet.

"The gossip was that Lincoln batted Amalie around. One of the girls said a friend of hers was in the restroom at some political function when Amalie was there. It was some affair at the Ritz-Carlton. She saw Amalie lift up her top to look at a huge black-and-blue bruise on her rib cage. She said she put a cold compress on it. She explained to this person that she had fallen off a horse. Then someone else said they used to watch how gingerly she walked, like she'd been hurt. My press secretary looked me right in the eye, Gabe, and told me Lincoln was, and these are her exact words, 'beating the hell out of his wife' in places where it didn't show.

"No one knows why. But all the ladies think Amalie left Lincoln. Think about it, Gabe, because I sure have. None of us have seen Amalie in over five years. Where is she?"

"When I ask, he says she's in France, that she doesn't like it here," Gabe said as he continued to chew his lip. "Why would he beat that beautiful creature? She's gentle, she's kind, she's sweet, and a wonderful person. He also told me more than once that his private life was none of my business. And he's right, it is not my business."

"I don't know the answer to that question, Gabe. I always liked Amalie. She was so shy, and I thought the two of them were in love. I should have known better. Lincoln Moss only loves himself."

Gabe tried to make sense out of what his wife was saying. "Why? I never had an inkling of any kind that he could or would do something like that."

"You don't live with him, Gabe. Amalie did. Nothing is as it seems, you know that. Lincoln is a control freak. I think Amalie was afraid of him. I'm thinking, and this is just my opinion, that she got fed up and just up and left. No one has seen her in over five years. At least no one who will admit to it.

"Five years is a long time, Gabe. Lincoln always has an answer as to where she is. Saturday night will tell the tale."

"Why do you say that?" Gabe asked, still trying to digest the fact that his best friend in the whole world was a possible wife batterer.

"Because there is a rumor going around that Amalie is going to attend the gala on Saturday night. Sans Lincoln. Just this morning, my personal secretary told me that Amalie Laurent will be the guest of the Director of the FBI. And that they will both be sitting at a table bought by the Countess de Silva? What do you think of that, Gabriel?"

They were back to Gabriel, with both feet in hot water. "Is that a definite or a rumor?"

"The RSVP came back from Director Sparrow with his name and his guest's name. It said Amalie Laurent, not Amalie Moss. Now, does Lincoln know that? I have no clue. If there's nothing else, I need to go to my meeting. I'm already a half hour late."

"Tell anyone who wants to know why you're late that I was chewing off your clothes and making wild passionate love to you. They'll cut you some slack then."

Emily laughed out loud. "Okay." She kissed him on the cheek before she left the kitchen.

Gabe missed his wife the moment the door closed behind her. He knew he was late for his next appointment, but he didn't care. He got up and cleared the table and washed the dishes. He knew how to do laundry, cook, and clean because his mother taught him how to take care of himself. He was even a fair-to-middling plumber. He wished right now he could go outside and mow the lawn. He loved the smell of new-cut grass. He looked around the kitchen to make sure it was clean and tidy. What the hell, why not? He started stripping off his clothes as he headed for the master bedroom, where he pulled on a pair of threadbare gray sweatpants and a muscle shirt. He tied up the laces of his Nikes, fished around in the closet until he found his Atlanta Braves baseball cap, and squashed it onto his head.

Outside in the corridor, the President's Secret Service men looked at him, their eyes popping. "Where to, sir?"

"The work shed. I'm going to mow the lawn."

"But sir . . ." Protests followed the President's long-legged stride all the way to the secluded work shed.

"No buts, gentlemen, I'm climbing up on that John Deere, and I am cutting the lawn. You can ride alongside or trot or watch me, your call."

And that's exactly what President Gabriel Knight did that sunny afternoon in July. Not only did he cut the lawn, but he sang, off-key, at the top of his lungs, as he tooled along at three miles an hour. Every news channel carried the event on the evening news. The commentators started off their hourly news by saying, "Hold on to your hats, ladies and gentlemen, what you are about to see is something never before shown on TV." The picture that popped up on the screen was the President waving to one and all as he buzzed around the White House lawn, a grin as wide as the Grand Canyon on his face. It was clear to one and all that he was having the time of his life. And as the news commentators said, why shouldn't the President have the time of his life. He was, after all, the leader of the free world.

The moment Lincoln Moss saw the picture flash on the screen, he went from placid to nuclear, knowing that a picture was worth a thousand words and that Gabriel Knight just jumped up twenty points in his approval rating. He smashed up his state-of-the-art kitchen, where he was eating his solitary dinner at the kitchen counter.

"Son of a bitch!" he cursed.

CHAPTER 17

The boys sat around Myra's kitchen table, drinking coffee. "I don't get it, why are we even here? What's going on? I feel like I should move my stuff here and take up residency," Dennis grumbled.

"Sometimes, it's good to be on the down low, kid," Ted said as he poured fresh coffee into everyone's cup. They were on their third pot since their arrival a little after sunup.

Harry, the only one not drinking coffee, looked at the tea leaves in the bottom of his cup as though the answer to all life's problems could be found there. He mumbled something that sounded like, "We're just the second string."

"How'd you guys like those pictures of the prez on the news last night?" Jack asked, grinning. "I actually did a double take. Good for him."

Ted joined in the laughter. "Those

pictures made it around the world in like sixty seconds. Feedback was positive the world over. That's what's been lacking in the guy's presidency, the human side of him. Not the side that Lincoln Moss wanted presented to the world. I gotta say, though, he can't sing worth a damn." Another round of laughter rang through the kitchen.

"Men perceived him like just a guy you could belly up to the bar for a beer with. Nikki said women would view it as if he was doing his honey to-do list. Just another guy mowing the lawn. Personally, I thought it was great even though I didn't vote for him, either time. I would vote for him if he were able to run again, though," Jack said. "You know what else, it wasn't a photo op. It wasn't staged. I think the guy just got a burr in his jockeys and decided to do what he wanted to do at that moment in time. That's what made it so great," Jack said.

"Moving right along here, what's going on in the war room that we can't be there?" Abner asked.

"They're plotting and scheming and strategizing, that's what they're doing," Ted said.

"Where are the two ladies?" Dennis asked, hoping he sounded nonchalant.

"Upstairs. I heard Myra tell them to stay

up there till they got back," Espinosa mumbled as he fiddled with his camera. "Anyone know what's in all those FedEx boxes piled up in the foyer?"

"I do believe but am not certain that those boxes contain the women's outfits for Saturday night. I looked at the return label, and even I know the names of Donna Karan and Vera Wang. I think Annie is friends with or knows them. Something like that," Ted said.

"What about us? Are we chopped liver?" Jack grumbled.

"I think the boxes labeled Hugo Boss are our designer duds. Something about Fergus knowing someone at that fashion house. Don't you guys know anything? It's not what you know, it's who you know, especially in the fashion business," Espinosa said.

"And you know all this . . . how?" Jack snorted.

"I know it because Alexis told me. Everyone knows Alexis has fashion sense and can create something out of nothing. I'm not being a wiseass either, Jack. What I said is true," Espinosa said, pointing his camera and snapping a picture of Jack with his mouth hanging open.

The talk turned to the new pool Nikki and

Jack were putting in on the property they were in the process of buying from Nellie.

"I never realized how much earthmoving equipment was needed to dig a hole for a pool. We have mountains of earth piled everywhere. Now it's mud, with all the rain we had. Things are at a complete standstill. We'll be lucky if it's finished by Labor Day, then it will be too cool to swim. But Nikki wanted a pool, so we're getting a pool."

"Does that mean you and Nikki are selling your house to Jack Sparrow?" Harry asked.

"Last week, Sparrow wanted to buy it. Then he changed his mind the other day, then he changed it back to wanting to buy it. He can't make up his mind if he wants to be a homeowner or not. The deal's on if he wants it," Jack said.

"Since we're obviously not needed here, why don't we head back to town and see if Sparrow can join us for lunch. I think we need to powwow with him in regard to Saturday night," Ted said.

Dennis was up and off his chair as he rinsed the coffeepot and turned it off. The rule was no one ever left Charles's kitchen a mess. As in ever. He hung the dish towel over the oven door on the handle, looked around, and announced that they were good to go.

"Should we leave a note?" Espinosa asked.

Jack scribbled a note and stuck it on the fridge.

"I just sent Sparrow a text, and he said he'll meet us at the Squire's Pub at twelve-thirty," Ted announced.

They all piled into the *Post* van. Dennis lagged behind, hoping he'd catch a glimpse of Rosalee, but the farmhouse remained quiet. No curtains moved, the dogs didn't bark. It was like there was no one home. Maybe later, if they decided to come back to the farm after lunch, which didn't seem likely since Ted was expounding on the afternoon schedule. He wished Rosalee had a phone so he could text her, but he knew his life would hang in the balance if he tried to sneak her one. He sighed mightily as he slid into his seat and buckled up. He did his best to shift his thoughts to the girls and what they were doing in the war room.

What the girls were doing, as a matter of fact, was staring at each other as they tried to come to terms with a resolution to what they called the Lincoln Moss Debacle.

The picture of Lady Justice on the big-screen plasma TV kept them on their toes as Charles and Fergus did whatever they were doing up on the dais. They could all hear the pings and whirring of the copy machine and fax as they tried to concentrate on the best outcome for Amalie Laurent and Rosalee Muno.

"The way I see it," Kathryn said, "we have two choices. Either we take him out at the Four Seasons on Saturday night, or we wait a few days and hit him where he lives. Secret Service will be crawling all over the Four Seasons, and we don't even know for sure if Moss is going to attend. When it comes right down to it, we don't know anything about the bastard other than that he went off on Maggie yesterday. That tells us he's on edge, so he's going to be superalert."

"I don't think he would expect anything to go awry at the Four Seasons for the very reason you just articulated," Isabelle said. "He knows now that Amalie is going to attend. Unless he thinks that was some kind of ploy to draw him out. But, having said that, he doesn't know we're after him."

"We could have it all down pat, get everyone in place, then he's a no-show. All that wasted time and effort. Personally, I don't think he's going to show," Yoko said.

"We need to start thinking the way Lincoln Moss thinks," Nikki said. "For starters, he thinks no one knows Amalie bailed out on him five years ago. He's managed to cover that all up. Now, suddenly, things have changed. First was the picture and article in the tabloid. At that point, he had to start thinking that someone knew what had happened. Without a doubt, he has hired the biggest and the best investigative agencies around. Abner verified that from his checking account. He's spent over a million dollars trying to find Amalie, all with nothing to show for it.

"I'm thinking he won't have the guts to show up Saturday night. But what I think he will do is be there in disguise, sitting in the lobby or hiding behind a palm tree or something. And if it isn't him in the lobby or behind a palm tree, it will be someone he hires, someone who will let him know if his wife really is attending the gala. For that matter, he could sit in the parking lot and watch unobserved," Nikki said.

"Wrong!" Maggie said. "Secret Service will be swarming all over the place. The guests of the hotel will probably be assigned a separate entrance, so that means no one will be hanging out in the lobby. Ted and I have covered enough of these events to know that that is how it works. However, there is a possibility, if Moss has the juice he says he has, that he could have booked a room in advance and, therefore, be a guest. With his clout, he could probably still get a room at the last second. Scratch the parking lot. I heard on the radio on my way out here this morning that the District police will be in charge of the parking lot. They said they were canceling all leave and bringing in everyone to help. Moss has got to know all that."

"Or he could do the unexpected and show up as himself and try to pull it off. As himself, he doesn't have to go through anything other than to show up. All it will take is one look to see if his wife is there or not. What he does from that point on will be a mystery to us, at least for now. My guess is he would leave ASAP once he saw his wife," Nikki said.

The women started to talk on top of one another, but in the end, they all agreed that Moss's showing up was the best working scenario that they could count on.

"If what you're saying is he's going to be in and out, there's nothing we can do in a room full of people," Annie said.

"Not so fast, Countess," Myra said. "We could surround him and *you,* my dear friend, can gush all over him. He'll be hard-pressed to dis *you.* But then what will we do? Remember, there will be well over a thousand people there if what Maggie said turns out to be true."

The women went back to jabbering and pointing fingers and at one point yelling at each other. Kathryn put her fingers to her lips and let loose with a bloodcurdling whistle. "Enough already! Obviously, it will be too dangerous to do anything at the Four Seasons, and by that I mean dangerous for us. I think we all realize that now. So now we have to make a plan to take him out at his home. I'm thinking we may need Amalie to guarantee that for us."

Yoko raised her hand. "I think it's a given that Moss is going to have some private-eye types casing the Four Seasons to see if Amalie does show up. He'll have her tailed at the end of the evening. It won't matter that she's with Jack Sparrow. What are we going to do about that? Where is he going to take her at the end of the night?"

"Off the top of my head, I'd say this is a job for Abner and Avery Snowden. Once Abner gives us the names of the detective agencies Moss used, Avery and his people can start tracking them. It will be a case of operatives trailing operatives. I'm almost sure that Director Sparrow will have some of his special agents on duty Saturday night also. I'm not worried about Amalie. Director Sparrow will get her to safety, I guarantee it," Annie said.

"Did we decide if Amalie is going as Amalie, the way she used to look before her surgery, with Alexis's help, or the way she looks now?" Nikki asked. "Maybe we should take a vote."

"Maybe we should ask Amalie what she wants?" Kathryn snapped irritably because her leg was starting to ache, which meant that rain was on the horizon. She apologized immediately for her sharp words.

"Right now, Amalie has no say in the matter. We make all the decisions. She's too vulnerable and fearful at the moment to know what is best for her. She'll do whatever we tell her to do because she just wants to put all this behind her and get her life back," Myra said quietly.

Maggie let out a whoop of sound. "Ooooh, wait till you hear this! Lisa from the paper, our girl Friday, just sent me a text saying the biggest flower arrangement in the world just arrived for me. She said there are six dozen champagne-colored roses in a decorative bushel basket sitting on my desk. And they are . . . drumroll, la-di-da, from Lincoln Moss! The note said he apologizes for his ridiculous threats yesterday and blamed it on a killer migraine. Well, will wonders never cease. Guess I can stop worrying about being on Homeland Security's terrorist list and sigh with relief that the IRS isn't going to come after me. I'm texting Lisa to divvy up the arrangement into separate bouquets and have one of the copy boys take them over to a hospice two blocks from the paper. I don't want any flowers from Lincoln Moss. I don't want *anything* from Lincoln Moss," Maggie said through clenched teeth, her eyes sparking dangerously.

"Good for you. I would have done the same thing. Just out of curiosity, Maggie, did you believe Moss's threats?" Isabelle asked.

"I did believe that he would try to do what he threatened to do. Because that's the kind of mean, spiteful person he is. I'm not above being scared out of my wits when someone threatens me. But did I think he would succeed? No, not really. Still . . ."

"Six dozen roses. That's seventy-two roses. Yep, guess he would need a bushel basket for that many." Maggie laughed, but it was a nervous laugh. "What's my next move, girls?"

"I guess calling him to thank him. I think I'd call him on his landline at home if I were you, though. Then throw him a bone and tell him he's inching up to the number one slot for your Man of the Year contest," Alexis said.

"Okay, I'll do that later. I don't want to appear eager or anything."

"Back to our game plan," Yoko said. "What is it?"

"We need to know first and foremost how serious Moss's security is at his home. How many guards there are for one thing? And is the security twenty-four/seven or just at night? Why does the guy need security anyway? And dogs, we need to know if there are dogs on the premises. Is his help live-in or do they go home at night? Amalie might know, but then again, things might have changed after she left," Nikki said.

"Not to change the subject, but do any of you read the financial page in the morning?" No one raised her hand. "Well, I do," Annie said. "Several days ago, there was an article about *La Natural* and how Moss's crown jewel of his holdings is tanking. The company lost its billion-dollar status and is now only a million-dollar company. Regardless, the company made him mega billions since he bought it. The bastard still has enough money to live a life of luxury over a thousand lifetimes."

"No! No! No, Annie! He only has the use of the money until my husband hits the one key that takes it all away." Isabelle chortled.

"There is that, you're absolutely right," Annie agreed, laughing. "I can't wait to see his face when he realizes it's all gone."

"Okay, girls, time to get to the *good stuff.* What is his punishment going to be?" Myra demanded.

Up on the dais, Charles and Fergus shivered at the evil laughter wafting their way.

The brainstorming went on for several hours but in low tones, so that neither Charles nor Fergus was privy to any of the actual decisions. From time to time, they would flinch when they heard the women whoop and cackle with delight. They did whisper to each other that the bloke had no idea what was coming his way. Both men almost jumped out of their skin when they heard Annie say, "That's it, then. We have a few days till we head his way, so I'll set the wheels in motion. Girls, I'm proud of us. I knew we could come up with something unique and deserving for that disgrace to manhood." The girls all clapped and whistled. Fergus peeked around the corner in time to see the women high-fiving each other. And to think his companion was the ringleader. He had the urge to step down and high-five her himself, but he knew that Charles wouldn't approve.

The women all shouted a loud good-bye as they trooped out of the war room. When the door closed behind them, Charles flopped down in his swivel chair. Fergus joined him in an adjoining chair. Both men looked at each other. "Whatever it is, it certainly pleased them to no end. I think that's the part they like the most, doling out the punishment they know the courts would never allow. I can't say I disagree with them, either. If Moss was taken into custody for spousal abuse, what's the worst thing the courts would do to him considering his position and the thousand-dollar-an-hour battery of lawyers he would have defending him? Not to mention the judges he plays golf with. Maybe probation. But more than likely, he'd get off scot-free, and Amalie would be the one who gets the short end of the stick. That happens to the victims a lot. Not with our girls, though. This time, Amalie will be the victor, and Moss will get whatever they think he deserves. How can we argue with that, Fergus?"

"We can't, Charles. We both did it back in the day when we had to. It's just, I don't know, strange I guess is the word I'm looking for, that women can do this."

Charles laughed out loud and slapped at his knees with his open palms. "Those women were born to do this. It took me a while, but I finally realized how very capable they are. Not to mention wily, crafty, downright devious, and in plain English, they don't give a good rat's ass who gets in their way if they are on a mission. Actually, I applaud them all."

Fergus felt his chest puff out. And Annie was the ringleader, his amour. He knew Charles felt the same way, and he also thought of Myra as the backbone of the Vigilante group. No doubt about it, the ladies had it going on.

"Well, Fergus, unless we plan on eating peanut butter and jelly sandwiches for our meal, we need to get moving here and see about dinner. Your tapioca banana pudding should be ready to go into the oven about now."

Fergus heaved himself up and looked around. "What about our guest in the cell down at the end of the hall, Charles?"

"What about her?" Charles asked.

"Should we check on her?"

"Why?" Charles asked.

"Okay, I get it, not our purview. I am getting hungry, so let's head for the kitchen."

"I'm right behind you, pardner," Charles cackled.

CHAPTER 18

"The day is still young. I think we should do something constructive," Annie said.

"What do you have in mind, Annie?" Nikki asked.

Annie shrugged. "Something has been bothering me about all of this, and no one else picked up on it so I thought . . . think maybe it doesn't mean anything."

"Talk to us," Myra said.

"Amalie and Rosalee both told us that when Lincoln Moss's beatings went over the top and he cracked and broke ribs and bones, he'd call a doctor to come to the house. Aren't doctors supposed to report abuse to the authorities, or is that just for people like teachers, where children are concerned? I'm sorry I'm so ignorant on the subject. And where did Moss get a doctor who if he didn't suspect what was going on, would keep his mouth shut? I think it's important.

"When Abner went through Moss's personal checking account, there were numerous checks made out to a Dr. Symon Mattison. I Googled him, and he's an internist with an excellent reputation. He has a private practice and admitting privileges at Georgetown University Medical Center. That means he has to be at their beck and call if a case needing his expertise shows up.

"He has a very big practice. A staff of six plus two associates. And he makes house calls!" Annie said, her eyebrows shooting up to her hairline at this unbelievable revelation. "I don't know a single doctor in this area who makes house calls. That's not to say there aren't any, but I think it would be newsworthy if there were. This is, after all, the nation's capital."

"And this means what to us?" Myra asked.

"What can we do with the information?" Nikki asked.

"Wouldn't it be nice to have all of Amalie's records so that when we take down Moss, we can shove them under his nose? And they might help Amalie get a quick divorce when there is no Moss around to consent to one after we make him disappear. Not to mention that Amalie might want to ask the good doctor why he didn't help her by reporting her various injuries."

"But she and Rosalee both said they lied to the doctor and said all those beatings were accidents, that she was accident-prone, blah blah blah," Myra said.

"The man's a doctor, Myra. He's trained to spot things like that. He chose, for whatever his reasons, not to say anything. Abner made a note saying Mattison has played golf a time or two with Moss and the President. That means they are at least quasi-friends. It also probably means the good doctor and his wife were probably invited to the White House. In this town, that would give the wife a certain amount of prestige among the other medical wives. By the way, the current wife is number four, just in case you're counting."

"Believe it or not, there are those among us who can look away when a prize is offered. Moss could hand out the prizes," Annie said.

"Let me guess. You want us to pay a visit to the doctor, right?" Nikki asked.

"The thought did cross my mind. It's only two-thirty. We have the rest of the afternoon in front of us. Everyone else is doing something. Alexis is going through all those treasure boxes that arrived. Isabelle is helping Abner, and she's becoming quite the hacker. Kathryn had to leave for therapy. Yoko said she had to be at the nursery because some shipment of something or other was due to arrive, and she had to be there to sign off on it. Maggie is back at the paper with the boys, working on her call to Moss and the Man of the Year contest. Harry has classes, and Jack is helping. That leaves the three of us, and I absolutely do not want to go home and look at those mountains of mud around the house," Nikki said.

"Let's do it," Myra said. She looked at Nikki and Annie to see if she thought they would pass muster for a trip to a prestigious internist's office. Satisfied with what she was seeing, she gave the pearls around her neck a jerk, and asked, "Who's driving?"

"Me!" Nikki said before Annie could get her tongue to work. "I want to get there in one piece. No offense, Annie."

Annie laughed. "None taken, dear. So, how do we play this. Do we go in, flash our gold shields, and play badass agents? Or what?"

"That sounds about right," Myra said. "I'm itching to take someone on right now."

"Whoa, Myra," Nikki said as she gunned her BMW and raced down the long road that would take her to the highway. "I need an address, ladies."

Annie flashed her phone. "I have the address right here. I'll program it into your GPS, and it will take us right to the door. The doctor owns the building. Eighteen thousand square feet. He even does minor procedures there. According to what I'm seeing here, we should be at the door in thirty-three minutes."

"That's if you were driving, Annie. Since Nikki is driving, add fifteen more minutes." Myra laughed. "Have you given any thought to the doctor's not being there? Then what do we do?"

Annie held up her hand. "Not to worry, he has office hours till four. I checked."

"I'm excited," Myra said as she fingered her pearls.

"You might want to ditch those pearls, Myra. I don't think special agents of the government wear pearls even if they are considered badasses when they do an insertion. That's what we're doing, you know." Myra dutifully tucked her heirloom pearls under the collar of the button-down shirt she was wearing.

"We should put our shields on a lanyard. Do you have any in the car, Nikki? This way, when we make our entrance, the shields will speak for themselves."

"Sorry, Myra, I don't carry lanyards in my car, but we can stop at the first drugstore we see and get three of them. Good idea, Myra. What your eyes see first is what sets the tone for what is to come. What do we do if there are still patients in the building when we get there?"

"We dismiss them and tell them to call to reschedule. I say we gather all the personnel together, scare the hell out of them, then zero in on the good, or not so good, doctor. As to the associates, if they're there, then we make short work of them. These shields will scare anyone into instant obedience," Annie said.

The women batted their entrance scenario around for the rest of the ride into the District. The stop at a Rite Aid drugstore barely ate into their time, and they arrived at Dr. Mattison's office right on schedule.

"Eleven cars in the parking lot. Six staff, the two associates, the doctor, and possibly two patients. Ooops, make that possibly one patient. Someone just got into one of the cars.

"Pricey real estate," Myra said. "Did Abner tell you what the doctor's income is?"

"Close to three million. He's up there with the movers and shakers. One of his usual golfing buddies is the President's personal physician."

The women climbed out of the car. Nikki locked it. And then, as if on cue, all three adjusted their gold shields hanging from leather lanyards around their necks.

"If I'm not mistaken, here comes patient number two. We are good to go, ladies. We can admire the architecture another time. Step lively now." They did wait at the door to see if the elderly gentleman was indeed headed to the burgundy-colored Saab in the patient section of the parking lot.

Annie opened the door and walked straight to the counter, where a young woman sat typing into the computer. She only looked up when Annie cleared her throat.

"Office hours are over, ma'am. I can make an appointment for you if you like."

"We don't need an appointment, young lady. We're here to see Dr. Mattison. Call him. Then gather up the staff and have them here front and center. Do it *now*!" Annie wiggled the gold shield for the receptionist's benefit. Her eyes grew wide, and she opened her mouth, but no words came out.

Nikki backed up and locked the door to the lobby.

"Now means *now*!" Annie said. "Or I can

do it for you."

"I think you should do it," Myra said.

Annie brought her fingers to her lips and let loose with a shrill whistle that was deafening. Running feet from every direction could be heard.

"There is an intercom, Annie, that could have gotten the same result," Myra said. Annie shrugged.

The lobby, which had looked so spacious, all of a sudden looked crowded as everyone skidded to a stop and stared at Myra, Annie, and Nikki, who all were holding up their gold shields for inspection. The questions that were about to erupt died in the staff's throats.

"What's the meaning of this intrusion? Who are you people, and what are you doing here?" a distinguished man dressed in a white lab coat barked.

"Dr. Mattison, I presume. We ask the questions, we don't answer them. Sit down and don't move until I tell you to move. And do not speak."

Nikki looked at the staff. "Gather up your things and leave the building. Listen to me very carefully now. You are not to speak to anyone about what you've just seen and heard. If you do, you will be arrested and held for seventy-two hours without the aid of an attorney. That means you are not to speak of this to your family, your friends, your spouses, or your partners. Raise your hand to indicate you understand what I just said." Every hand in the room shot in the air. "If you do speak and mention this, you will need to engage the services of an attorney at the end of the seventy-two hours, and that will cost you, bare minimum, fifty thousand dollars. I doubt very much that your boss, Dr. Mattison, will want to spring for your retainers. Raise your hands to tell me you all understand what I just said." Again, every hand in the room shot up in the air.

"Before you leave, each of you write your name, address, phone number, cell-phone number, the make of your car, the license-plate number, and make a photocopy of your license and one credit card. Hop to it, ladies. You too, gentlemen," she said, addressing the new young associates.

Dr. Mattison started to mutter and mumble. Myra raised her index finger for silence as she watched the staff scurrying about under Annie's and Nikki's watchful eyes.

The two associates, both young men, kept glancing at their boss to see his reaction and wondering if they would have a job the following day. One of them looked at Nikki and asked if they should report to work in the morning. Nikki laughed out loud. The associate's face turned red as he shot an ugly glare at his boss.

Annie carefully scrutinized the paperwork she was holding. Satisfied that everything was in order, she stuffed it all into a manila folder she picked up from the desk. "Get your things, people. Do not leave anything behind. One more time, do you all understand the rules as I've presented them to you? Raise your hands." Again, every hand in the room shot upward. She nodded to Nikki, who unlocked the front door and waited till everyone was out of the room before she closed and locked the door and lowered the blind over the door.

"Show time, Dr. Mattison!" Myra said, a lilt in her voice. "Take us to your office, please."

"What gives you the right to invade this office?"

"This is what gives us the right," Nikki said, shoving the gold shield up against the doctor's face. "The lady told you to move, so move, or I will move you myself."

Mattison was a tall man, probably in his midfifties, with a full head of iron-gray hair, blue eyes that owed their color to contact lenses, tanned, and sculpted. Some kind of facial surgery to tighten up his features, Myra thought. He was wearing a spotless, crisp, white lab coat with a stethoscope hanging out of one of the pockets. He wasn't exactly eye candy, but he was easy on the eyes. And he did look every inch like the professional doctor he was.

"Whatever this is all about, I would like to have my lawyer present, if you don't mind. I have some very influential friends in this town, and I resent this invasion. You have no right to do this, and I don't care what those things around your necks say."

"Unfortunately, Doctor, what they say is we're in control, and you aren't. There's no one here but you and us. No lawyer. As to all those influential friends in this town, how's that working for you, Doc?" Nikki asked. "Oh, feel free to vent, resent, whatever you want. Now, this is what we want from you. A list of each time you treated Amalie Laurent Moss. By that I mean those secretive house calls you made to Glenwood Drive when Lincoln Moss called you. Shame on you, you didn't report even one of those visits."

Mattison's eyes almost popped out of his head. "I don't know what you're talking about."

"Really! Well maybe this will refresh your memory." Annie slapped down a sheaf of papers, printouts, thanks to Abner, of Lincoln Moss's canceled checks, the dates, and the doctor's personal bank-account statements.

"Where did you get these? That is personal, private, and privileged information. I want a lawyer."

"We hear that a lot. About wanting a lawyer. This," Nikki said, waving the gold shield, "allows us to do whatever we want. For instance, if I suddenly get the crazy urge to find out if you wear boxers or tighty-whities, this shield will let me march into your house and go through your dresser drawers. Not that I would ever want to do that, I'm just saying. Now, we want Amalie Laurent Moss's medical records. Hit the keyboard, Doc."

"I will do no such thing. A doctor's records are sacred. I will tell you nothing. It goes under patient-doctor privilege. Even a court order won't make me tell you."

"You sure about that, Doctor?" Annie asked. "Or are you protesting because Amalie Laurent Moss's records are not in your computer since you did not want anyone to know about those little visits out to Glenwood Drive? We can just take the whole computer with us when we leave. Oh, did I mention you will be going with us?"

Symon Mattison licked at his bottom lip. Clearly, he was agitated, and he also clearly did not know what to do. Finally, he came to some kind of decision and nodded.

"We know you like going to the White House. We know your wife likes to boast to her fellow bridge players that she gets invited there. We get all that. What we don't get, Dr. Mattison, is why you did nothing to stop the abuse. Amalie Laurent, she doesn't like to be called Moss these days, is prepared to testify against you. She said you did what her husband told you to do. You could lose your license; your new trophy wife, social climber that she is, will divorce you; and your children will become outcasts. That is the reality of what you are looking at. Ask yourself if your friendship with Lincoln Moss is worth the loss of all you hold dear," Annie said.

"Has something happened to Amalie?" Mattison asked nervously. "I haven't seen her in over five years, maybe longer."

"Are you asking us if he killed her? That's always been your fear, right. Still, you did nothing. That's what you're thinking, isn't it? He finally did it, that kind of thing."

"There was always an excuse, a reason

305

given by Amalie herself for her injuries," Mattison whispered. "Lincoln said if I ever told anyone, he'd ruin me. I kept a separate file on Amalie."

"To cover your own butt, right?" Nikki bellowed.

"Yes, but for Amalie as well. I knew in my heart someday that this might happen."

"You could have reported him anonymously," Myra said.

"No, I couldn't. I was the only one who knew other than the little Mexican maid. And she was too scared to even look at me. I don't even know if the maid spoke English because I never heard her speak. She seemed to understand when I told her what she had to do for Amalie, however."

"And you just walked away and took his money and kept silent."

"Yes. And I am not proud of it. I did what I could for Amalie. Not that this means anything, but I despise the bastard."

"Where are the records?" Annie asked.

Symon Mattison pulled a key ring out of his pocket and opened his bottom desk drawer. He pulled out a thick file folder. He stared at it for a long moment, drew a deep breath, and handed it to Myra, who was the closest to him. "What happens now?"

The three women looked at one another.

"We can't tell you that, Doctor. But would you like some advice?" He nodded.

"If I were you, I'd pack up that trophy wife of yours, close down this office, and get the hell out of Dodge. You're a wealthy man; it's time for you to give back. Do what you do and expect nothing in return. The advice is free. And the same thing applies to you, Doctor, as the advice we gave to your staff. One word, and we'll be back. No matter where you go, we can find you. We *will* find you if you open your mouth about any of this to your buddy Moss."

"He's not my buddy, so please stop saying that. Okay, okay, I'll do what you say."

"Don't get up, Doctor, we can find the way out. By the way, nice digs you have here. Should bring a pretty fair amount to your coffers when you put it up for sale. That's not a suggestion, it's an order. Remember, *we will find you,*" Annie said coldly.

Outside in the hot, humid air, the three women looked at one another. "It's just another nail in Lincoln's coffin. It pains me to see how thick this file is," Annie said.

"It went well, all things considered. The man will be on a plane somewhere with or without the trophy wife by this time tomorrow. By Monday morning, this building will

307

have a FOR SALE sign on it, and the staff will be on the unemployment line." Nikki looked at Myra and Annie to see if they agreed. Both women nodded. Myra yanked at her pearls and removed the lanyard, then stuffed it along with the gold shield into her pocket.

"Let's go home, girls."

"I'm driving," Annie said, making a beeline for Nikki's Beemer. The only other car in the parking lot was a silver Porsche. She jerked her head in the direction of the parked car, and said, "Betcha we could get that set of wheels for pennies on the dollar tomorrow."

"That's a sucker's bet, and you know it," Myra said, laughing so hard Nikki had to push her into the backseat.

CHAPTER 19

Clyde Entwhistle, President Knight's chief of staff, looked up at the President and did a double take. The leader of the free world looked . . . *Presidential.* Today POTUS was dressed in a Savile Row suit, the crease in the trousers knife sharp. He was wearing a blood-red power tie. The shirt under his jacket was blinding white. Entwhistle looked down at the floor. The shoes were new, too, John Lobbs if he wasn't mistaken. What the hell happened overnight that he wasn't privy to? Gabriel Knight just looked so damn *Presidential.* It must be true what the fashion magazines said, clothes did indeed make the man.

What Entwhistle found the most startling though was what else he was seeing. A certain quietness of the man who was suddenly in total control of his whole being and his emotions, something he'd never seen before.

It wasn't that the President never dressed well, he did. Today, though, there was something different about his boss. He wondered if that ride on the John Deere had anything to do with it. Or the absence of Lincoln Moss at the White House of late. Then again, maybe the First Lady had gone shopping. It was a well-known fact that Emily Knight did all the President's shopping. Probably all of the above, Entwhistle decided.

Rarely was Entwhistle at a loss for words or anything else for that matter, but this morning he felt flummoxed for some reason. He looked over at the President, and because he couldn't think of a thing to say, said, "You're early this morning, Mr. President."

"I know. I took the liberty of ordering coffee and pastries. I guess you're wondering why this meeting is being held here in your office instead of the Oval Office."

"The thought did occur to me, Mr. President."

"This is how I see it, Clyde. Everyone knows this is where it all goes down. The Oval Office is for show. That's where we do meet and greets, shake hands, smile, do photo ops. This office, your office, is where we get down and dirty, where we get to play

310

hardball and piss everyone off. Today, I am going to unpiss off a lot of people, and I wanted it to go down here. That okay with you, Clyde?" The President's tone clearly said he didn't give a good rat's ass if Clyde liked it or not, this was where the meeting was going to be held and where he was going to unpiss everyone off.

Entwhistle nodded. "It might help, Mr. President, if you told me what this sudden meeting is all about. I am your chief of staff. You're supposed to clear these things with me first, and as protocol goes, I set up the meeting."

"I just did," the President said calmly.

And that was the end of that.

This all must have something to do with that lawn-mowing stunt the President had pulled before anyone could stop him, Entwhistle decided. "Can I at least ask who is coming to this meeting?"

"You'll see when they get here. Stop acting like some old fuddy-duddy, Clyde. I'm not going to press the red button, and I'm not going to mow the lawn again. I have to say, though, that ride on the John Deere took fifty pounds of stress off my shoulders. I felt like a human being for two whole hours. Do you mow your lawn, Clyde?"

"Don't have one, sir. I live in a condo."

311

The President himself opened the door when he heard the soft knock to admit one of the stewards pushing a linen-covered dolly. Cups of fine china were set up on the conference table at the far end of the room. Followed by fine china plates, sterling silver, and linen napkins with the Presidential seal embroidered on one corner. Three platters of pastries sat under crystal domes, with a set of sterling silver tongs next to each.

The President eyed the chairs at the table. Satisfied, he nodded to Entwhistle to escort the attendees to the room. He moved to the head of the table, where he always sat, but waited until everyone was in the room before he sat down. There was no tried-and-true seating arrangement, but the people in the room had been there often enough that they always took the same seats.

The President looked around and greeted each person by name. Gerald Bryce, the National Security Advisor; Louella Laird, the first female Director of the CIA; Jack Sparrow, Director of the FBI; Harold Montgomery, the Secretary of State; Mitchell Palmer, the Secretary of Defense; General Dylan Davis, Chairman of the Joint Chiefs of Staff; and, of course, Clyde Entwhistle, chief of staff.

All the chairs at the table held a body

except for the one to the right of the President's chair. As much as the people seated at the table tried not to look at the empty chair, their eyes kept going to it.

The chair that Lincoln Moss always sat in. While it was a nice chair, softly padded with shiny wood armrests, it now looked like some ugly thing that didn't belong. No one said a word when the President's leg shot out from under the table, giving the chair, which was on wheels, a fierce kick and sending it rolling back to the wall, where it bounced, then slid farther down the room out of sight. The gesture was enough to inform the others that Lincoln Moss would not be attending this particular meeting.

The President took his time as he looked at the people, good people, loyal people in the eye, and said, "I want to apologize to all of you. Just because I'm the President of the United States doesn't mean I don't make mistakes. I'm here today to tell you I've made some serious ones, but I recognize that now, and I'm not too proud to admit them and to ask for your help. Starting today, things are going to be different around here. Better late than never.

"Now listen up, people, this is how we're going to start running this administration.

313

We've got two more years to do things the way they should be done. For starters, we're going to settle this Venezuela and Iran business, then I'm going to tell you how from here on in this White House is going to run. One last thing, I hope all of you here today will change your minds about turning in your resignations. Yes, yes, I've heard all about it. You should know there are no secrets in this town. All I'm asking is for you to help me out here, so we can get back on track and run this country the way it should be run. From this point on, we do not look back. It's full steam ahead."

The look of relief on everyone's face was all President Knight needed to shoot his fist in the air.

Maggie Spritzer rolled out of bed, beelined for the bathroom, took a quick look in the mirror at her bed hair, and winced. She quickly brushed her teeth, then ran downstairs to make coffee. The clock on the kitchen range said it was 6:20. The perfect time to call Lincoln Moss. With any luck at all, she wouldn't have to speak to the man and could simply leave a message. Then again, she'd read somewhere that he got up at four-thirty in the morning and by six-thirty he was raring to go. When asked where he went that early in the morning, he'd snapped, "The White House." End of story as she remembered it.

Maggie scrolled through her address book until she found the listing for Lincoln Moss's home landline. She punched in the numbers and waited. Did the man answer his own phone or did he have some housekeeper or secretary do it for him? She had no clue. She waited, counting the rings, five, six, seven, and the call went to voice mail. Maggie felt herself relax immediately. The message was the same as all voice-mail messages. *This is Lincoln Moss. Obviously I'm not home, so leave your name, your number, and I'll return your call as soon as possible.*

Maggie spoke quickly to be sure she got her entire message across before the voice mail kicked over to the next call. "Mr. Moss, this is Maggie Spritzer from the *Post*. I'm calling to thank you for the lovely flowers. That wasn't necessary, and I appreciate the thought. Also, I'm calling to tell you that yesterday you were in the lead for our Man of the Year contest, but overnight, the Director of the FBI, Jack Sparrow, has taken the lead. Just so you know we are aware of the adversarial nature of your relationship with Director Sparrow, so we will have to address that, and the fact that he is the one escorting your wife to the First Lady's gala on Saturday night. This is just my personal opinion, Mr. Moss, but I think you could regain your lead if you would agree to a sit-down interview with me, and I can assure you, you'd win if your wife was at your side. The interview would have to take place either late today or early tomorrow morning. Of course, the decision is entirely up to you. My colleague, Ted Robinson, has been granted an interview with Director Sparrow for sometime around noon today. You can reach me at the *Post* or call me back at this number." Maggie rattled off both numbers, before breaking the connection. She had a vision of Lincoln Moss sitting in a chair listening to her speak and giving her the famous single-digit salute.

What Maggie did not know was that Lincoln Moss was doing exactly what she envisioned, but instead of giving her the single-digit salute, he was occupied putting his fist through the kitchen wall next to the bar stool he was sitting on. The cook, who had just served him his breakfast, ran for cover as if her life depended on it, squealing prayers of mercy.

A ten-minute rant, and after playing Maggie's message four more times, Moss stomped his way to the second floor, where he kept a compact office. Just as he sat down at the computer, the office phone rang. He blinked at the caller ID. The White House. He chewed on his lip for a moment before he picked up the receiver and announced himself in what he hoped was a businesslike voice, and then he listened.

"Mr. Moss, this is Darrel Honeycutt from the *New York Post.* I'm calling you from the pressroom at the White House to ask why you were not present at the meeting that was suddenly called at the White House this morning. Would you care to give me a comment? If not, I'll have to run with the wild speculation that's going on here."

Moss struggled to find just the right folksy tone. "Now, Darrel, you and the rest of the press know I never make comments. Today is no different. In the end, you guys print pretty much what you please anyway. Have a good day."

Moss would have put his fist through the computer screen, but his knuckles were already raw and bleeding. He thought about the phone call then, playing it over and over in his mind. Suddenly called meeting. For what? Who was there? He wished he had someone to call to ask, but there was no one. At least no one who would give him that kind of information.

317

Moss stewed and fretted for another hour before he clicked on his computer address book for the detective agency he'd used to try to find Amalie. There were over a dozen listed, none of them worth the name on the door except for one called Universal Privacy and a man named Gunter Wolf. Wolf was discreet. In fact, Wolf didn't talk at all, he just listened. He didn't take notes either. That's one of the reasons Moss liked him. What Moss didn't like were his enormous fees, but he paid them without a whimper.

"This is Lincoln Moss, Mr. Wolf. We need to talk. I have a rush job for you. Are you available to meet me in thirty minutes at the Knife and Fork?" Wolf assured Moss that he would be at the greasy diner at the appointed time. "Bring your checkbook." Like Moss didn't know that already.

Moss was a whirlwind then as he washed his hand and poured an antiseptic solution all over it. It still looked ugly and sore, but there was nothing he could do about that short of bandaging his hand, and he didn't want to do that. He changed his clothes because there were blood streaks on his Izod golf shirt and a few spots on his khaki slacks. He jammed his personal household checkbook into his hip pocket.

In keeping with his down-home, just-another-guy persona, Moss drove the gardener's battered pickup truck to the meeting.

Wolf was already in one of the cracked red-leather booths in the back of the diner, where he was guzzling coffee and preparing to chow down on what looked like a bacon, egg, and cheese sandwich. He looked inquiringly at Moss to see if he was going to order anything, but Moss shook his head.

Gunter Wolf was a tall man, bony, with hollow cheeks and deep-set eyes. His forehead was like a shelf over his eyes. His nose was too small, and his lips were thin slashes across his face. He had beautiful teeth, and from time to time, Moss had wondered if they were his own or false. He shaved his head, and it was shiny bright. He dressed well in custom-made clothes to cover his extreme thinness.

"Talk to me."

Moss talked, his voice even and flat. "That's all I know at this moment. Some of it could be rumor, but I don't think so. I want pictures, and I want to know where my wife goes, if she does attend with Director Sparrow, at the end of the party. I don't want you to do anything, I just want to know where she goes."

"You really want me to go up against the FBI?"

"What? You're afraid of the FBI! I'm not asking you to intervene or accost him or my wife. All I want you to do is follow them. Stake out the Four Seasons. If you see them entering, take a picture. You must have a camera with long-range capabilities that you use when you track all those errant husbands."

"Just like that, with all the Secret Service swarming all over the place, you expect me to take pictures and call attention to myself. There's no place to stake out around the Four Seasons. I'll stand out like a sore thumb, and I'll get hauled in for questioning. I do not like having that happen. If you think this is all so damn easy, why don't you do it yourself, Mr. Moss?"

"At this point in time that is simply not possible. Look, Gunter, if you don't want the job, say so right now, and I'll find someone who will take it."

"This is not something easy you're asking me to do, you know."

"So that's a no then," Moss said, preparing to slide out of the booth.

"It's not a no, Mr. Moss. I'm simply telling you what I'll be up against, so you don't piss your pants when I tell you I want a hundred grand up front as a retainer. And there are no refunds in my line of work. If I fail to get you the information you want, it won't be because I didn't try my best, it will be because of the Secret Service and federal agents. That's why my fee is so high. Take it or leave it, and I do not haggle."

Moss whipped out his checkbook so fast one could be excused for thinking that he was making a profitable investment in a sure-thing acquisition. He scribbled off a check and didn't bat an eye. "Gunter," Moss said, using the detective's first name again to show how serious he was, "I want to remind you that you have failed me twice. First with my wife, then with the woman who started this whole mess. Keep in mind that I can ruin you if I want to. Because of your ineptness, I've had to write off that young woman. I want you to pay attention now. I want solid confirmation by the close of business today that my wife is definitely accompanying Director Sparrow to the First Lady's gala at the Four Seasons on Saturday evening. Once I have that information, I will know better how I will proceed. Can you guarantee me this information by the close of business today?" Moss didn't realize he had been holding his breath until Wolf nodded.

He watched as Gunter Wolf popped the rest of his breakfast sandwich into his mouth and dabbed his thin lips with one of the tiny paper napkins that were in a stainless-steel holder on every table.

The terms were agreed upon, and the meeting was now over.

Lincoln Moss left the diner without another word. He wondered if he had just paid for a pig in the poke.

CHAPTER 20

"You're early this morning, Annie," Myra observed, looking at the kitchen clock, which indicated that the time was ten after seven.

"Blame it on Fergus, Myra. For some ungodly reason he said that he told Charles he'd be here at seven. So you have to put up with me, or I could turn around and go back home. What's for breakfast?"

"Toast or Pop-Tarts, take your pick."

"I suppose I have to make it myself, eh?"

"That's how it usually works. The butter is soft, and the jam is room temperature. Does that help?"

Annie rolled her eyes. "Is it going to be one of those days, Myra?"

Myra knew exactly what Annie meant by one of those days. It meant she was jittery, and nothing would go right until she figured out a way to make things work the way she wanted them to work.

"Okay, let's hear it," Annie demanded as she dropped four slices of thick bread into the toaster.

"Last night, after you all left, I went down below to talk to Jane Petrie. All she kept doing was yammering for a lawyer. I really wanted to give her a good swat. I gave her every opportunity, Annie, to show some remorse, but that young woman just laughed in my face. She's all about money, vacations, and designer clothing. She earns a decent living, and she has a profession, but she's greedy."

Annie reached for the toast that popped up and lathered an inch-thick coating of butter and jam over all four slices. "So, what did you do?"

Myra clenched her teeth. "I made an executive decision all on my own. I called Abner and told him to erase her identity. I also told him to clean out that robust brokerage account of hers. As of this moment, she no longer exists. Then I called Avery Snowden and at two o'clock this morning, he and his team came to pick her up."

Annie stared at her friend over the top of her coffee cup. "Where did they take her? Never mind, I do not want to know."

"I told them to give her some cash and to

take her somewhere where she could put her profession to use. We'll probably never hear from her again, and that's a good thing. Annie, she did not show one iota of remorse. Even when I described in graphic detail what Moss had done to Amalie. What she said was, 'Tough for her. It's a dog-eat-dog world we live in, and only the strong survive.' Can you believe that?"

"Yes, I do believe it. Well that takes care of that loose end, and I can assure you no one will care that you made that executive decision on your own. Oooh, a text is coming in from Maggie."

"What's she saying?"

"That she called Lincoln Moss and left a message she knows he is not going to return."

Myra reared back as she, too, received a text from Abner, alerting her to the fact that Lincoln Moss had just called a company called Universal Privacy. She showed the text to Annie and frowned. "I know that name from somewhere," she said.

"It's one of the dozen or so detective agencies that Moss used to try to find his wife. I recognize the name. That has to mean he's up to something, or he's really worried. Probably both," Annie said, finishing the last of her toast. She carried her dishes to the sink, rinsed them, then set them in the dishwasher before pouring herself another cup of coffee.

"So, what does all this mean to us?" Myra asked fretfully. "The gala is just two days away."

Annie drummed her fingers on the tabletop. "Let's look at the worst-case scenario, Myra. Let's assume, for the sake of argument, that Moss somehow, some way, got his hands on his wife. What do we think he would do? We never discussed that aspect. Lock her up and throw away the key, kill her, what?"

"Good Lord, Annie, I haven't the slightest idea. What I do know is that we cannot let that happen. Not in a million years."

Annie was a dog with her favorite bone. "But, Myra, what if it did happen?"

"Then I guess we call the police, the feds, anyone we can think of. What? Do you have an idea?"

"I don't, that's the problem. Always remember, what can go wrong will go wrong no matter how hard you try and no matter what you do. Things happen to thwart the best-laid plans. I'm nervous, I admit it."

"It's raining out," Myra said inanely.

"So it is," Annie said just as inanely.

"Where is everyone?" Myra asked fretfully.

"Probably still sleeping. Even our guests, I assume. We really should go get our nails done, Myra," Annie said, holding out her hands to show the condition of her nails, which had not been rectified since the day Pearl Barnes interrupted their session at the Beautiful Nails Salon. "If we leave now, we can be the first customers when they open at eight o'clock."

Myra looked at her fuzzy nails and winced. "Let's do it."

Maggie Spritzer met up with Ted, Espinosa, and Dennis for breakfast at a small café in Georgetown. She briefed them on her early-morning phone call to Lincoln Moss and the message she had left for him.

"He's not going to do the interview so why are we even discussing the matter," Ted said sourly.

"I think I boxed us into a corner. At the time it seemed like the thing to do."

"I got a text from Abner on my way here," Espinosa said. "He's been monitoring Moss's accounts and phone usage, and he said he contacted Universal Privacy. That's a private detective agency Moss has used in the past to try to find his wife. Probably the same agency he sicced on Jane Petrie, too. Might I add, with no known results."

"How does that help us?" Dennis asked.

"I don't know, Dennis. I'm just talking to convince myself I'm still alive until our food arrives. I'm starved," Ted said.

"I don't think you need to be a rocket scientist to figure out what he's up to. Now, if we'd been really smart, we would have put a tail on Moss," Maggie said.

"What do you mean, Maggie?" Dennis asked.

"What I think it means is he's hired the company to do surveillance on the gala Saturday night to see if Amalie really shows up. If she does, the guy or gal, whoever he hired, will be tailing them to see where they take Amalie, then he'll swoop in and try to snatch her. That's just my personal opinion."

Dennis snorted to show what he thought of Maggie's personal opinion. "No one in their right mind would do something so stupid right under the feds' noses."

"Whoever said or even alluded to the fact that Lincoln Moss was in his right mind and that he wasn't stupid?" Espinosa snarled. "That guy thinks he's a law unto himself. Right now, his feet are to the fire." Dennis leaned back in the booth and thought about what Espinosa had said. He shrugged. Everyone, he thought, was

328

entitled to his or her own opinion.

"Listen, guys, I heard something earlier. I got it on the down low, so who knows if there is any merit to it. I have a friend in the White House press corps and we . . . you know . . . trade info from time to time. He woke me up this morning to tell me there was some kind of hush-hush meeting in the President's chief of staff's office at the crack of dawn, and Lincoln Moss was *not* there. The scuttlebutt is that the President showed up looking like a movie-star President dressed in a Savile Row suit. Now, my buddy doesn't know Savile Row from a Target suit that comes with three pairs of pants, but a colleague, Katie O'Brien, told him the prez was wearing a Savile Row suit, a Hermès tie, and John Lobb shoes.

"And he tore into everyone who was there and said today was the beginning of something new. Or words to that effect. And, this is the best part, the prez kicked Moss's chair, the one he always sits in, clear across the room."

"And your buddy knows this . . . how?" Maggie demanded.

"He butters up the kitchen stewards and slips some green under the table. You gotta do what you gotta do in cases like this. We

329

all do it, so don't look so shocked, Dennis," Ted said.

"What good is it if you can't print it?" Dennis grumbled.

"You see, kid, here's the thing. When gossip like this hits the fan, it grows legs, then someone in the know has to come front and center and either deny it or explain it, then the reporter gets to expand on the gossip angle without getting the steward in trouble. You getting it now?"

"Yeah, yeah. So that means Moss is out as in *out*?" Dennis asked. "More to the point, does Moss *know* he's out?"

"He has to know. This town has been buzzing for weeks now about a mass resignation. I don't think Knight had any other choice but to do what he did if he did indeed do it. Remember, this is all Capitol Hill gossip," Maggie said.

"You know what they say, where there's smoke, there's fire," Espinosa said, just as platters of omelets and bacon were set down on the table.

For the most part, the little group ate in silence, with only a few comments about yet another day of rain and what it was going to do to Nikki's and Jack's efforts to install a swimming pool. "They're living in a world of mud, that thick gray kind that grabs you like a million leeches that won't let go once you step into it. Nikki said she's glad Nellie isn't around to see what's going on.

"So where does this all leave us?" Ted asked.

"Right where we were when we came in here for breakfast. The way I see it is that there is nothing for any of us to do until Saturday evening. Other than the fittings we have to have for our party duds tomorrow."

"We go back to the paper?" Dennis asked, hoping the answer was no, and that they were going out to Pinewood, where he could see Rosalee. His hopes were dashed when Maggie said yeah, they did have jobs and had things to do. He took it all with good grace and paid the breakfast bill since it was his turn.

Myra and Annie left the Beautiful Nails Salon, admiring their new glossy manicures. "Lunch?" Myra asked.

"Only if it's a hot dog," Annie said.

"Okay by me," Myra said, opening her umbrella. They walked along, huddling close under the umbrella until they got to a newly opened hot-dog joint, where Annie started smacking her lips in anticipation. "The works on two dogs," she told the pert

331

waitress, "and two double Orange Juliuses."

"We are living dangerously, aren't we?" Myra giggled.

"Sometimes you just gotta do it, Myra. Otherwise, what's the point in getting up in the morning?"

"Guess that's as good as any excuse I could come up with," Myra said, gulping at her Orange Julius.

Annie held up her Orange Julius, and said, "Here's to Lincoln Moss's downfall! At our hands!"

"Hear! Hear!" Myra said, taking another big gulp from her tall drink.

Lincoln Moss was sitting in front of his computer, the word *downfall* on his lips. How in the hell did this happen? How had he gone from being the number two man in Washington and the Knight administration to . . . this? How?

When he first got wind of the rumors about the mass resignations on the horizon, he'd actually laughed. Not for one nanosecond did he take them seriously. And here he was, two weeks later, at the threshold of oblivion. In his mind, it was all because of his wife and her sudden reappearance. If it was even true and not some trumped-up trick.

Moss bent down and opened his bottom drawer and pulled out his little black book. He thumbed through the pages, smirking at what he was reading, thanks to Universal Privacy and the Pinkerton Agency. Right now, all he had to do was start making phone calls to every name in the book and watch what happened. Or better yet, he could call one of those reporters, anonymously, and spiel off the contents and sit back to watch the fireworks. But did he really want to open that can of worms?

Moss leaned back and closed his eyes after he replaced the book in the bottom drawer. Hell, he even had the goods on his best friend, Gabriel Knight, President of these here United States. He smirked as he wondered, and not for the first time, what Gabe would say if he knew that Moss had kept a record of his short stint as a cat burglar, stealing priceless paintings and jewelry, then fencing them. He conveniently ignored his own role in the heists as being inconsequential. How else were they to get the money to dive into the stock market? Working a nine-to-five job simply wasn't in the cards for either one of them. They both wanted success ASAP, not years down the road. And it had worked because of his own cleverness.

333

All water under the bridge as they say, he thought. It was over, and he knew it. The way he saw it, he could go quietly, fade away into the night, or he could go out with a bang and take everyone out with him.

Moss looked over at the door and the bag that had sat there for years. His GO bag as he called it. It contained cash, some files, memory sticks, and four different cell phones, which were activated but had never been used except to charge them from time to time. Plus three different sets of documents attesting to the fact that he was someone other than Lincoln Moss. Each packet contained a new name, a driver's license, a passport, two credit cards, and a voter registration card, along with a library card and several other pieces of ID that would help him blend in and start a new life anywhere in the world.

The way he looked at it, he was standing in front of a speed bump at the end of the road.

What to do?

CHAPTER 21

"Okay, ladies and gentlemen, listen up!" Alexis bellowed to be heard above the kitchen chatter. "It's three o'clock, and that means it's time for everyone to get made up for tonight's gala." She looked pointedly at the boys, and said, "Right now, you are definitely not needed. That means you can go out on the terrace, dry off the furniture since it stopped raining, and moan and groan to your hearts' content. A suggestion if you are interested. Eat! Unless you want to chow down on the kids' menu at the gala. Your duds are in the spare room at the top of the stairs. Everyone is to be down here ready to go at five-fifteen, when our limousines arrive. If any of you have questions, ask someone else because I'm too busy to answer them. Now *GO!*" She winked at Espinosa, who burst out laughing.

"At least it stopped raining," Myra said. "We should be thankful for small favors. I

335

for one hate going to a black-tie affair in the rain. So, who is going first?" The women squabbled good-naturedly for a few minutes before Yoko stepped forward. No one objected.

The dining-room table was full of pots, jars, flats of makeup that resembled an artist's palette, bottles, and brushes by the dozen. The women could only stare in amazement at what they were seeing and how Alexis moved from one brush, pot, bottle, or jar to another at the speed of light. And then there were the spray bottles and cans that spewed out glitter and flakes of something that shimmered and twinkled under the lights of the chandelier. Next to the dining-room table was a serving cart that held Myra's and Annie's jewelry, which Tiffany's would have envied. Noticeably absent was Annie's multimillion-dollar tiara. The girls were told to pick what they wanted but to make sure whatever they chose would go with their evening gowns, to which Kathryn replied, "You're joking, right? Diamonds go with *everything.*"

"Where's Amalie?" Nikki asked.

"Upstairs. Alexis wanted her separate and sitting quietly so all that adhesive and stuff she mixed up dried properly. She'll be down shortly," Isabelle said, looking at her watch.

"I saw her, and let me tell you, she looks exactly like she did before her surgery. Even if her husband went nose to nose with Amalie, he wouldn't be able to see the difference. Alexis is a miracle worker, there's no doubt about it. Wait till you see her. Better yet, wait till Jack Sparrow sees her."

Annie was busy checking her cell phone. "I thought Mr. Snowden would have reported in by now." She clucked her tongue to show she was not happy with knowing what was going on. "He's got round-the-clock surveillance on Lincoln Moss. His last text at noon said Moss hadn't left the house." Everyone just shrugged as they went back to choosing their jewelry for the evening.

"I talked to Amalie earlier, and she was telling me how many people worked for her husband while she lived there. A very large staff, but Abner said that according to his checking-account records, Moss only has a housekeeper, at least he assumes it's a housekeeper, and one other on his actual household staff. Two women. He pays them weekly out of a separate account. The same account he used when he had a full in-house staff. He has three people for the grounds, who maintain everything outdoors, a quasi-chauffeur who he calls on from time to time and, of course, four security guards who work rotating shifts. That means to me he has two people on security at all times. I guess you could say he downsized once Amalie left," Kathryn said.

"That means if we hit him at home, we only have to worry about two guards, right?" Nikki asked.

"That would be my assumption. Amalie said the housekeeper and the cook go home at night, as do the maids and the gardeners. The quasi-chauffeur lives in a cottage on the premises, as does his personal trainer. No one is inside the house after six o'clock except Moss. Unless he entertains. Amalie said that was rare. She said Moss was a fanatic about everyone's leaving the house on the stroke of six. Rosalee was the only one permitted to remain since she was Amalie's live-in personal maid," Kathryn said. "Also, I suppose he realized that someone needed to take care of his wife after he got through beating on her. I cannot wait to get my hands on that bastard."

"I know this is a shot in the dark, dear, but did Amalie by any chance say if she knew the code to the electronic gate?" Myra asked.

Kathryn laughed. "She was never allowed to leave on her own, so no, it was never given to her, but Rosalee said she saw out of the corner of her eye as one of the guards punched in the numbers, and it was four zeros. Moss might have changed it since then. We won't know until we try it I guess."

"Maybe what we need is an electrician or someone who can turn off the power to Moss's house or maybe a few houses to make it look like there's a malfunction somewhere," Yoko said. "The alternative is I could scale the gate, slide down, and open the gate for you from the inside."

"Now that sounds like a plan," Annie said.

Maggie spoke up for the first time. "Mr. Moss never did respond to my voice mail. How rude to blow me off like that." The others laughingly agreed that it was indeed rude on Moss's part to blow off and tick off Maggie at the same time. There was no doubt in anyone's mind that Moss would pay for that big-time.

The remaining hours and minutes ticked by until the clock on the dining-room buffet indicated that it was already four-thirty.

"Time's up. I want each of you to check yourself in that mirror in the corner, the lighting is just perfect. Tell me if you approve or if you want anything extra done," Alexis said, her hands on her hips as she surveyed her handiwork. She grinned at the ooohs and aaahs.

"We look like models!" Annie laughed in delight. "I love it that you were able to fill in all my wrinkles and cover up those ugly brown spots. Just love, love, love it."

Myra seconded Annie's glowing testimonial. "We certainly do," Myra said, patting at an errant curl by her ear.

"Hollywood, eat your heart out," Nikki said, peering at herself in the mirror, where nary a blemish could be seen. She quickly put on a pair of diamond-teardrop earrings that could have fed a third-world country for a year. When she was done admiring herself, she clasped a diamond choker around her neck and swooned. "This stuff is insured, isn't it?"

"Absolutely it is," Myra said.

There was a mad scramble as the girls dove into the pile of jewelry.

"Time to get dressed, girls. I still have to make myself up and check on Amalie. Someone tell the boys to get dressed. We'll all meet up in the kitchen. Hurry, girls!" Alexis chortled happily. She did love it when things worked out so perfectly.

"We look like a bunch of penguins," Ted announced as he walked around checking everyone out. "Pretty spiffy if I do say so myself. Just out of curiosity, when was the last time any of you guys looked like this?"

Harry barked, "*NEVER.* And you won't see it again anytime soon."

When Harry spoke, the others realized that their own comments or opinions didn't matter. The room went silent until they heard Annie shout from the hallway, "Everyone stand back, here we come."

And in they came sparkling, glittering, and shimmering, with enough jewels, beads, and glitter to light up a room. One by one, the girls sashayed around the massive kitchen, showing a generous amount of leg, skin, and cleavage. And they smelled as good as they looked. To say the men were dumbstruck would be putting it mildly.

When they finally got it together, Jack let loose with a shrill whistle that said it all. The women all giggled while the guys just gawked. In stupefied amazement. Or as Yoko said later, their expressions were the ultimate compliment, and who could ask for anything more.

"Okay, everyone, partner up and let's get this show on the road," Annie said, reaching for Fergus's arm. Myra followed suit by taking Charles's arm and heading out to the waiting limousines. The others followed.

The three long stretch limousines were

their own parade into the District and to the Four Seasons, which was lit up like the Fourth of July. The media and security were everywhere.

Invitations clutched in hand, the girls and boys of Pinewood exited the limousines as the hawkers who always appeared at functions like this whistled and shouted their approval of the women's attire.

Inside, after going through three different security checkpoints, the group made it to the ballroom and were told to go to their assigned table, which they did. Fortunately, Dennis's Welmed table was right next to Annie's table on the left, and the *Post*'s table on the right.

"I do believe we have it covered, people," Annie said.

"The acoustics in here are terrible," Myra said as she strained to hear whatever it was that Nikki was saying. Finally, she gave up and shrugged.

"A drink would be nice," Jack said. Almost immediately, a juice box was placed in his hand by a hovering waiter. "This isn't exactly what I had in mind," he grumbled. Harry laughed out loud.

"There's no bar. They want everyone seated, so nothing can go wrong," Nikki said. "Canapes should be coming soon."

When a silver platter was set down in the middle of the table next to an artful arrangement of orchids, the group all laughed, Harry the loudest. Staring up at them was an assortment of small pretzels, gummy bears, Hershey's Kisses, and marshmallows.

Annie poked Myra in the arm and tilted her head to the side so she could look at the Director of the FBI and his date for the evening. Sparrow looked like a deer caught in the headlights, and Amalie looked like she was frozen to her seat. Her eyes were on the entrance to the ballroom, and even if her partner for the evening said anything, she wouldn't have heard a word he said.

At six-thirty, the First Lady entered the room. Everyone stood, and she motioned to everyone to sit down. She walked over to a temporary podium and adjusted the microphone. She thanked everyone for coming, then went into a short speech about how desperately the children of the world needed help. Twice her voice cracked when she spoke of certain children and what they had to endure until help was forthcoming. The last thing she said before stepping down was to plead for all the guests to be generous at the end of the evening. "All of us here tonight are fortunate that when we leave here, we'll be going to our homes, to sleep in nice beds with pretty linens and air-conditioning. Before you close your eyes, think about some child going to sleep in a ditch because there is nowhere else to sleep. Be generous. I'm begging you. Please, make me proud of all of you here tonight." There was a standing ovation for the First Lady that went on for a full five minutes.

Then came the usual speeches, all of them short and poignant by heads of different organizations that helped children. The last speaker was the President. "Don't get up, please. I just want to second the First Lady and thank you all for coming and to say I do not think there is anything more important in this world than our children. Having said that, I know you are all counting the seconds till your food arrives. Enjoy, everyone."

The five-second speech called for another standing ovation as the waiters and waitresses started serving dinner.

"I think half of Hollywood is here. A pity we don't know any of those people. I would have thought since this is an older crowd, they would have called on someone like Barry Manilow or Tony Bennett," Annie sniffed.

Nikki leaned across the table. "There's a reason for the young entertainers, Annie.

They're the ones who get the message out there. Think social media. The young are born to it. The world follows their every move. I think the First Lady is trying to sign them up to work on her behalf. Pretty good thinking on her part if you ask me. The President's being here to shake hands and do photo ops with them certainly can do wonders. With young Hollywood, it's who you're seen with. This is a really big coup for those who are here. Tomorrow, their pictures will flash around the world at the speed of light and call attention to this event."

"Forget tomorrow. Try five minutes after they leave the stage," Maggie said.

Myra looked at Annie, and said, "Do not say we are old and don't know who Bouncy is or that skinny one who got beat up by her boyfriend. We know. Thank you, Nikki, for clarifying all of that because it does make sense. I hope they donate as well."

"Oh, trust me, that's part of the gig. They'll all make huge donations. I'm liking these SpaghettiOs." Nikki giggled as she popped a tiny meatball into her mouth. "You used to serve these to Barbara and me for lunch on rainy days, do you remember, Myra?"

"I do remember, dear. You were both also

partial to those gummy bears, too."

Nikki laughed. "This is like a trip down Memory Lane."

"Lincoln Moss is not here," Isabelle said as she craned her neck to look over at the table he had purchased.

"I know. All you have to do is keep watching Amalie, who has not taken her eyes off the entrance door since she sat down. People keep staring at her. Someone needs to tell her to lighten up and pretend she is interested in the director. Without even trying, she's going to blow this whole deal."

Kathryn leaned over and spoke to Dennis, who in turn alerted Rosalee, who then whispered to Amalie, who looked shell-shocked. She glanced over at the Welmed table, where Annie and Myra were sitting. Both women gave a curt, no-nonsense nod and narrowed their eyes at the stunning young woman, who immediately pasted a smile on her face and said something to Jack Sparrow, who blushed ten shades of red.

"Oh, dear, I don't think our plan is working too well with those two," Myra whispered to Annie.

"Well, we'll just see about that," Annie said, getting up and walking over to her own table, where she bent over and whispered in Amalie's ear. It was anyone's guess as to what was said, but both women smiled.

"What did you say to her?" Myra asked when Annie returned to her seat.

"What do you think I said, Myra? I told her if she didn't start acting like she was having the time of her life and start flirting with Director Sparrow, I was personally going to deliver her with a big red bow on top of her head to her husband at the end of the evening."

Myra gasped. "Tell me you didn't say that?"

"You want me to lie to you, Myra?"

"Good Lord, no. Well, she does look like she's enjoying herself."

Annie smiled.

As the evening wore on, the group relaxed. Moving about, however, proved to be a challenge, what with all the Secret Service. One by one, the members of the group got up, took bathroom breaks just to head to the spacious lobby to see if there was any sign of Lincoln Moss or anyone who looked like he didn't belong. All reports were negative, which then caused anxiety on Annie's part.

Isabelle nudged Yoko, and whispered, "Check out the director and Amalie. Tell me that isn't love about to bloom." Yoko giggled. "And look at Dennis and the sappy expression on his face. He's already in love with Rosalee. That's a good thing. Dennis needs someone to love, and it sure looks to me like Rosalee is returning his affection." Yoko continued to giggle.

Harry got up and said he was going outside to get some air. He looked pointedly at Jack, who quickly agreed that he could use some air, too.

Outside, the night was sticky hot. "Let's take a walk, Jack," Harry said, striding off. Jack had no other choice but to follow. "What's up, Harry?"

"Think about it, Jack. I've got eyestrain right now from staring at everyone inside that hotel trying to see who didn't belong. As in someone Moss sent. He isn't here, that's obvious. We both know he wants to know if his wife showed up. How else is he going to find out unless he's got someone here doing surveillance. I haven't seen anyone like that, have you?"

"No, and if Snowden has people here, I haven't been able to spot them either. So we are meandering around hoping to . . . what, spot someone with a camera that has long-range optics?"

"Something like that," Harry muttered.

"We should be smoking a cigarette or a cigar, something, so we don't stand out.

Two guys in tuxes strolling along is going to raise eyebrows. People might think we're gay." Jack expected Harry to make a comment, but he didn't.

"Pay attention, Jack, your four o'clock, guy in a Tommy Bahama shirt across the street. I say we pretend to have too much to drink, and we go down one block, cross over, sneak up on him, and take him out."

"Works for me, Harry," Jack said, picking up his pace. It only took five minutes of staggering down the pavement, pretending to hold each other up, and extolling the virtues of the smoking-hot babes inside the Four Seasons. The man standing against a building, well out of sight, dropped the camera he was holding to his side and waited for the two drunks to pass him.

"Well, well, well, if it isn't Gunter Wolf. How's it going, man?" Jack said happily, as Harry reached for the detective's camera.

"You know this guy?" Harry asked.

"Oh, yeah," Jack drawled. "When I was a prosecutor, he was a regular in court testifying in divorce cases, usually battery. He's a pro. Who you working for, Gunter?"

"C'mon, Emery, you know I can't tell you that. Client privilege."

"That's crap, Gunter. How about if we tell you who you're working for, and you take it from there. If you don't help us out here, you're going to find yourself in a world of pain. Lincoln Moss."

"I am neither confirming nor denying. You can't intimidate me, Emery. This is not a court of law. You don't have any jurisdiction here. I'm not breaking any laws, I'm not loitering either. Buzz off, buddy."

Jack crossed his arms over his chest. "Gunter, that isn't working for me. Last chance, what's your deal? Pain is . . . a terrible thing, and you're so bony to begin with. I bet your joints would snap in a good wind."

Harry's foot, in his shiny, patent-leather shoe, shot out and smacked into Wolf's knee. Jack thought he heard a bone snap as the private detective toppled over groaning in pain. "Good shot, Harry."

"I know," Harry said.

"One knee down and one to go, Gunter. Talk to us."

"Okay, okay, you sadistic bastard. Yeah, it's Lincoln Moss. I've worked for him before; he pays real good. Hard man to deal with. Jesus, my leg hurts. Will you call an ambulance or something. You busted my kneecap."

"In your dreams. Keep talking."

"All right, all right. Moss called me

yesterday to meet him and paid me a hundred grand to come here and find out if his wife showed up. He wanted pictures." He moaned some more but stopped the minute he saw Harry lift his foot. "Okay, okay, I tried to find her over the years, but she disappeared into thin air. Couldn't find a trace of her anywhere. Then he calls again out of the blue, and I didn't want to take the job, but the money was too good to pass up. I'm supposed to get pictures. I got some, but I don't think he's going to approve. I was supposed to check in an hour ago. I didn't. I didn't want to listen to his threats. Besides, there are some newspeople in there taking pictures of the guests. If she's in there, and I think she is, it will be on the ten o'clock news. Damn, my leg hurts. You bastard, you shattered my kneecap."

"Yeah, I did. You want to go for two?" Harry asked. Wolf just moaned.

"Where's your phone? Don't make me ask again," Jack said.

Jack reached for the phone and started scrolling. "He's sent you nine texts in a little over an hour and a half. Are you lying to us that you didn't respond? Or are you telling the truth?"

"I didn't respond. Man, would you please call a doctor for me. This pain is killing me.

C'mon, give me back my camera; that cost some big bucks."

"In your dreams. Possession is nine points of the law. Anything else you want to tell us while you can still talk?" Jack snarled.

"What the hell does that mean, while I can still talk?"

"It means I am going to bust up your other knee if you don't tell us what we want to know," Harry said.

"I told you everything. The pictures I managed to get suck. I know Moss won't be happy with them. The man is crazy, he wants instant results. I tried to explain to him that this was a tricky job, but he didn't care. That's it. Now will you please call a doctor or EMS for me. I'm going to black out."

Harry looked over at Jack, who was busy sending a text to Lincoln Moss. He was also grinning like a Cheshire cat.

"Tell me how this sounds, Harry. 'Subject entered Four Seasons on the arm of the Director of the FBI and a large party that seemed to be all together. Subject was laughing and looking like a movie star. She was dressed to the nines and sported enough jewelry to light up the night. Pictures to follow shortly.' "

"Works for me." Harry laughed.

"That guy is going to frigging kill me when he finds out I didn't send that text. Look, forget the EMS, help me to my car. I need to get out of here."

"See ya, pal," Jack said as he walked away with Wolf's phone and camera, Harry right behind him.

"Where are you going to stash the camera and the phone? We can't take them into the ballroom."

"The courtesy desk, unless you have a better idea. Our limo has moved on and won't be back for another hour."

"Let's do it," Harry said happily as he smacked his hands together.

Jack loved it when Harry was in a good mood.

Back at the table, Jack and Harry both whispered about what had gone down to Nikki and Yoko, who in turn passed it on to the others.

"Oh, look, the First Lady and the President are making the rounds of the tables, so pictures can be taken. I think after that happens, we can leave," Myra said. "I think it will go quickly. We're Table Four, so another thirty minutes, and we're gone. Kathryn, call and alert the drivers."

Myra turned to Annie. "I never had my picture taken with a President and First

Lady before. I know you have. How did you feel?"

"Like I met two new people. Okay, watch, Myra, they're heading for Sparrow's table. Keep your eye on Amalie."

Myra did just that. She wished she could hear the conversation, but the music was so loud that all she could do was watch what was happening at the table she had purchased.

"How nice to see you again, Amalie," President Knight said, bending low to hug the young woman. "It's been a long time."

"Yes, Mr. President, five long years. Congratulations on your second term. It's good to see you, too. This is a lovely affair. I hope the donations flow freely."

"I'm sure they will. People are generous when it comes to children. I don't see Lincoln. Where is he, or did I miss him?"

"I wouldn't know, Mr. President. I haven't seen Lincoln since the day I walked away from his house five years ago. I thought you knew that."

The President recovered quickly from the shock of her words and smiled at a nudge from one of his Secret Service agents that it was time to move to the next table. Amalie was left with a quick greeting by the First Lady. They smiled, touched hands and cheeks. The First Lady leaned close, and whispered, "Just so you know, I'm on your side, my dear."

And then it was time for Table Four, the Welmed table, to have their picture taken. Smiles, pats on the shoulder, a few personal words. "Countess, I was delighted when I heard you were going to attend this evening. I looked forward to seeing your tiara, but you aren't wearing it." The First Lady smiled warmly.

Never bashful no matter whose presence she was in, Annie quipped, "I didn't want to upstage you this evening." Both the President and the First Lady laughed out loud.

Annie stood and eyeballed the First Lady. "Now, tell me what I can do to help you with this very worthwhile cause you are so dedicated to." Soft brown eyes grew moist as the First Lady stared at Annie. "If I give you a phone number, can you remember it without writing it down?" the First Lady asked quietly. Annie nodded as she committed to memory the number the First Lady rattled off.

"Call me next week, and we'll do lunch. I always wanted to say that for some reason, but the time was never just right. But" — she wagged a finger under Annie's nose —

"promise me you'll wear your tiara and let me try it on. I'll even have the White House photographer take a picture of us each wearing it."

"Deal." Annie grinned. The two women touched cheeks, then the First Lady moved off. Annie sat down, still grinning.

"What'd she say, what'd she say," the girls yammered.

"She asked me to lunch next week and told me to wear my tiara and asked if she could try it on."

"And you said what?" Myra demanded.

"I'm no fool, Myra. I said yes."

CHAPTER 22

Lincoln Moss at best was a teetotaler. He'd only been drunk once in his life, thirty-four years ago at the age of twenty-one. He rarely drank, and when he did, he would nurse a glass of wine all evening long. Right now, though, he was stinking drunk thanks to Gunter Wolf and the media. The minute the ten o'clock news came on, he was glued to the eighty-six-inch plasma TV in his family room. It was now past midnight. For company, he had a bottle of Jim Beam, who was now his best friend. Through his blurry gaze, he could see that there was barely an inch of alcohol left in the bottle. His curses were ripe, loud, and long.

Moss knew he was drunk and out of control, something he never allowed to happen. But he *had* let it happen. Now he was in this sorry condition. Right now, he wasn't worth a good spit. And where the hell was that piece of crap Wolf? Where were the pictures he was supposed to send? Not that he needed them now. For the past two hours, he'd done nothing but stare at his beautiful wife. The picture that almost made him put his foot through the television, assuming he could even lift his foot that high in his present condition, was the shot of the President hugging his wife, then the shot of the First Lady whispering in his wife's ear. He should have killed the bitch.

Moss took another slug from the Jim Beam bottle and reached for his phone. If he squinted, he could almost make out the letters that seemed to be running all together. None of the texts looked like anything he was interested in. Certainly not that crazy woman from the *Post,* who said she and her colleagues would be out to see him tomorrow afternoon. Like that was really going to happen. Not. He scrolled down and saw another text he must have missed, from Gunter Wolf, who said he was in the hospital with a shattered kneecap, and for him to shove his job up his ass and never contact him again. And then another line, which read, *and don't expect a refund.* "Well screw you, Gunter Wolf," Moss bellowed to the huge, empty room. "Did you hear me, Wolf, screw you and the horse you rode in on!"

Moss upended the Jim Beam bottle and emptied it. Now he was never going to find out where his wife was. He should have killed her. He wondered why he hadn't. Maybe what he needed to do was go to bed and sleep off this drunk. In the morning, he could make some final decisions. He struggled out of the recliner he was sitting in, took two steps, fell flat on his face, and passed out cold.

The night guard on his hourly patrol around the mansion stopped and looked through the French doors. He saw his boss lying on the floor, the empty Jim Beam bottle next to him. He grimaced. As far as he knew, the boss never drank. He debated if he should enter the premises, but negated the idea almost immediately. He hated the man, as did the other guards, but it was a cushy job and paid three times what he would or could make elsewhere in the private sector. The job also provided good health benefits. He turned around and kept on with his hourly patrol.

The gang always loved Sunday brunch at Pinewood, where Charles outdid himself with a tremendous buffet. Today, they were eating in the dining room because that was the only room that could seat everyone at the same time, and the buffet could be set up on the sideboard.

It was noon, and everyone had arrived. The talk, as everyone knew, would be about the First Lady's gala and how it all went down.

"We're going to talk and eat at the same time, Charles, just so you know," Myra announced. Charles nodded. He hadn't expected anything else. Sometimes, like now, it simply did not pay to argue.

The conversation flowed freely as the group ate, laughed, and talked about how exciting it was to meet the President and First Lady even though no one at the table had voted for Gabriel Knight either time he ran for the office of President. There was much ado about Annie's upcoming luncheon with the First Lady and her having been instructed to wear her tiara.

Through it all, Dennis and Rosalee could have been on another planet because they were totally oblivious to everyone else. And they didn't seem to care.

Amalie and Jack Sparrow sat side by side, and while they weren't obvious about it, their attraction was there for all to see. Right off the bat, Sparrow had announced to one and all that Amalie had gone home with him to Georgetown and had slept in the guest room. They smiled at each other a lot. It was clear to everyone that their friendship would continue somehow, some way.

The rest of the afternoon was spent indoors because the day was overcast and so humid it was difficult to breathe outdoors.

When the clock struck five, everyone but the girls left. No one asked questions. The minute the electronic gate closed behind the last car, the women hurried to the living room, where Myra pressed the ornate rose that would open the secret door to the dungeons below the house.

"It will be nice and quiet now that Jane Petrie is gone," Nikki said. "That young woman sure had a set of lungs on her. I hope wherever she ends up that she puts those lungs to good use."

"Let us not go there, girls," Annie said, sitting down at the table. "We need to make some decisions right now. I want to go on record as saying the longer we delay our punishment for Mr. Moss, the longer he has to make his own plans to depart the area. I don't think we should wait beyond tomorrow. He now knows Amalie is in town. What he can do about it is anyone's guess, but none of us thinks like he does. So, let's talk about all this."

"Well, people," Kathryn said, "I sent Moss a text last evening and told him that I and my colleagues would be out there today. This is already today, and we aren't going out there. Now he might not have taken me seriously. Or then again, he might have and already split. That means to me, we hit him tomorrow. Having said that, I'm okay with doing it tonight after dark, too. Whatever you all think will work for you will work for me."

Isabelle spoke next. "I talked to Abner, and he came up with the blueprints online for Moss's house. The breaker box is inside in the laundry room. That's only a help if we can get inside the gates. He said he doesn't have any sources at the power company, and if we want the power off, we'll have to do it ourselves. Yoko said she's willing to climb the fence, and if we use parabolic cameras, we can tell where the guards are. She's quick and fast, so she should be able to get in and out within minutes. And, Abner said, there are no dogs. That in itself is a relief."

"We have to take out the guards. There are only two per shift. Harry and Jack can take them out with stealth. No noise, no scuffling. Once that happens, we have a clear field. Again, darkness will be our friend," Nikki said.

"How are we going to know if Moss is really inside? What if he packs up and leaves today or tonight or tomorrow during the day?" Kathryn asked.

"Avery Snowden has men out on the service road. They know the make and model of all of Moss's vehicles. They'll follow him, and if they think he's on the run, they will arrange something so he has to return to his house. We're good there, I think," Myra said.

"It breaks down to do we go tonight or tomorrow night," Annie said. "Let's take a vote."

"The question to me is are we good with all our gear or do we need to do a practice run? I know, I know, we work well together, but we did not do any practice runs, and that's always been crucial to our success, as you all know. We need to be able to anticipate each other and know each other's jobs plus our own," Alexis said.

"I vote for tomorrow night," Yoko said. "Not so much for us but for the boys. They don't move in sync like we do. I'm sure you've all noticed that. I can go over the fence at dusk and hide out on the grounds till you're ready to enter."

The vote was taken, and they all agreed

on Monday night based on Yoko's reasoning.

"Then I vote to adjourn and get a good night's sleep. We will have all day tomorrow for our dry runs and practice sessions," Annie said.

Lincoln Moss looked at the clock on his nightstand. Almost twenty-four hours had passed since his booze bender, and he didn't feel one bit better than he had when he woke up this morning. Right now, he felt as limp as a wet noodle, and he knew that if he crawled out of bed, he'd fall flat on his face. He probably had alcohol poisoning. He closed his eyes, so the room would stop spinning. And yet people drank like this every day and still managed to function. He swore then that alcohol would never again touch his lips.

Moss cursed then, every dirty, filthy word he had in his vocabulary spewing from his mouth, which tasted like a barnyard in the heat of summer. He'd lost track of how many times he'd brushed his teeth and showered, yet he could still smell the alcohol leaking out of his pores.

He wished now he hadn't sent his housekeeper home. Maybe coffee or toast would help him to get back on track. Or maybe tomato juice with Tabasco sauce in it. His gut told him if he did that, he would just puke it back up, and right now his stomach muscles were just one giant knot of pain. Even the light sheet covering him was painful.

"Son of a bitch!" he seethed.

This wasn't getting him anywhere. He owned the sorry condition he was in, so he had to make the best of it. He forced himself to get out of bed. He gripped the edge of the night table until the dizziness passed. Then he shuffled to the bathroom, where he turned on the shower full blast. He stepped in, clothes and all, and stood under a freezing torrent of water. When he couldn't stand it a moment longer, he turned the knob to steaming hot and almost passed out. He went back to cold, then hot, then cold again until he thought his body was frozen. Then he turned the knob to warm and literally swooned at how good it felt. He managed to strip off his boxers and T-shirt and poured shampoo all over his body. He just couldn't make his hands work with a bar of soap and a washcloth. The shower filled with bubbles. Sounds that could have been laughter escaped his lips. Bubbles. And they smelled good.

Finally, Moss stepped out of the shower

and into a thick terry robe. He sat down on the edge of the hot tub to wait to see how he felt. Better than before but still not human. He got up, walked over to the sink, and stared at his reflection. Plain and simple, he looked like shit. He still felt like shit, too. He brushed his teeth, rinsed his mouth, then gargled. He did it three times. At least his mouth didn't taste like a barnyard anymore. He should shave. With his stupid luck, he'd probably slit his own throat. He reached for his electric razor and ran it over his face several times. Not a clean shave but good enough.

Barefoot, he made his way to the elevator that he had never used, not a single time, got in, and rode down to the narrow hallway outside the kitchen area. He looked around the spotless room and made his way to the built-in coffeemaker. All he had to do was press a button because his housekeeper always prepared the pot before she left at night.

Moss reached into the cabinet for a cup and filled it. His hands were shaking. In the whole of his life, he couldn't ever remember seeing his hands shake. He was more certain than ever that he had alcohol poisoning. He sipped at the hot coffee, certain he was burning his throat. But he didn't care. He

366

waited to see if French roast would bubble up and out. When it didn't, he drank more until the cup was empty. Then he tottered over to the small powder room off the kitchen and reached for the aspirin bottle. He swallowed a handful, wondering if he would die from an aspirin overdose, if that was possible. Maybe his stomach would rebel from the aspirin, and he'd bleed out right here in the kitchen. At the moment, he didn't care about that either. He sat down with a second cup of coffee and waited to see if he was going to die. When nothing happened, he sat up a little straighter. The awful pounding in his head was lessening, and his vision seemed to be clearing somewhat. Maybe he would live after all. Right now, right this minute, he wasn't sure if he wanted to live or not.

Moss immediately talked himself out of that doomsday thinking and looked over at the clock on the range. He had to squint to see the digital numbers — 2:22 in the morning. Triple deuce. It had to mean something. What, he had no clue.

The coffee had stayed down, and he wasn't feeling nauseous. Good sign. His head just ached now, and his vision was starting to sharpen. Maybe he was going to live after all.

When the sun finally crept above the horizon, Moss decided he was going to live after all. He felt almost normal in the bright light of the day, which just went to prove the wisdom of that old adage that things always looked darkest in the night. Thankful that his personal trainer was on vacation and the cottage on the premises in which he lived was empty until he got back, Moss got up and headed for the elevator, rode to the second floor, and got dressed in khaki cargo pants and a brand-new Polo T-shirt. He slipped his bare feet into boat shoes and made his way to his home office. His legs were steady now, almost as steady as his hands. He had things to do.

Moss booted up his computer, then unlocked the bottom desk drawer and pulled out his black book. Before he did anything, before making his final decision, he brought up the newest blog of Dominic Sludge, not to be confused with the Drudge Report, the blogger who was fast overtaking every other blogger reporting on the D.C. politicians.

Moss put on his reading glasses and perused the blog. It was all about the First Lady's gala and his wife's attending the event with the Director of the FBI. *Noticeably absent was the beautiful model's husband, Lincoln Moss. I also want to report that the lady's husband, who has had 24/7 access to the White House from day one, has not been seen in over a week at the famous address. Which raises speculation that the rumors of a mass resignation of President Knight's advisers are all true, as first reported here on the Sludge Blog. Calls to Moss's home were not returned before press time.*

Moss clenched his fists as he read the report several more times until he had it committed to memory. No sense getting upset, he knew this was coming. Now it was payback time. Moss pressed keys, clicked an arrow here, and pressed more keys until he was satisfied he was on a secure server in Bucharest that could never be traced to him. Then he started to type, copying all the pages from his black book. It took him an hour before he was done. Only one entry remained, the one about Gabriel Knight. He stared down at the printed words with narrowed eyes. Spare his best friend? Well, that really wasn't an option anymore since Gabe was no longer his best friend. He started to type.

When he was finished, he looked at the long narrative. His finger hovered over the SEND key. Instead, he moved his fingers, selected the final entry, and hit the DELETE button. "You're off the hook, Gabe," he murmured to himself as he hit the SEND key, turned off the computer, and took it apart. Carrying the computer hard drive and the rest of the guts of the computer in a plastic bag, he made his way out to the yard, where just days ago he had been mixing cement for his new flower beds.

He worked like a beaver, sweating out all the toxins in his body as he mixed fresh cement and poured it into the molds he'd made weeks ago. The computer parts were at the bottom of the cement, where no one would ever find them. When everything was set to his liking, he proceeded to break up the chunks of cement he'd let dry the day the *Post* reporters had come to call. He loaded the cement into a wheelbarrow and trundled them off to a rock pile behind a small fence where the gardeners kept a compost pile. Let them cart it away.

He should have killed Amalie and buried her under the concrete the way he'd just buried his computer's guts. If he'd done that, none of this would be happening. Well, that was all water under the bridge now. Now he had to get ready to leave this place and the life he had created for himself in Washington, D.C.

Once more, he trudged into the house.

And this time took the steps to the second floor instead of the elevator, where he hit the shower full blast. When he emerged, he was ready to give himself a clean shave and dress the way he normally did. He headed back to his office, where he opened his locked desk drawer again and withdrew a burner phone. He called the airlines and, using one of his aliases, tried to book a late-afternoon or early-evening flight for Argentina. He was told the earliest he could get a flight was 7:00 A.M. the following morning. They were booked solid. He then tried three other airlines with the same result. He finally booked a red-eye out of Dulles for midnight tonight.

Time to put his house in order, so that whoever came to go through his things would find nothing. In the end, they'd say the man just walked out of the house and never returned. He felt so smug he decided to go downstairs and make himself a soft-boiled egg. Like Gabriel Knight, he knew how to cook; he just didn't like doing it.

While he was puttering around in his kitchen, Moss thought about his staff and how loyal they'd all been to him. He hated that he was going to leave them high and dry, but if he paid them a bonus or left money, then the scenario that he just walked out the door and never came back wouldn't work. He finally solved the problem by telling himself he would take all their names and addresses and in a few months he'd send money orders to their homes or envelopes full of cash by overnight mail.

It was all doable. All of it.

CHAPTER 23

It was just a few minutes before full dusk when Maggie Spritzer sent Lincoln Moss a text asking if she and her crew could stop by even though the hour was late. There was no response. As she explained it to the crew, it was just to confirm Avery Snowden's earlier text advising them that Lincoln Moss had not left the premises in two whole days. Unless he was dead, he was inside the house healthy and whole.

Little did they know.

It was barely dark when they all piled into the *Post* van and Espinosa's new Hummer, which he doted on and which still smelled brand-new. The third vehicle was driven by Dennis and was a Jeep whose cargo hold was full of their gear. The last vehicle belonged to Myra's gardener and was driven by Annie. Occupancy in all four vehicles was crowded, but no one complained.

It was totally dark and getting darker by

the minute when the caravan reached Lincoln Moss's home. The air was hot and humid, and the threat of still more rain was in the air. The lead vehicle didn't stop but slowed, so that Yoko and Harry could drop out and scale the fence. Down the road, a block and a half away, all the vehicles came to a halt. Cell phones were an open line so that Yoko and Harry could communicate.

First order of business was to take out the two guards, or as Harry put it, put them to sleep, nothing more. They were just doing their jobs and didn't deserve to be caught up in Moss's mess.

Inside the gates, Yoko went one way and Harry the other. Within ten minutes, both guards were leaning against a tree and sound asleep.

"You do good work, silent work, my husband," Yoko said, blowing Harry a kiss.

"And so do you, my little lotus flower," Harry said, blowing a kiss in return. Yoko giggled, and Harry laughed out loud. He just loved, loved it when he could make his wife laugh or smile, and a giggle was the best.

"I'll open the gate. You alert the gang to come on through." Yoko sprinted off to open the gate. She looked around with the aid of a small penlight for the manual switch that was at the bottom of the left side of the gate. She switched it off. Now the gates would stay open, with or without power. She was back at Harry's side within moments and headed for the rear of the house, where they planned to enter through the kitchen door.

"It's Annie's job to pick the lock, so we have to wait till she gets here," Yoko said. No sooner were the words out of her mouth than Annie appeared at her side, lockpick in hand. Five seconds, and the kitchen door opened on its well-oiled hinges.

Harry looked around and winced. They were a scary-looking lot. He hoped Lincoln Moss had a strong heart. The second everyone was standing in the kitchen, Harry held up his hand for silence as he waited for Abner, who was monitoring Moss's whereabouts inside the house with a heat sensor.

The one thing they didn't want to do was give Moss even a second to hit 911 on his speed dial. Quick, fast, and dirty, was the way Annie put it.

Harry held up his hand, and whispered, "He's in the family room watching television. His phone is on the table next to where he's sitting. He almost looks like he's asleep. Quiet now. Yoko, you go first, come up behind his chair, and snatch the phone.

Jack, you follow Yoko and grab him by his neck. We are then good to go."

And it worked out just the way Harry said it would. Yoko slid Moss's phone into her pocket just as Jack cut off his air supply. In the back of the room, Myra turned on the overhead lighting, and the opulent room came to life.

Moss's eyes almost popped out of his head when he saw all the black-clad figures standing in his family room. Jack released the hold he had on Moss's neck and stepped back.

Moss sputtered and gagged as he struggled to figure out what was going on. He finally blurted, "If this is a home invasion, be aware that I have security outside." He started to cough and gag from the pressure Jack had applied to his throat.

"Not anymore you don't. Ain't no one here but us badasses," Jack said.

"What . . . what do you want?" Moss gasped. "Who sent you here?"

"That's two questions," Ted said. "We want you and your money. Your wife sent us. How's that for a payback, Mr. Moss?"

The group had separated on entering. They now started to report their findings.

"No computer or laptop. The wires are still on the desk in his upstairs office. He must have gotten rid of it," Nikki said.

"He's going on a trip. Look at this," Kathryn said, as she held up a canvas tote. "No clothes, but there is a razor and a toothbrush. Memory sticks, checks, bank statements, brokerage statements, and some papers that look like they belong to his cosmetic company, something about a wrinkle filler. You know, like Botox. Guess it's important, or he wouldn't have it in the bag. And by the way he is . . . excuse me, was, headed for the airport to take a flight to Argentina under the name of Lynus Placid. Says he is a software developer. No imagination there."

Moss sucked in his breath, knowing he wasn't going anywhere. At least for now. And he sure as hell wasn't going to help these creeps figure it out. Well, he did have one ace in the hole. Everything on the memory sticks was password-protected and installed by the best spooks in the business, the CIA. Let them kill themselves trying to figure it all out. He was glad now that he had transferred monies to different parts of the world, so when he showed up, he would be able to simply pick up on his life. Still, he had well over a billion dollars locked up tight and spread all over the globe.

"His backyard is not going to work,

people," Annie said. "We need to load him up and go to Plan B. While the trees are in full leaf, they're spindly at the top. Light shows through. His neighbors just might be the nosy types who can't sleep, and one of us might make a noise that isn't familiar to them."

The gang moved with their usual efficiency and had Moss flexicuffed with his mouth taped shut. Espinosa threw him over his shoulder in a fireman's carry and hustled out to the parking area outside the kitchen. He dumped him in the backseat and told Dennis to watch him. Dennis paled and was about to discuss the point, but one look at Harry and he changed his mind. He felt important when he said, "You got it."

Isabelle was the last to leave Moss's house. It was her job to turn off all the lights and the TV and to make sure the kitchen door was locked when she closed the door.

Plan B was now in effect. Plan B required a trip to Nikki and Jack's farmhouse. Located across the fields from Pinewood, it was also known as the mud pit with the half-finished swimming pool that was full of muddy water.

A light rain was falling when the caravan arrived in Nikki and Jack's driveway. Jack took charge of Moss while the others unloaded the Jeep. It was totally dark, the only light coming from small Maglites the group held low to the ground. The only sound that could be heard was the sucking sound when they lifted their feet out of the thick, smelly mud.

When the group reached the rim of the pool that was still under construction, Jack ripped off the tape on Moss's mouth. He was rewarded with curses he'd never heard before. He casually backhanded Moss with a swat across the face. "The only thing we want to hear out of your mouth are your passwords and why you beat the living hell out of your wife. We aren't going to make nice either, so be forewarned."

"Screw you, whoever you are. What dark alley did my wife find you in? You can't make me do anything I don't want to do. And I am not giving up my pass codes to you or anyone else." That said, Moss lashed out with his foot and connected with Dennis, who yelped in pain.

Dennis's brain went into overdrive, and suddenly everything Harry had taught him about self-defense rose to the fore. He didn't stop to think, he just went into action, and in the blink of an eye, Moss was facedown in the thick, gooey mud that smelled like vomit.

"Nice going, kid," Harry said, clapping Dennis on the back. Dennis beamed his pleasure. Life didn't get any better than a compliment from his idol, Harry Wong.

"Now, here's what we're going to do, Mr. Moss. As you can see, the rain looks to be picking up, and none of us really wants to catch a summer cold. You, we don't care about, but none of us wants to get sick. Now, having said that, this is what you're looking at. You're going in that hole, which will hopefully someday be my swimming pool. It's full of mud, water, and a few dead animals that drowned during that horrendous rain this past week. You won't be able to climb out once you're in there. Did I mention that the pool, this monster hole in the ground, is fourteen feet deep all around?

"If you don't answer us, we're going to push you in the pool. And then we're going to give you some company."

Nikki turned to Kathryn and told her to bring the special bins to the side of the pool. The girls hustled to give Kathryn a hand.

"Do you want to see what's in the bins, Mr. Moss?"

Moss raised his head and wiped the mud out of his eyes and mouth. His heart rate ratcheted up. He struggled to appear uncaring but knew he wasn't pulling it off. "Not particularly. Probably something insane because you are all insane to kidnap someone like me. I'm a public figure."

"No you are not. At this point in time, you are a public joke. This whole town now knows the story of your wife. What kind of man beats a woman and holds her prisoner? Only a sick, demented person like you, you filthy son of a bitch. You are a power-hungry mongrel," Annie said loud enough to be heard above the rain, which was coming down even harder. "Go easy on yourself and tell us the passwords."

"Go to hell," Moss bellowed.

Annie threw her hands in the air. "Well, we tried to be nice. Show him what's in the bins, girls! Be careful now," she warned.

The girls advanced close to the pool and undid the heavy-duty lids of the hard plastic bins. But they didn't remove them. They waited expectantly.

Myra stepped forward. "Bin One is full of water moccasins. Bin Two is full of rattlesnakes, and Bin Three is full of copperhead snakes. We weren't sure if cottonmouths were the same as water moccasins, so we got some of those, too, because they do look different. They are in Bin Four. There are twelve of the pesky little devils in each bin. They go in the pool with you. Do you want to rethink your attitude and co-operate or not?"

Jesus Christ, Moss asked himself, *who are these looney tune people?* Moss could feel his insides start to crumble. He could hear the rattlesnakes rattling inside the bin.

"Time's up," Harry said as he shoved Moss into the muddy water.

Moss bellowed and cursed as he flailed about in the smelly muck. "Beg, Moss, like your wife begged you to stop beating her. I want to hear you. I want you to feel the fear she felt. Throw in the water moccasins," Annie said.

"Jesus God, no," Moss said as he struggled to get away from where the moccasins hit the water. He had never experienced such panic in his life. He felt something brush against his leg. "Oh, Christ, what was that?"

"They swim fast, just so you know," Annie called down. "Just say the word, and we can scoop you right out of there with the pool pole. Your call."

"Throw the rattlers in," Annie ordered.

They all watched as Moss tried to climb up the muddy side of the pool, only to flop back into the water. He was hoarse from bellowing.

"Tell us, is what you're feeling now what

Amalie felt when you came up to her with your clenched fists? Do you feel the fear?" Myra shouted.

Goddamn right he felt the fear. "Get me out of here. You win."

Jack leaned over and shined his light down into the muddy water. "You know what, who cares? We'll get our people to figure out the passwords. You aren't worth standing out here catching cold. Dump the cottonmouths and the copperheads, and let's go dry out. I know this all-night pizza place. Close up shop, people."

Moss let out a scream that could be heard in the next county. He begged, he pleaded, he promised a full confession, and if he had had children, he would have given up his firstborn.

"The passwords. Now," Jack ordered. Moss rattled them off. Ted recorded each and every number.

"Someone call Snowden," Jack said. Maggie obliged.

"Get me out of here," Moss bellowed. "You promised."

"Yeah, well I lied," Jack said happily. "See ya on the other side someday, Moss."

The gang trooped off and didn't speak until they were at their designated vehicles, and that's when they started to laugh. "Too bad he doesn't know all those critters we tossed in that pool are *mechanical,*" Annie said, laughing. "He'll be a raving maniac by the time Avery and his people pull him out of there."

"We did good, people," Myra said.

"You know, I wasn't kidding about that pizza place down the road. What say we hit it?" Jack said.

"Last one there pays," Harry said, climbing into the car with his wife.

Annie and Myra were the last to leave the area.

"We do good work," Annie said.

"Can't argue with you there, my friend. When you're right, you're right."

"And everyone is going to live happily ever after."

"Not till tomorrow, when Abner starts doling out all of Moss's money to worthy causes. That's when everyone will be happy."

"Like I said, when you're right, you're right." Myra laughed.

EPILOGUE

Six weeks later

Labor Day ushered in the end of summer, or, as Nikki put it, "I just knew when the pool would be finished, it would be by Labor Day. We can't even take a dip, the water's too cold, so the pool people installed a cover, and now we have to wait till next summer. The good news is that Jack and I are no longer living in a world of mud. I have grass!" She announced this like she'd just been handed the Holy Grail.

The gang, or as Charles referred to them, all his chicks, were on the terrace waiting for the holiday barbecue to get under way. Conversation was about everything and anything, none of it important in the scheme of things. Everyone was just glad to see one another and to unwind.

The gang had gone their separate ways after dumping Lincoln Moss in Nikki's unfinished swimming pool. Kathryn had signed herself into the hospital and had the titanium bar removed from her leg. She'd been right all along, to the chagrin of the surgeons. She was allergic to the bar. She'd spent the entire six weeks, as she put it, working her tail off in therapy, and she was now good to go with nothing more than a slight limp. The good news was she was pain-free. And just as good was that Bert had finally managed to take some time off from Annie's Las Vegas casino and was at Pinewood for the Labor Day holiday.

Isabelle had hunkered down with Abner and was still learning the tricks of his trade. Abner said she was a natural and was already almost as good as he was at the hacking game. They'd weathered their personal marital storm and were closer than ever.

Because of changes at the monastery that the monks wanted the parents to approve, two days after they walked away from Nikki's pool, Yoko and Harry had gone to China for a rare visit. After their initial visit with Lily, which lasted only six hours, the two of them had toured China. They had just returned home ten days ago, sad yet happy.

Alexis and Espinosa had driven out West and gotten engaged all over again, but they were still shy about setting a wedding date. They were home now and raring to go, as Espinosa put it.

Nikki and Jack had taken care of business at her firm and spent long weekends touring the various countrysides, followed by a trip to the Big Apple just for fun. A totally uneventful six weeks, according to both of them.

Annie got a decorating bug, and she and Fergus took two classes on how to hang wallpaper. Annie's house was now floral in design, which meant she had to buy all new furniture to go with the wallpaper. The bottom line was she was no longer sure if she liked the wallpaper, saying maybe she should have gone with stripes instead of flowers. Fergus said it didn't matter as long as he wore sunglasses.

Myra went back to her knitting, determined to finish her "five-mile-long scarf," which was now almost ten miles long. She trundled it around with her in a red wagon. "My knitting teacher, Claudeen, told me she thinks I should give it up and find another hobby. I'm not giving up, I'm going to make her proud of me yet." No one said anything, even when she produced the red wagon with the monster scarf. She was satisfied with Charles's comment that it was "impressive." Like she didn't already know it was impressive. Even Claudeen said she didn't know anyone who had ever knitted a ten-mile-long scarf.

Jack Sparrow had finally signed the papers, and Nikki and Jack's house in Georgetown was his. He'd even furnished it, with Amalie's help. Amalie had moved into the spare room and paid Sparrow rent while she went house hunting after her return from visiting her family in France. She had finally found a house to her liking two streets over on P Street in Georgetown. They were an item, but only in a platonic sense. But that was rapidly changing, as was the relationship between Rosalee and Dennis West.

Rosalee would start her nursing classes in a week, thanks to a mysteriously financed scholarship that offered a full ride plus a stipend for living expenses. Everyone knew they were already "an item," and everyone heartily approved.

Maggie and Ted, still reestablishing their relationship but hesitant about taking the final plunge, finished off the summer by simply working because, as the world knows, the news never rests. It was their job, a job they took seriously, to keep the public updated on world affairs. Neither was complaining.

It seemed like no one wanted to bring up the subject of Lincoln Moss, possibly because Amalie, the newest member of the family, was present. And yet it all hung out there like some unseen bad wind. Finally, Maggie said, "Okay, people, let's talk about it, then we can move on.

"I'm not sure if any of you know this or not, but Avery Snowden had Mr. Moss sign over his power of attorney to Nikki. It was the only way he would agree to pull him out of the pool. When those critters we dumped in the pool brushed up against him, they, for want of better words, sparked and stung him. He thought he was being bitten and was going to die. Mr. Snowden said he never saw such fear in a man. Said he was so far gone, he could barely tell them his name when they finally yanked him out.

"Abner, with Isabelle's help, donated his money to so many worthy causes I lost track, but it's all documented. With Lizzie Fox's help, we set up trusts for Rosalee, her family, Amalie's family, and, of course, for Amalie, who said she didn't want a penny of her husband's money. Mr. Sparrow had a long talk with her, reminding her of all the modeling work she had done as the face of *La Natural,* work for which she had never

389

been paid since her husband owned the company, and she finally agreed to a revocable trust that she herself would manage.

"We donated to all the usual, the Red Cross, the Heart Fund, various cancer research projects, animal causes, children's causes, especially the one the First Lady is working on, and one for building homes for returning veterans. Weekend Warriors will never have to worry again; nor will St. Jude's Hospital for children. Doctors Without Borders was a grateful recipient, and by the way, I do not know if this is true, but I heard from someone who should know that a nurse by the name of Jane Petrie is working with them. Oh, and last but not least, we helped ourselves to a very generous chunk of Moss's fortune for future . . . um . . . missions."

"Is it true, does anyone know for sure, if Moss was the one who outed all those politicians by informing Dominic Sludge?" Kathryn asked. "This whole town went crazy with all those resignations."

"They're saying it but can't prove it. The hot gossip was about where did Lincoln Moss disappear to? Again, there was no answer. It's all speculation. The good news is that President Knight is now his own man and is running the country the way it should be run and not the way Lincoln Moss wanted it run," Myra said.

"That's enough, folks. The past is prologue. We're here to enjoy a family day, so let's enjoy it. You all know what you need to do, so let's get that grill fired up," Charles said, like a commanding general, handing Bert a plate of chips.

Annie and Myra followed Charles and Fergus into the kitchen, where they took up their favorite spot by the kitchen window to observe their family. "Two new members to our family, Annie. How great is that?"

"Personally speaking, my dear friend, I don't think it gets any better than that." Annie smiled. "We did good, Myra. By that I mean we all did good. Look how happy Amalie is! And she's going to be even happier when she ties the knot with Director Sparrow. It's just a matter of time. And I guarantee that by the end of the year, young Dennis and Rosalee will be engaged."

Myra laughed out loud. Always and forever the matchmaker. "Someday, I want you to tell me how you pulled off that nursing scholarship for Rosalee."

"Whatever do you mean, Myra? Look," she said, trying to divert Myra from her question. "Is it my imagination, or do Jack and Harry look . . . off their feed, anxious. Something is off. I just can't put my finger on it."

"I did notice that. I've never seen Harry agitated before. Never. He looks agitated to me. And Jack looks . . . I don't know, *antsy* is the only word I can come up with. But does that answer your question?"

"Not really," Annie said, a frown building on her forehead. She continued to watch Harry and Jack through the window, while Myra turned away to do something for Charles. A shiver ran down her spine. She wished she could hear what the two of them were saying. Something wasn't right.

Annie was correct, she just didn't know it.

Jack tapped Harry on the shoulder. "Hey, Harry, let's go for a walk. I need to talk to you." Harry suddenly looked like a deer caught in the headlights. He didn't say anything but fell into step with his best friend in the whole world.

"Listen, Harry, I . . . this is going to sound really crazy, and I can't help it, so will you hear me out?"

"Yeah, what's up?"

"I woke up this morning at 3:33. I never wake up at 3:33. I was wide-awake, like someone punched me in the gut. My head was buzzing with . . . thoughts. And then . . .

and then . . ."

"You heard the name Cooper, is that what you were going to say?" Harry asked in a strangled-sounding voice.

"Yeah. Jesus, Harry, how did you know?" Jack asked, his voice sounding even more jittery than Harry's.

"Because the same thing happened to me. Exactly the same thing. I was trying to get up the nerve to tell you all day. Spooked the hell out of me."

"That dog is not . . . Cooper is . . . I don't know what the hell Cooper is."

"I have a text coming in," Harry said, feeling his cell vibrating in his pocket.

"Aren't you going to answer it? No one ever texts you except . . ."

"I know who it is," Harry said in a choked voice.

Jack licked at his dry lips. "I know who it is, too."

"Are we sure I should . . . ?"

"Yeah, Harry, I'm sure."

ABOUT THE AUTHOR

Fern Michaels is the *USA Today* and *New York Times* bestselling author of nearly 150 novels and novellas, including *Perfect Match, Eyes Only, Kiss and Tell, A Family Affair, Blindsided, Classified, Gotcha! Breaking News,* and *Tuesday's Child.* There are over 160 million copies of her books in print.

Fern Michaels has built and funded several large daycare centers in her hometown, and is a passionate animal lover who has outfitted police dogs across the country with special bulletproof vests. She shares her home in South Carolina with her five dogs and a resident ghost named Mary Margaret. Visit her website at www.fernmichaels.com.